THE NEW WORLD

Scott K. Andrews

HODDER &
STOUGHTON

First published in Great Britain in 2017 by Hodder & Stoughton
An Hachette UK company

1

A CIP catalogue record for this title is available from the British Library

Trade Paperback ISBN 978 1 444 75213 7
Ebook ISBN 978 1 444 75214 4

Typeset in Sabon LT Std by Palimpsest Book Production Limited,
Falkirk, Stirlingshire

Printed and bound by Clays Ltd, St Ives plc

Hodder & Stoughton policy is to use papers that are natural,
renewable and recyclable products and made from wood grown in
sustainable forests. The logging and manufacturing processes are expected
to conform to the environmental regulations of the country of origin.

Hodder & Stoughton Ltd
Carmelite House
50 Victoria Embankment
London
EC4Y 0DZ

www.hodder.co.uk

THE NEW WORLD

About the author

Scott K. Andrews is the author of three novels in Abaddon's Afterblight Chronicles series – *School's Out, Operation Motherland* and *Children's Crusade* – which follow the adventures of a group of schoolchildren trying to rebuild society after a viral apocalypse. He has also written audio dramas, comics, episode guide books and was the lead writer on Rebellion's Sniper Elite: V2 computer game.

For Kitty and Thomas, for all time.

Previously . . .

Three teenagers – Dora Predennick from the 1640s, Kazic Cecka from the early twenty-first century, and Jana Patel from the mid twenty-second century – have somehow acquired the ability to travel through time using the power of thought. They have been on many adventures . . .

In 2014 they were kidnapped by another time traveller, Henry Sweetclover, lord of Sweetclover Hall in Dora's time. After being interrogated about their roles in future events, they were freed by the intervention of a mysterious person from their future, who they only know as Steve.

Following Sweetclover's trail back to 1645, they encountered his wife, Quil, the badly injured leader of an army engaged in a terrible war in the twenty-second century. Quil was assembling an army in the cavern that lay beneath Sweetclover Hall, a cavern that also contained a mysterious, glowing rock. The three young people barely escaped with their lives.

Next they travelled into the future where they met Professor Kairos, a physicist who was waiting for them in a quantum bubble – a safe place outside the flow of time – that he had created for them below Sweetclover Hall in 2158. The quantum bubble existed in the second before Sweetclover Hall was destroyed by the timebomb – a temporally unstable asteroid that Quil had discovered in mysterious circumstances years earlier and fashioned into a weapon.

Our heroes then tried to change history by saving Kaz's mother from a car bomb in 2010, but they were thwarted by Sweetclover and Quil, and Kaz's mother was lost in time.

They next travelled to a peace conference in the capital city of Mars, Barrettown, in 2158, where Quil and her army of clone soldiers were meeting to discuss peace with a unified Earth government. Kaz, Dora and Jana believed that by preventing an assassination attempt on Quil's life they could change history and prevent her becoming their enemy.

But things went terribly wrong on Mars – Barrettown was completely destroyed, and Quil was taken prisoner by the Earth president, who was revealed to be Quil's mother. Jana and the others were then horrified to learn that Quil was a clone of Jana, created after Jana first jumped into time.

Deciding that they could still salvage events, Kaz, Dora and Jana staged a daring attack on Sweetclover Hall, now a top-secret holding facility where Quil was being held. They were successful, and together with Kairos, they created the quantum bubble that their younger selves had once sought refuge in.

They discovered that Quil had been poisoned by an Earth spy, so as to make her paranoid and unpredictable and trigger her downfall, weakening her army. After receiving the antidote, Quil turned out to be surprisingly reasonable. She took Jana, Kaz and Dora on a journey through time to show them her life and explain her war.

We do not yet know what secrets Quil revealed to them during this time-trip, only that they returned to the quantum bubble determined to stop the Earth president, Jana and Quil's mother, at all costs.

However, time had played a cruel trick. Jana believed that

by giving Quil the antidote to the poison they had changed history, preventing her travelling back in time to become their enemy. In fact, their creation of the quantum bubble had split Quil in two. One version of her, still poisoned and still mad, had travelled back in time to marry Sweetclover and become their enemy; the other, reasonable one had remained in the quantum bubble to become their friend.

When the mad version of Quil tried to return to the future, she was pulled into the quantum bubble and the good version of her was erased from the timeline. Even worse, Kaz's mother appeared in the quantum bubble at exactly the wrong moment, and died as Quil made her escape.

The quantum bubble then collapsed and the timebomb destroyed Sweetclover Hall, with our heroes still inside it . . .

Now there is only one Quil left, our heroes' implacable foe who, together with her husband, has returned to 2158, unleashed her army from the ground beneath the ruins of Sweetclover Hall and ordered them to kill <u>everything</u> . . .

Prologue:
Philadelphia, 27 May 2155

The crowd appeared quickly, quietly and with no warning. A thousand men and women, all dressed in plain black clothes, wearing white porcelain masks, filed into Independence Park and stood in a block, facing Independence Hall, their featureless faces a silent rebuke.

Security was tight around the Hall because the president was visiting to inaugurate the new mayor, a close political ally. There were snipers on the roof, Secret Service guards at all the entrances, drones and helicopters in the sky.

So at first, the security teams, although alarmed by the mysterious protestors, did not believe there to be a real and present danger. But then all the agents with embedded ENL chips went into a fugue state. Those agents not affected panicked, drew their weapons and began shouting and calling for backup.

The crowd stood motionless while these events unfolded.

When the chipped agents regained control of themselves five minutes later – insofar as they were able, given the vomiting, the crying, the shock of what they had experienced during those minutes – attention quickly turned to the protestors, who had begun chanting, 'We're not monsters.'

The panicked agents put the call out for tactical support.

Those police with chips had also experienced the fugue, so the response time was poor. It took fifteen minutes for them to secure all the exits to the square, and in that time a large, angry mob of ordinary people had joined the mysterious masked protestors. The crowd was now louder and less predictable. The agents called for the National Guard, but they did not arrive in time to have much impact on the chain of events.

The police were heavily armed but budget cuts meant they did not carry the latest laser weapons. They aimed their old-fashioned projectile weapons at the crowd and waited.

The stand-off lasted for about ten minutes. The crowd were defiant, but peaceful. The police and secret service were afraid and twitchy.

Then someone in the crowd fired a gun into the air. A laser gun. The beam lanced into the sky and began sweeping down towards the roof of Independence Hall.

This gave the police and secret service the excuse they needed.

They opened fire.

The massacre began.

Part One

Breathing space

1

The first thing Jana became aware of was the keening.

From far, far away the long, slow, desperate howl of pain sliced through the post-explosion deafness that muffled all other sound. It was hardly a human noise; it was more primal than that. Animal. The sound of a fox caught in a trap, realising that it would have to gnaw its own leg off to survive.

Or of a boy who'd just seen his mother sliced in two.

The sound tugged at Jana, pulling her back towards consciousness.

She was lying on her stomach.

Smell returned – the earthy scent of the mud that caked her face.

She blinked her eyes, which teared up as they washed the mud away; the grit lacerated her eyeballs as she blinked. She could make out only an impression of light; a hot, orange glow that surrounded her. Her nose was blocked. Her mouth was full of blood.

She pushed herself up, bringing her knees forward, planting her feet in the mud and attempting to stand. She had only risen to a half-crouch before the ground seemed to crumble beneath her and she felt herself falling, arms and legs flailing as she crashed and tumbled down a slope.

She fought unconsciousness, even as she knew she would lose.

The first thing Jana became aware of was movement.

She was shaking from side to side, like a passenger on a rickety old bus navigating a potholed side street. It took a moment for her memory to return, but then she gasped in alarm as she remembered the explosion and the fall.

The keening sound had stopped. She did not know whether that was a good or a bad sign.

She felt sick, nauseated; her head was swimming with dizzy abandon, and when she opened her eyes all she saw were strobing patterns of light, zigzagging left and right.

There was a muffled sound that accompanied the shaking; a repeated throb of white noise nagging her back to life. As she once again reclaimed her limbs, the noise gained clarity – someone was calling her name.

As soon as she realised that, she understood that someone was shaking her, trying to rouse her.

She again pushed herself up with trembling arms, and tried to get to her feet. The blurred world swayed and rocked, but this time Jana felt hands beneath her arms, helping her, lifting her. When she was upright, an arm snaked around her waist, and she felt herself being propped up and forced to walk. She allowed herself to be steered, completely helpless, aware that if the person helping her were to step away she would collapse in a heap.

She could not find the words to warn her carer before she vomited, so she threw up while hobbling, violent and wrenching, her bile spattering her clothes and probably also those of the person helping her.

That person did not pause as Jana was racked by heaves

and her stomach did its very best to pull itself up and out of her throat. They kept shambling forward into the hot orange murk.

When she was done vomiting, Jana spat and coughed and blinked her eyes over and over, willing herself to ignore the grains of dirt that ground between eyeball and eyelid. She forced out tears in a hurried bid for some kind of sensory input she could use to anchor herself.

Everything was the colour of fire. No, not fire – lava. Something hot but not flaming. It was bright and painful and it obscured details. Oddly, there was no heat to help her locate the source of the glow. Whatever it was, it wasn't hot.

The ground beneath her changed as she and her helper began climbing up a slope. Dirt and stones shifted beneath Jana's feet, threatening to unbalance her and send her tumbling again, but together she and her unseen companion were able to find a rhythm and maintain it. They were obviously working their way up the slope she'd fallen down the first time she'd regained consciousness. Thankfully, it was not too steep.

As she climbed her vision gradually sharpened. She was climbing up a slope of recently overturned earth, and the orange glow was coming from behind her. She did not think it wise to risk looking back over her shoulder – it would most likely send them both tumbling again. She glanced to her right and recognised the person aiding her. It was Professor Kairos, the temporal physicist who had helped her and her friends Dora and Kaz in their struggle against Quil, Jana's unhinged clone.

No, that was where they had got it wrong, she reminded herself. Their real enemy hadn't been Quil; it had been the relentless inevitability of time itself.

Which is why they had lost so completely.

Kairos was covered in dirt, and there were red streaks of

drying blood running from his ears and nose, but he otherwise seemed in better shape than Jana. He guided her to the top of the slope and helped her steady herself. His mouth moved but all she heard was a buzz of static. She was wobbly on her feet, but she risked turning to look back at where they had been, and her bleeding eyes opened wide in surprise.

She was looking down into a vast crater, at the middle of which sat a glowing orange rock she had seen before. It was the warhead of the timebomb, shaped from an asteroid found in the far future and then launched at the Earth government's secret holding centre in England by Quil's clone army. It lay, burning bright orange, in the wound left by its explosive journey backwards through time from the moment of its impact, in 2158.

As if that were not staggering enough, Jana became aware of the landscape beyond the crater. She knew this piece of ground would eventually become the site of Sweetclover Hall, that she was standing on what would one day be Cornwall. But those days were far away judging by the lush, almost tropical forest that surrounded her.

How far back in time had they been blown?

She flinched as she felt hands on her head, pulling away from Kairos in alarm to see him brandishing a handkerchief. He mimed wiping out his ears and handed it to Jana, who did as she was bid. The white cotton square came away caked with fresh red blood mixed with dark chunks of coagulation. She gagged briefly, before evacuating her other ear. There was still a dull, ever-present whine, and Kairos's voice sounded like it was softly echoing to her down a hundred metres of metal tubing, but she could make out his words now; he was asking if she could hear him.

'Thank you,' she said, offering him the bloodstained hankie

and then, when he waved it away, shrugging and dropping it on the ground. She winced at how her voice sounded when heard mostly though her skull. 'Yes, I can. Where are Kaz and Dora?'

Kairos pointed over her shoulder and Jana turned – too quickly; she wobbled, almost fell, reached out to grasp Kairos's hand and right herself – to see Dora sitting at the crater's edge, cradling Kaz's head in her lap. He was curled up, foetal, his body shaking as though he were sobbing. Not an unreasonable response to seeing your mother murdered, thought Jana. Dora was stroking his hair, looking up at Jana, her face a dirt- and blood-streaked vision of helpless fury.

A flash of movement beyond Dora and Kaz caught Jana's eye and she refocused as best she could on the treeline. There was something there, the shadows of the trees shaded orange by the glow from the warhead. She squinted, craned forward, trying to make out what it was.

She took a step closer, then another, trying to extract meaning from the interplay of light and shadow in the dense foliage.

When she realised she was looking into a large yellow eye, she felt a jolt of fear that rooted her to the spot.

Was she . . .?

She was.

She was sharing a moment with a dinosaur.

Being careful to move slowly so as not to startle her new acquaintance (as if she could move quickly anyway, the state she was in), Jana reached her hand out behind her, beckoning Kairos forward as she tottered towards her two friends. The professor knelt beside her and she took his hand as she crouched beside her wounded friends and placed her other hand gently over Dora's.

She looked up and winked at the creature observing them curiously from a distance, then, connected to her three companions, sparks dancing around the small areas of personal intersection, Jana closed her eyes and dreamed of safety.

Kinshasa, Democratic Republic of Congo, 2 June 2120 – 38 years to timebomb impact

Jana's head was still ringing from the detonation three days after they left the Jurassic.

Those three days had been spent recuperating in the Kinshasa medical centre that was swiftly becoming her home from home. The injuries that had landed her here the first time had been more severe, but conversely easier to fix; surgery to repair a knife wound, it turned out, was simplicity itself compared to fixing the variety of injuries she and her friends had suffered when blown back through history by the timebomb.

She totted up her new aches, pains and encumbrances as she sat in the dining area sipping her tea, waiting for Professor Kairos to debrief them.

Worst was her hearing – she had lost sixty per cent in her right ear and seventy per cent in her left. Kaz, Dora and Kairos were similarly affected. The consultant told them they would have to wait at least a week for their individually tailored gene therapies to be programmed and prepared; until then, all three were wearing custom-moulded in-ear hearing aids to compensate for the damage. Even after the gene therapy, there was a good chance they would still have to wear them, because one hundred per cent restoration was unlikely.

Less dramatic, but more noticeable, was the damage to her eyesight. Whereas her hearing was just absent – no tinnitus, happily – her sight was a mess. Her cornea had been flash-burnt, leaving her in constant pain, hiding behind shades because light made her wince, squinting to make out details with her blurry vision. As with her hearing, another few days would be required to prepare corrective treatment, but happily this was likely to effect a perfect recovery. She thought she and her friends looked comical in their dark glasses, sitting in the half-light of the dining area with the curtains drawn against the sunlight.

The permanent headache was ongoing, rising and falling from uncomfortable to unbearable and back again depending upon how many painkillers she could safely take. She'd exceeded the dose twice already, and was probably going to do so again in another hour if the intense pressure behind her eyes continued to build. This would probably self-correct once her eyesight was mended. Probably.

There had also been some weirder side-effects, like the way her bones ached. Kairos had proposed a theoretical explanation involving the effects of time dilation on calcium, which had made no sense to her at all. Whatever the cause, the upshot was that she and her friends were temporarily arthritic, creaking around the clinic like septuagenarians.

Finally, her sense of smell had completely gone, and everything tasted like porridge.

Turns out, it was no fun being blown up.

'Well,' said Professor Yasunori Kairos, taking his customary verbal run-up to an explanation, causing Jana's hearing aid to whine and make her jump as if someone had shoved a hot skewer through her frontal lobe.

'Shh, Professor,' whispered Dora, beating Jana to it.

Kairos was wincing too, as if he had startled himself with the volume of his pronouncement.

'Sorry. Yes,' he continued, softly. 'When the Godless fired the timebomb at Sweetclover Hall they could not have known exactly what effect it would have. By its nature it was a one-off, and had not been tested outside of mathematical projections. As Quil herself told you when she took you back into her timeline, she developed it as a weapon of last resort, a threat she could use to subdue resistance once her fleet had encircled Earth.

'In the event, the projections were useless, because the warhead did not hit stone and earth and concrete, as they expected. Instead, it blew down through Sweetclover Hall into the cavern below and smashed straight into its older self. This magnified the explosion tenfold, but also focused most of the energy backwards in time.

'The resultant temporal explosion had two immediate effects. One, the "older" warhead was destroyed.' Kairos used his fingers to draw air quotes as he spoke.

'Two, the "younger" warhead was blown back in time, fracturing the structure of causality as it spiralled back into the distant past. The explosion finally burnt itself out in the Jurassic and the warhead came to rest in what would one day become Cornwall. And there it sat for thousands of years, waiting for its younger self to come along and destroy it.'

'And that's where we woke up?' asked Dora. 'Jurassic Cornwall?'

Kairos nodded. 'Because of your unique abilities, you were

swept backwards in time on the shockwave of the temporal explosion. And because you had the presence of mind to grab my hand, Dora, I was also pulled along safely.' He smiled and nodded his thanks to Dora.

Jana was surprised to see genuine affection in the smile Dora flashed back at the ageing professor. Another welcome chink in her ninja-façade.

'You said the "older" warhead was destroyed,' said Jana, sifting through the possible implications as she spoke.

'That is so,' confirmed Kairos.

'And it was the warhead that acted as a lodestone, preventing us from arriving in deep space, pulling us to Earth when we jump through time.'

Kairos nodded.

'So that means we can only travel in time between two very specific dates,' concluded Jana. 'We can't travel to any time earlier than the moment we arrived in the Jurassic . . .'

'And we can't travel any further forward in time than 8.22 a.m. on the seventh of April 2148,' said Dora, nodding as she locked into Jana's line of reasoning.

'So how do we kill her?'

Jana looked across at Kaz, surprised by his interruption; she had not thought he was listening. Like all of them, he was in bad shape – dark circles under his eyes, a raggedy growth of stubble and bloodshot eyes. But his wounds were more than physical. His gaze lacked any spark of the boy who she'd come to think of as her best friend.

'Excuse me?' asked Kairos.

'Because we can't change events we've been part of, the only time and place left for us to kill Quil is on Earth, after the timebomb exploded,' said Kaz, his voice toneless and dead. 'How do we get to her, if we can't jump there?'

Jana could see that Kairos was both discomfited by Kaz's bluntness, and confused that he would ask such a simple question.

'We jump forward to just before the explosion, somewhere outside the blast radius, and wait for time to pass,' said Jana, trying and failing to avoid a tone that added an implicit 'you moron' to the end of her answer.

'But we have no advantage, if we do that,' said Dora. 'We would be three ordinary people in the middle of a war zone, trying to assassinate one of the best-protected people on the planet. We wouldn't stand a chance.'

'I don't think we need to kill her,' said Jana carefully, aware that Kaz was unlikely to be receptive to the alternative plan she was beginning to formulate. 'We just need to stop her.'

'How?' asked Kairos.

'Why?' asked Dora.

'Excuse me?' said Kaz, sitting upright angrily. 'Did you ask why?'

Dora leaned forward, hands clasped on her knees, and spoke directly to Kaz.

'Why have we done any of this?' she said. 'Quil and Sweetclover sought us out. They kidnapped us, they interrogated us. They did this partly because Quil was obsessed with accessing Jana's chip and filling in the missing gaps in her memories. But also because of our role in the events on Mars. We went to Mars to try and save lives, and stop her. But it turned out she wasn't the villain there. She was poisoned and tricked by Earth's president.'

'Or as I call her, Mom,' interjected Jana dryly.

'We failed on Mars,' continued Dora. 'In fact we became a key part of the events we were trying to prevent. Classic predestination paradox. We made it worse.'

'So what's your point?' said Kaz, impatient.

'We don't know what happened after the detonation, but my guess is that Quil's too busy fighting her war to bother coming after us any more,' said Dora. 'She spent twenty years in the past preparing an attack on the future. And it looks like she pulled it off. We were just a side project, a distraction. If we leave her alone now, I doubt we'll ever see her again. We can just walk away.'

'She killed my mother,' said Kaz through gritted teeth.

'Yes,' said Dora softly. 'She did. But she wasn't in her right mind. The Quil who pursued us through time is suffering the effects of the poison she was given on Mars. She's paranoid and psychotic. But that's not her fault.'

'It's my mom's,' said Jana.

'Exactly,' agreed Dora. 'So we let them deal with each other. If Quil wins her war, she'll kill the person who drove her mad, the person really responsible for all of this mess.'

'And if she loses?' asked Jana. 'If my mother kills her?'

Dora shrugged. 'Do we really want to pick a fight with the president of the whole planet? She doesn't even know we exist. Why paint another target on our backs? Look at us.' She gestured around the room. 'We're wrecked. We're all damaged nearly beyond repair, it's a miracle we're alive at all. We've been running ever since we all found ourselves in Sweetclover Hall that night. We can stop now. We can pick a time and a place – any time, any place – and start new lives. None of us have to worry about money, or jobs, or natural disasters. We can live long, happy lives on completely our own terms. If we just walk away, right now.'

Jana felt the pull of Dora's argument strongly. Would it be too wrong to turn their backs on Quil and her mad crusade and just get on with their lives? She thought again about her plan to travel back through time, writing and researching ancient civilisations. It was a seductive idea.

'But I feel responsible,' she said sadly. 'Quil is a monster, and yes, our mother made her that way. But so did I. She's my clone. Created to be the better version of me. She only exists because of choices I made. She's my monster too.'

'You can't blame yourself for her actions,' said Kairos.

'But I do.'

'And what about justice?' said Kaz, still angry, still barely holding it in. 'For my mother? For your parents, Dora, and everything she put them through? For the people she slaughtered in Pendarn?'

'Justice?' replied Dora. 'Or vengeance?'

'Same damn thing,' said Kaz, standing and stalking out of the room.

Jana, Dora and Kairos sat in silence for a while after his departure, each wrapped up in their own thoughts.

'Whatever I decide,' said Jana eventually, 'will completely change the course of my life. I know I could have the kind of life you describe, Dora. But I'd never be able to enjoy it. Not really. I'd always have the nagging feeling that I'd betrayed myself. I can't walk away. I have to finish this. Quil's story is, kind of, my story too.'

'You'll die, you know,' said Dora, sadly.

'Probably,' agreed Jana. 'But I've done it twice now. It ain't so bad.'

Dora nodded her understanding. 'Then I'm coming with you.'

'You don't have to do that.'

'I know.'

Jana reached out her hand to Dora, who took it. She squeezed it tightly, feeling the warmth of her friend, and felt a flutter of butterflies in her stomach as it occurred to her, not for the first time, that maybe Dora could be more than a friend. But she dismissed the thought. If we survive, she told herself. Maybe then we'll see.

'And Kaz?' asked Jana.

Dora shook her head. 'I don't know,' she said. 'He's unstable right now. He needs to grieve. If we try to involve him in any kind of plan to take down Quil—'

'And my mother.'

Dora cocked her head in surprise at Jana's mission creep, then nodded. 'And your mother,' she agreed. 'He'd get himself killed. And us too, most likely.'

Jana knew Dora was right. 'I'll talk to him,' she said, giving Jana's hand a final squeeze before releasing it and standing to leave.

'Do you have any kind of plan?' asked Dora as Jana pushed open the door.

Jana stopped and looked back over her shoulder.

'Of course not,' she said.

She found Kaz outside, walking as quickly and angrily as he could manage – which was in fact a kind of determined, hunch-shouldered shuffle – in the gardens that surrounded the clinic. Her arthritic joints made it hard to catch up with him, but she eventually managed to pull level and fall into step alongside him.

He did not acknowledge her presence.

'I agree with you,' she said. 'We need to stop them. Both of them, my clone and my mother.'

Kaz shuffled on for a while before finally replying, 'Good.'

'But we have to get better first,' said Jana. She steeled herself for his reply before she added, 'In body and mind.'

'What does that mean?'

'It means, Kaz, that you're a mess, and not just physically. You've been through a terrible ordeal and you need time to work it out. Heal properly.'

'Screw that,' growled Kaz. 'Kill first, deal later.'

Jana put a hand on his arm and gently drew him to a halt. It took him a minute of standing motionless before he would meet her gaze, and when he did his hollow, broken gaze made her heart ache for him.

'Listen,' she said softly. 'I know I was pretty hard on you before, when I accused you of running away as soon as things got tough. I was being selfish, and I'm sorry. I should have seen the effect all this was having on you. You *should* run away. Take some time for yourself, recuperate. Let the clinic fix you up, then step away for as long as it takes to get your head straight. You won't be delaying us – you can jump back to us the second after you leave. Quil isn't going anywhere.'

Kaz shook his head. 'No. As soon as I can walk properly, I'm going after her, with or without you.'

Jana clenched her jaw, biting back her frustration at his self-destructive pig-headedness.

'If you go after her in this state, you'll only end up getting yourself killed.'

'Then come with me,' he pleaded.

'Of course we will. We're your friends, we wouldn't abandon you. But you'd get us killed too. You're no use to us like this.'

Kaz broke her gaze and stared at his feet. Jana silently willed him to give in.

'OK,' he whispered, his spirit seemingly broken. 'We get ourselves fixed up here, and I'll go away and get myself together. But when I come back, we hunt Quil down and finish this.'

Jana reached out and held his hand.

'Deal,' she said, awash with relief. With Kaz on form, they stood a much better chance of surviving.

'Now we just need a plan,' he replied ruefully.

'We need more intelligence first,' said Jana. 'If only we knew what Quil and Sweetclover were up to.'

Io Scientific,
22 August 2014, 3:50 P.M.

Henry Sweetclover paced the floor outside the doctor's lab, adrenalised and scared. He had wanted to stay while the doctor conducted his examination of Quil, but he had told him to relax, go grab a coffee; she was fine and having him hovering with a face like <u>that</u> wasn't going to help.

He told himself over and over again that the doctor was right, that whatever had happened to his wife in the future hadn't harmed her. The opposite, in fact. She seemed invigorated and oddly youthful, her face smoother, her body rounder and more supple. Once the initial confusion had passed, she had seemed clear-headed and cogent.

That still did not alter the fact that something inexplicable had happened to her. If he were of a more religious bent he would have sought a spiritual explanation for what it was – she had, after all, been literally transformed into a pillar of fire and what or who could do such a thing but the Lord Almighty? But he had seen too much and travelled too far to fall back into superstition at this stage. His wife had assured him that there was a scientific explanation for what had occurred; they just needed to work it out. And when it came to such matters, Henry had long since accepted his basic uselessness.

During the years of Quil's recuperation in the seventeenth century, she had sometimes tried to explain the details of her predicament, talking to him of quantum physics, higher mathematics and the like. These discussions had always left him feeling confused and slightly ashamed at his inability to comprehend her. He could grasp the basic thrust of time travel and its wider implications, but only by thinking of it as witchcraft. His wife laughed and swore to him that it was not magic, it was science, but apart from not needing to make compact with the devil in order to gain her powers, the end result seemed basically the same to him. His incredible wife could break the laws of nature, and the how was less important to him than the fact of it.

Upon setting up home in the twenty-first century, he had attempted a more formal education, hiring a series of tutors to school him in history, mathematics and the sciences. He had done well enough, had passed the same examinations as children of this time period, but he had not excelled, and the higher levels of study left him cotton-headed and confused. The day his mathematics tutor had introduced algebra was the day all sense had fled from the world. He was, above all else, a practical man.

So now, when his wife had fallen prey to some strange scientific conundrum, he felt powerless, which made him feel angry.

The door to the lab opened and Quil emerged, dressed now, and looking healthier and more vivacious than he had ever known her. Was it possible that she had been made younger?

Seeing the confusion and frustration on his face, Quil laughed and stepped up to him, planting a kiss on his lips and then smiling up at him with the same indulgence one bestows upon a pet. He felt uneasy.

'What did the doctor say?'

Quil linked her arm through his and led him away from the lab. 'He said I've got the face of an angel and a body made for sin, you lucky, lucky man.'

'Quil . . .'

'All right,' she said, rolling her eyes. 'He can find no evidence of the damage done to me all those years ago. It is as if I was never caught in the timebomb's blast, never blown up on that boat, never forced to spend all those years healing in your undercroft. My body, it seems, is that of a much younger woman. My face is my own again, not the reconstructed version I had come to accept, but the original, unblemished.'

He looked down at her as she fluttered her eyelashes at him, flirtatious and amused.

'How?' was the only response he could muster.

Quil shrugged. 'Your guess is as good as mine.'

'I very much doubt that.'

Quil laughed. 'Tell me again what they said. Exactly.'

'They said it was nothing they had done,' he explained. 'They seemed . . . concerned about you. Solicitous. And Jana asked which one you were.'

'Huh,' said Quil, brow furrowed, thoughtful. 'What else?'

'Kaz demanded to know if you had received surgery for the burns on your face. When I confirmed that you had, Jana said that meant you could be "either of them".'

'Either of who, I wonder?'

'Then the man they called Professor said something I could not make out. Something about amalgamation, I think.' Henry shrugged. 'I was not paying them much mind, my love. You were my only concern.'

'And then they asked whether I knew who you were,' said Quil. 'And they only raised their weapons with intent when I said that I did. I wonder . . .'

'What?'

'It would make sense, I suppose,' said Quil, more to herself than to him. She looked up at him and winced. 'I am sorry but I do not think you would understand the science. There is a possibility I had not considered. I think that, for a time, there might have been two of me. One in the future with them, one in the past with you.'

Henry did not even bother to ask how such a thing was possible. He knew she was right – her answer would only confuse him.

'It would explain their concern,' she continued. 'If they had somehow befriended this other version of me. Fooled her into thinking they were her allies. Then, when we arrived, the other version was cancelled out. But no, if that was true then I would be unchanged. We must have fused in some way. Unexpected, but I suppose I should be grateful. It's undone years of damage.'

'All I care about is that you are safe,' said Henry, but Quil was so engrossed in her deductions that she did not acknowledge his comment.

'They said that anybody trying to travel through time beyond the moment of the timebomb's impact would be sucked into their little trap, yes?'

Henry nodded.

'Then we can still continue with my plan,' said Quil, smiling. 'We just travel to a few minutes before and wait for the detonation. We are free to proceed as planned. I worry though.'

'About?'

'If I'm right, if there was another iteration of me in the

future with those kids, I worry about what she might have done.'

'You think this other version of you could have been working against us in some way?'

Quil shrugged. 'I don't know. It's not impossible, I suppose. Who knows what lies they spun this other me. If only I knew what she'd told them.' She shook her head, dismissing her speculations.

'It doesn't matter,' she said. 'She's gone now. Wiped from existence.'

Henry pondered his wife's words, unable to disregard her speculations so easily. The idea that there could have been another version of her, perhaps travelling through time with their enemies, revealing all the secrets of her life, both chilled and intrigued him.

There was so much he did not know about his wife. He wondered what hidden truths her vanished quantum double might have revealed to their enemies . . .

Part Two

Flashback – Hidden truths

2

Brooklyn, America East, 9 September 2128

'I thought the point of this trip was for me to tell you about my life,' said Quil, impatiently.

Jana sighed. 'And as I have explained more than once, there are some facts about mine that I think you need to know first, so please just trust me. Do you remember this?'

'I try not to,' replied Quil, not bothering to hide her annoyance.

The house was large and old. Not Sweetclover Hall old, but it was impressive by American standards and had more history than most. White clapperboard walls clad the exterior over two storeys and small windows poked through the high shingled roof, telling of a spacious attic or third storey. The grass out front was well kept but covered by a thin carpet of autumn leaves, dropped from the oranging boughs of a pair of large oaks that stood at either end of the lawn as if guarding the house.

A driveway ran up one side of the structure to a large

garage. A smart black towncar was parked outside it. Jana could see the chauffeur in the driver's seat, waiting patiently.

The air was crisp with autumn chill and a light rain was falling, but it was not yet winter-cold. Jana enjoyed the freshness of it, even as it reminded her of things she preferred to forget.

'This is where you grew up?' asked Kaz.

'Yes,' replied Jana and Quil simultaneously. *Awkward.* Jana looked across at Quil and saw that she was equally embarrassed and slightly uncomfortable.

'Huh. Well, *she* did,' said Quil. 'I just thought I did.'

'We lived here until I was seven years old,' said Jana. 'And I was happy. We all were, I think. There's a big garden to run around in, a small lake to go boating, my best friend lives four doors down.'

'Katie,' said Quil. 'I . . . you liked her. She was fun.'

'And my parents . . .' Jana trailed off, unwilling to finish the thought. 'What happened today— what *happens* today, changes everything.'

'Someone's coming out,' said Dora.

Jana looked to the front door and saw her mother stepping on to the front step, briefcase in one hand, the other holding her coat tight around herself. She never did like the cold.

'She looks so young,' said Quil, awestruck.

Jana nodded her agreement; this was her mother before the change. Tall and thin, with her hair in a bob and her glasses perched on her long thin nose, Abhilasha Patel was simultaneously gamine and bookish. Her clothes were chic but not showy – tailored and fitting, garments that bespoke professionalism and calm assurance. As Jana watched, her mother turned to kiss her father, Prabal, goodbye. It was a brisk, unsentimental on-the-move kind of kiss, and it did not linger.

Jana craned to look for her younger self, but she was not there to say goodbye to her mother. It was early; she was probably still in bed.

Hurrying away from the front door, face scrunched up in disapproval at the rain, Jana's mother walked quickly to the car and climbed into the back seat before the chauffeur had time to register her approach and step outside to hold the door open. The car pulled out silently and cruised away, heading for the city.

'It's a Sunday but there she goes anyway,' said Jana.

Kaz picked up on her accusatory tone and rolled his eyes. 'Plenty of people have to work weekends, Jana,' he said. 'It doesn't make her a bad parent.'

Jana did not take the bait. 'Dad and I will be out soon,' she said. 'Then we can go in and take a look around.'

They sat in awkward silence for another hour until the door opened again and Jana's father ushered out little Jana. He turned to close the door behind them, then took her hand.

Bundled up against the cold, young Jana was little more than a face peeking out of a coat, but she skipped and smiled and hung off her father's hand, eagerly dragging him after her.

'Off to the market,' said Quil softly.

'He likes to check the produce before he buys it,' added Jana. 'Can't make a good pie with bad fruit.'

'I remember him saying that,' said Quil, but there was little affection in her voice.

The quartet watched until Jana and her father rounded the corner.

'They'll be out for less than an hour,' said Jana as they left the van. They crossed the road and walked down the side of the house. The electronic lock on the garden gate was easily bypassed, and Jana ushered everyone through and closed it behind them.

The garden was large but crowded. While all their neighbours favoured well-kept lawns and carefully tended flowerbeds overseen by armies of gardeners, the Patel garden was wilder and more exciting. Trees of all sorts stood higgledy-piggledy, forming a haphazard kind of orchard. The grass was ankle-high in some places, although paths had been cut through it to form a curving, looping maze between the trees.

Jana pointed out the various types of trees as they walked.

'Cooking apples, eating apples, plums, peaches, pears, cherry, apricot, greengage, pomegranate, pawpaw.' They walked through the orchard and reached a large greenhouse. 'And in there you've got lemon, orange and lime.'

'This is amazing,' said Kaz, smiling. 'This is your dad, right?'

Jana nodded. 'He loved to make things grow and he liked trees because he said they didn't need as much tending as flowers or shrubs,' she said. 'Mom wasn't the only workaholic in the family. I saw more of Dad than Mom, yes, but days like today, when he'd stay home and make time for me, were the exception not the rule.'

'He was kinder,' said Quil. 'At least he was here sometimes.'

Jana did not respond. Instead she said, 'Come on, let's get inside.'

As they walked back up the garden Dora fell into step beside Jana.

'This is a lovely orchard,' she said. 'You are lucky to have grown up in such a place.'

Jana smiled and nodded. A year ago she would have scoffed and replied, 'It isn't the place that's important, it's the people,' but she'd seen enough on her travels through time to know that such thoughts were best kept to herself. No one wanted to hear the sob story of the poor little rich girl, least of all someone who'd grown up with little but servitude to look forward to.

They reached the patio doors, where Dora made short work of the lock and pushed them open, gesturing everyone inside. Jana paused on the threshold and turned when she realised Quil was not beside her. Her older clone was standing in the grass staring up at the plum tree, lost in thought as she contemplated the heavy boughs, weighed down by fruit ripe for harvest. She reached up, pulled a heavy purple plum from the tree and bit into it with relish, closing her eyes in ecstasy as the juice dripped off her chin.

Jana wondered how much Quil really remembered about this day.

'Stop lollygagging,' she said, half irritated, half indulgent.

Quil looked around, startled by Jana's nagging, and for a second Jana caught the irritated, imperious look of a woman unused to being spoken to in such a manner. Jana reminded herself that despite everything they had in common, for all that this was not the poisoned, insane version of Quil who had caused her so much grief, this was still a woman who had waged war across the solar system. It was probably best to keep that at the forefront of her mind.

'You should try one,' said Quil coldly as she walked past Jana and into the house, tossing her a plum as she did so.

Jana dropped it as if it were a hot coal and followed her inside.

The kitchen was spacious and well appointed, and Kaz was eyeing the coffee maker greedily when Jana entered.

'We leave no trace,' she said firmly, causing him to pout

resentfully. 'Put one camera there' – she indicated a shelf of cookbooks – 'and another there.' She pointed to a dresser with a fancy wooden top, the curlicues of which would hide the lens.

Dora rummaged in her bag, removed the first camera and got to work.

Quil hovered impatiently by the interior door. 'Are you ready to explain why you brought us here yet?' she asked.

Jana shook her head. 'You have to wait and see it. We place the cameras, then head back to the van. We can watch from there.'

'Don't we get the grand tour?' said Kaz.

'I said—' began Jana, but Quil had already opened the interior door and was ushering Kaz through it.

'Dammit, Quil,' muttered Jana, but her older alternate self silenced her with a look. Sighing her resignation, Jana decided to follow.

'We don't have that much time,' she offered lamely as she did so. 'They'll be back in about half an hour.'

Jana had not wanted to venture any further into the house than necessary. These were memories she did not want to dredge up. She was here out of necessity only, and wanted to minimise the experience as much as possible.

'It is different for me,' said Quil, guessing Jana's thoughts as they walked to their father's office. 'You have actually been here. For me, this house is a phantom memory. I recall everything about it intimately, from the height marks on the study wall that chart my growth, to the creaky floorboard on the landing. But I have never set foot in here before. It's like walking through a dream. I have your memories in my head but there is something missing from them, some sense of it, the muscle memory of walking up the stairs perhaps. It's in my mind, but not my body. It's hard to express.'

Jana thought she'd done a pretty good job of expressing it. In fact, she knew exactly what Quil meant, but she didn't say so. She did not want to dull the surprise of what Quil would shortly be seeing.

Quil led them into the large ground-floor room their father had used as a library and workplace. A handsome wooden desk and chair sat by bay windows looking out into the garden. The walls were lined with fitted oak bookcases, heavy with texts on legal and financial history, case precedents and textbooks. It was a warm room of earth tones, leather and wood. Jana felt instantly safe in here.

'Your father is a lawyer?' asked Kaz, browsing the books.

'Professor,' said Quil. Jana detected a hint of pride in her voice, which surprised her. It seemed to surprise Quil too, because she darted a quick glance at Jana after she spoke and shook her head slightly, as if in self-reproach.

'He specialises in scientific legislation,' explained Jana. 'Mostly medical ethics and copyright issues.'

'Much good it did him,' muttered Quil darkly. Jana flashed her a quizzical look.

'You'll see,' was all the answer she got.

'What about your mother?' asked Dora; she was just coming in the door, having placed the cameras.

Quil wordlessly led them across the hall to their mother's home office, which could not have been more different. Sparsely furnished and functional, it was an austere space of clean lines and order. The furniture was steel and glass, square and simple. There was only one shelf, and that held paper copies of books to which Jana's mother had contributed.

'So your parents are the opposites-attract types, huh,' said Kaz.

'Yeah, and how well does that ever work out?' replied Quil caustically.

Jana winced at that, remembering the awkward distance between Kaz's military father and journalist mother. But of course this version of Quil knew nothing about them.

'Your mother is a lawyer also?' asked Dora, staring at the certificates framed on the wall.

'Only as a means to an end,' explained Jana. 'Her ambitions were always political. She used to say there were only two ways to the White House—'

'Profiteering or professional arguing,' finished Quil.

'And she always did love an argument,' said Jana, scowling as she turned and left the room. She had never liked it in there.

'So your bedroom must be up here then?' said Kaz, enthusiastically bounding up the stairs. Jana knew he was delighting in winding her up, and forced herself not to rise to it.

'What dark delights lurk in the bedchamber of little Jana?' whispered Dora as she climbed the stairs alongside her, smiling as she joined in the fun.

The landing was long and wide, with five rooms leading off it, but it wasn't hard to spot Jana's door.

'Flowers. And. Ponies,' said Kaz in open-mouthed astonishment as he saw the bright pictures papered over the bedroom door of six-year-old Jana.

'Not ponies, Kaz,' said Dora, looking closer at the door and admonishing him with obvious glee. 'I think you'll find they're unicorns!'

'I was six!' Jana shot back at her giggling friends.

As Kaz and Dora pushed the door open and stepped inside, Jana turned to look at Quil, who was being very quiet. Quil stood beside her, staring at the bedroom door, her face white, her eyes wide and brimming with tears. Jana was taken aback by such a display of emotion and instinctively reached out to take her hand, only retracting her arm when sparks arced between their fingers.

'It's so *normal*,' said Quil softly. 'I remember it, of course. But I was never here. The first room I could really call my own was a squalid little storage cupboard on a mining asteroid. That's what's real. Not this. This is somebody else's life, not mine. Never mine.'

So saying, she turned and walked back down the stairs. Jana wanted to follow her, to explain why they were here. But, she reminded herself, she had decided to play this a particular way and she was still sure it was the right thing to do. So she let her older clone go. She would understand soon enough.

Kaz appeared in the doorway to her bedroom holding a Barbie doll in a billowing pink ball gown, pointing to it, his face a mask of joyful reproach.

Jana decided to hit him.

Twenty minutes later, having forcefully ejected Kaz and Dora from her bedroom – and made them put all her dolls back exactly where they'd found them – Jana was sitting in the back of the van they had parked across the street from her house. Dora had provided it that morning, greeting Jana's questions as to its provenance with a small, crisp shake of the head.

Equipped with all manner of surveillance technology as it was, it was a tight fit for all four of them, but they crowded around the monitors, watching the feed from the cameras Dora had placed in the garden and kitchen.

There was still no sign of her father or her younger self,

but she knew they'd be home shortly. The details of this morning were indelible in her memory.

'I never figured you for a Barbie girl,' teased Kaz. He was proving tiresomely unable to reconcile the young girl whose room he had ransacked with the glowering young woman sitting across from him.

Jana flashed a glance at Quil, hoping for solidarity, but she was lost in her own thoughts, distant and unresponsive.

'My mom was very trad,' said Jana, making a show of being patient through gritted teeth. 'She liked girls to be . . . girly. Like, really really girly. And I was six, and it made me happy to play with dolls, so shut up or I'll pop off and visit the bedroom of your six-year-old self, see how you like it when the shoe's on the other foot.'

'I'm thinking action figures,' said Dora, considering Kaz with obvious amusement.

'And stuffed animals,' said Jana. 'Lots and lots of stuffed animals.'

'OK, OK, point taken,' said Kaz, smiling but knowing he was beaten. 'Shutting up now.'

'Here they are,' said Quil, cutting through the merriment of the three teenagers, coldly impatient. 'Now what is it you brought me to this time to see?'

Jana took a deep breath and steadied herself. This was going to be hard to watch.

'As you can see, it's raining today,' she began. 'Not heavily, but enough that I'm wearing my rainboots.'

Six-year-old Jana was skipping alongside her father as he walked up the side of the house and entered the kitchen, carrying a bag of groceries, oblivious to the cold and damp.

As her father began unloading the groceries onto the kitchen table, young Jana sat and began to take off her boots.

'Leave them on, sweetheart,' he said. 'We might as well get all the wet jobs out of the way.'

Young Jana looked up smiling. 'Oh, are we going to do the plum tree?'

Her father nodded.

'Then can we make jam?'

Again, he nodded. 'And cobbler and pie and muffins!'

Jana clapped in glee.

'I used to love cooking with him,' said Jana, watching her younger self's joy with an ache in her heart. 'He didn't get much time to spend with me, but when he did, it was so precious. We used to spend afternoons making cakes and bread, jams and preserves.'

'It's the time I remember being most happy,' said Quil. 'It was the hardest lie for me to let go of.'

'Me too,' said Jana, unthinkingly. She sensed that Quil looked at her sharply after she said that, but she did not meet her gaze.

'Plums, of course,' whispered Dora. 'On Mars. That's why she poisoned them.'

Quil nodded. 'Yes,' she replied. 'She knew I'd eat them first.'

'The kitchen floor,' Jana continued, 'is marble tiling. Very expensive. Very beautiful. And very slippery.'

Jana knew she was conjuring a sense of foreboding in the van, that all trace of the merriment that had reigned only moments ago was gone.

They sat in silence watching young Jana and her father in the garden. He stood on a stepladder, picking the plums and passing them down to her so she could collect them in a bucket.

She remembered the next moments so vividly, she couldn't bring herself to look at the screen. She closed her eyes as young Jana turned and ran inside, carrying the first full bucket with both hands, struggling to carry the weight of all that fruit.

She remembered pulling off her boots and kicking them behind her on the floor, discarded and forgotten in her excitement to cut open the first plum of the year, scoop out the stone and bite into the soft flesh.

She remembered straining to reach the sharp knife, the one her dad always told her not to touch, and the thrill of triumph as she grasped it in her cold, damp fingers.

She remembered turning towards the bucket on the floor, stepping backwards as she did so, her foot landing on the discarded boot, which skidded out from under her, slippery on the slick wet floor.

She remembered falling awkwardly, the knife still in her hand. She remembered that she did not realise for a few moments that she had stabbed herself – the pain in her teeth from the crack of her chin on the floor was sharper and more immediate. But then she remembered trying to cry out and finding that no breath would come, the room blurring, the stickiness of her fingers, still clasped around the knife handle . . .

'Oh God,' breathed Dora behind her.

Then the cries of alarm from her father. The shouts for help. The frantic call for medical assistance. The ambulance that came so very quickly but was too late nonetheless.

The siren and then the silence.

'And that,' said Jana, finally, 'is how Yojana Patel – the original, natural-born daughter of Abhilasha and Prabal – died.'

Jana felt Quil grasp her arm tightly, ignoring the sparks, digging her fingernails in, oblivious.

'You mean . . .'

Jana looked up and met her gaze at last. 'I'm no more Yojana Patel than you are, Quil,' she said, aware that there were tears streaming down her cheeks. 'I'm a clone too. We're both of us just echoes of that poor little girl.'

Jana stirred sugar into her coffee as she prepared to answer the barrage of questions.

'When did you know?' asked Quil.

'That I wasn't like other girls?' replied Jana, surprising herself with sarcasm. 'I developed a huge crush on Jeanette Gonzalez when I was thirteen and I never looked back.'

Nobody laughed or scoffed. Jana looked up and saw three faces full of sympathetic curiosity.

'Sorry,' she said softly. 'I've never told anyone before. It's not easy.'

'We understand,' said Kaz.

'No, *I* understand,' said Quil, turning on Kaz with unexpected venom. 'You just think you do. But you really, really don't.'

'Don't do that,' said Jana to Quil, firmly. 'These are my friends. If I'm honest, they're the first real friends I've ever had.'

'You'll learn,' said Quil bitterly.

'What's that supposed to mean?' asked Dora.

'It means that deep down you don't think we're real people,' spat Quil, years of resentment bubbling up. 'Fakes, copies. God, Jana, you even said it yourself – we're echoes. I've never met a womb-born who didn't think the Godless were an abomination, and here you are parroting their prejudice.'

'Oh give me a break,' said Jana. 'I'm not part of your war, Quil. And you'll have time to tell us your story so we can understand exactly why you are . . . like you are. But I'm not you, I'm not Godless. I'm just Jana. And I have friends now, so back off.'

The bar was not busy, but there was enough hubbub to swallow the slightly raised voices coming from their table as they sat contemplating their drinks. Jana and Kaz nursed black coffees, Dora a green tea, and Quil a double bourbon. It had been Kaz's idea to seek out this place, and he seemed comfortable here in a way that reminded Jana of how relaxed he'd been in the bar on Mars before everything went to hell there. After witnessing Yojana's death, they had not travelled in time, but had crossed into Manhattan and wandered for a while before Kaz had pulled them in here. Nobody had said much of anything until their drinks had arrived.

'When did you know?' repeated Quil, neither proffering an apology nor softening her tone.

'I knew something was wrong immediately,' replied Jana. 'I woke in the hospital two months later. Private clinic, flowers and cards and toys from well-wishers and extended family. The doctors told me I'd been in a coma but that I'd made a miraculous recovery.'

'So what tipped you off?' asked Kaz.

Jana struggled to articulate it. 'You've got to remember, I was six years old.'

'You were a month old at most. Use your proper birthday, have some pride,' said Quil.

'Again – not part of your movement, thank you very much,' said Jana, beginning to get properly angry at Quil's strident tone.

She took a gulp of coffee and gathered her thoughts.

'They chipped Yojana very young,' she continued. 'Three, I think. And they paid for the deluxe service, full backups. So when she died they had all her memories in storage, and ready in case of emergencies. When I woke up in the clinic, they had filled my brain with her life experiences. I remembered everything she did. As far as I was concerned, I was Yojana Patel, six years old, waking up after an accident. I didn't know it was my first real day of life.

'But everything was slightly wrong. My muscles felt withered, I felt awkward and uncoordinated. My right kneecap kept popping out for weeks. The doctors told me it was normal after two months of complete bed rest for the body to have lost muscle tone, and I didn't argue – I was six, after all. But it was like I had to relearn how to use my body, like it was *almost* right, but there were tiny recalibrations my brain had to make. I didn't question the explanation I was given, not consciously. But I felt like . . . like a passenger in somebody else's vehicle.

'And that was nothing compared to my parents. They were weird as hell from the moment I woke up. Dad just couldn't meet my eye. I didn't understand why, but . . . he used to be so affectionate. Lots of cuddles and kisses and holding my hand. But now it was like he couldn't come near me. At the time I thought it was my fault. Of course I did, I mean, I was just a kid. For years I thought he blamed me for the accident with the knife and that he was punishing me for disobeying him. Nothing I've ever gone through, or could ever go through, was as painful as the sudden loss of his love.

'Now I understand that I didn't lose anything, because I never had it in the first place. I think it was guilt, really. And bereavement. He was mourning his daughter and here I was, some imitation, like a ghost haunting the house reminding him that his little girl died on his watch. It must have been awful for him.'

Quil scoffed. 'You are the victim here, Jana, not him. Don't make excuses for him.'

'God DAMN it, Quil, will you shut up and let me talk?' shouted Jana, her anger finally besting her control. 'Not everything is black and white, you know? It's not always victim and oppressor. Sometimes it's just messed-up people trying their best but screwing it up. He was not a bad man. He held his daughter as she died, for God's sake. Have some compassion.'

Quil sneered but fell silent.

'And your mother?' asked Dora.

'She was different too,' continued Jana after another sip of coffee. 'But in a different way. She'd never been what you'd call motherly. She was always focused on her work, she didn't really spend much time with me. She was nice enough, but it was a succession of nannies that really raised me, raised Yojana, until the accident. After that, though, Mom was more, how can I say it? Proprietorial. She bossed me about more, barked orders at me like I was a servant. I was expected to behave a certain way, to meet all her expectations and requirements. She'd never been like that before.'

'Because that's what you were,' said Quil, moderating her tone with a touch of sympathy. 'You weren't her daughter. You were a possession, bought and paid for. And just like any *thing*, you had to perform to spec.'

'What I don't understand is why,' said Kaz. 'Why create a clone? Why not just bury their daughter and move on?'

Jana shrugged. 'I've wondered that for years. Guilt? A refusal to let go? I don't really know. Maybe it was just that they had the money and the connections and did it in a daze. Maybe they thought they were really bringing her back. Whatever the reason, I think it was my mother's idea. I don't think she gave my dad much choice. He was never comfortable with me, but she came to see me, I think, as a tool. Something she could use to paint the picture of a perfect little family, help her create a narrative that supported her political ambitions. I became a prop in a performance.'

'I'll tell you what I think,' said Quil. 'I think revealing that her child had died would have shown weakness. She thought nobody would trust her with political office if she couldn't even keep her daughter alive.'

'Wow,' said Jana. 'You really think she's a monster, don't you?'

'You'll see,' Quil said.

'Anyway,' said Jana, picking up the threads of her story. 'From my perspective, my life changed the day I fell on the knife. My parents pulled away, started treating me differently. My body felt like it wasn't really my own, and didn't for years. And then there were the dreams.'

Quil looked up at her sharply and then nodded, understanding. 'You didn't have any,' she said.

Jana nodded. 'Not a single one. I can remember what dreams are like, I can even remember a few specific ones, but they weren't mine, they were Yojana's. It took a long time for me to notice the absence, but I felt it, I think, for a long time before that. And it was when I was thirteen, flicking through the channels on the net, and I stumbled across a piece about cloning and it mentioned that they don't dream. And I just knew. Instantly. Everything suddenly made sense.'

'I can't imagine what that must have been like,' said Kaz.

'I can,' said Quil, fully sympathetic now.

'You'll get your turn, this is my story,' said Jana, determined to finish what she'd started and tell her truth wholly and completely for the first time. It was almost as if she was feeling physically lighter the more she revealed.

'Of course,' said Quil.

'What did you do?' asked Dora. 'Did you confront them?'

Jana shook her head. 'No. Never did, never have. I just started ignoring them. Stopped doing as I was told. I still went to school, I didn't want to get sent away to a boarding school or something, but I couldn't be bothered studying. I didn't see the point of any of it. I wasn't real, you see? Not a person at all. So why pretend to be one? I'd not found it easy to make friends after my accident, birth, whatever. But now I just started looking at people as experiments, toys, things I could manipulate. I wasn't like them, wasn't one of them. I decided I was better. Smarter. Superior.'

Jana turned to Quil. 'I bet you can empathise with that.'

Quil smiled and nodded.

'I just treated everything as a game,' said Jana. 'School, family, relationships. I toyed with them.'

'Sounds like you were depressed or dissociated or something like that,' said Kaz.

'You think?' said Jana, rolling her eyes.

'How did your parents respond?' asked Dora.

'Dad was hardly ever around by this point. He'd got a professorship across the country and he just kind of moved out. He still lived with us, officially, but I hardly ever saw him. With every year the sight of me just got more painful for him. And I think he resented my mom for having me made in the first place. He just couldn't take it any more.'

'And Mother?' asked Quil.

'Mom cracked down,' said Jana. 'Rules, curfews, you name it. I ignored them all. Eventually she hired security guards to keep an eye on me, follow me around. I kind of enjoyed that, it added to the fun. It was a laugh finding new ways to give them the slip, humiliate them, make them feel useless. Which they were.

'But the big break-up came when she found out I liked girls. One of the lunkhead security guys caught me making out with Jeanette and told Mom. Wow, she was incandescent. I couldn't figure it. I mean, it's not really a big deal. I know it is in your time, Kaz, in some places anyway, but in my time it's just not a thing. But I soon worked out what it was that really got to her.'

'She thought she'd been sold faulty merchandise,' said Quil coldly.

'That's what I reckon,' agreed Jana. 'I didn't speak to her again after the fight. It was only a few days later when evil twin Quil sicced her goons on me and I jumped off a roof to escape them. And Mom. And all of it. Just . . . all of it.'

'And you met us,' said Dora, smiling kindly.

'And I met you losers,' agreed Jana, smiling.

A waiter came to take their cups and glasses, so they ordered another round and sat in silence as it was prepared and brought to their table. Jana took a big sip of her second coffee and waited for an onslaught of further questions, but they didn't come. As Jana sat looking at her two friends, with whom she'd been through so much, she realised something surprising – her story hadn't changed their view of her at all. They still accepted her for who she was. Which made her feel more herself than anything that had ever happened to her.

When Kaz resumed the conversation by firing questions at Quil instead, it almost made Jana tear up. She wanted to hug him to death.

'So let me get this straight in my head,' he said, eyeing Quil suspiciously. 'Yojana dies, aged six. Your parents—'

'They aren't our parents,' said Quil. 'The individuals from whom we are cloned are our progenitors. But we have no parents.'

'OK, so what do we call them?'

'Parents,' said Jana, impatient with Quil's complicated, politicised linguistic rules.

Quil took a deep breath and continued, not rising to the provocation. 'All right, for the sake of this story, our parents.' But she made a face of disgust as she said the word, as if it tasted sour in her mouth.

'Right,' continued Kaz. 'So your parents commission a clone of Yojana, pop her memories in and pretend she never died. That's you, Jana. I'm guessing this would have needed a lot of money and contacts, because, I hesitate to ask this, but what happened to Yojana's body? There wasn't a funeral, and the doctors who attended her on the day she died must have been paid off.'

Jana looked at Quil, but she shrugged. 'No idea,' she said.

'Then they had to find and pay someone to grow you, Jana,' Kaz went on. 'And after all that effort to preserve their family, they can't cope. Your dad basically moves out, your mum wants even less to do with you than she did when you were alive.' Kaz paused. 'Which you weren't, of course. Man, it's hard to talk about this stuff, isn't it?'

'It requires new terminology,' agreed Quil pointedly. 'As I've been trying to tell you. *We* call the life you remember, but did not live, your ghost life.'

'Right. So things get so bad that you actually seem kind of pleased when you're given an excuse to jump off a roof,' continued Kaz.

'Not pleased, exactly,' said Jana. 'More like relieved.'

'And then, after you've disappeared – the clone they couldn't live with, and that your mum thought was faulty – they go and do it all again? Cover up your disappearance, commission another clone? That's nuts.'

'But by that point the stakes were even higher,' said Quil. 'When Jana took a swan dive, the mother of our progenitor was already being tipped as a future president. Scandal was the last thing she needed. Remember, as far as she was concerned Jana had just run away. *There was no body.* She was a tearaway, an embarrassment, an aberration.'

'Thanks,' said Jana drily.

'She saw an opportunity to fix the mistakes they'd made when they created Jana,' explained Quil. 'I'm not just another clone of Yojana, with her and Jana's memories in my head. I was *engineered* to be the perfect politician's daughter.'

'We've compared notes, and our memories aren't the same,' explained Jana.

'I've no recollection of the accident that killed Yojana,' said Quil. 'My ghost life was happy, warm, loving. In my simulacra, I never rebelled, never realised I was a clone, never jumped off a roof.'

'Simulacra?' asked Kaz.

'It's our word for the memories that are preloaded when a clone is created,' explained Quil. 'They are the closest thing the Godless have to dreams: stories in our minds that feel real but never actually happened.'

'So when you woke for the first time,' said Dora, 'in your head you believed you were a seventeen-year-old girl who'd lived a stable, happy life with loving parents.'

'Exactly,' said Quil. 'From my perspective, I went to sleep in my nice warm bed, safe in the bosom of my family, and woke up naked, in a bucket full of bodies, six weeks later, halfway around the world.'

'Oh, and you're straight!' said Kaz, eyes widening as he realised. 'The other version of you is in love with Sweetclover. You're not bisexual, right, Jana? You told me you were gay, not bi.'

'Yup, girls only,' confirmed Jana.

Kaz looked at Quil and Jana, horrified. 'Your mum had you *fixed*,' he said, aghast.

'It seems that way,' said Quil. 'I was surprised when Jana told me she was gay. That is certainly not part of my design.'

'I'm a little bit angry about that,' said Jana as calmly as she could, mentally patting herself on the back for her admirable self-control.

'But none of this makes sense,' countered Dora. 'If your mum thought Jana had simply run away, having another clone made would be really risky. Jana could have turned up again at any point and blown the whole thing.'

'Maybe that's why she had second thoughts,' offered Kaz. 'Had Quil grown in secret and then, at the last minute, changed her mind and had her, um, thrown away.'

'Perhaps,' conceded Quil, but she didn't sound convinced. 'It's one of the questions I mean to ask her when I get the chance.'

'That must be the reason the version of you we met in 2014 was so keen to get her hands on my chip,' added Jana. 'I think she wanted to compare her memories with mine, to see how much of her simulacra was real and how much was an invention.'

Jana was keeping her fingers crossed. If this trip down memory lane worked, if telling her all these things now changed her actions in the future, the woman sitting opposite her would never travel back in time and become the obsessed monster they had encountered. This was the crux of their plan – to educate this Quil out of becoming their enemy and change the timeline. She wondered – had they already done enough?

'We're missing something,' said Dora, shaking her head, unsatisfied. 'Your mother's actions after Jana's disappearance do not make sense. There's some fact we're not in possession of.'

Everybody nodded in agreement, but nobody offered any possible explanations.

'There is one time and place we can find some answers,' offered Jana, holding out her hands to her companions.

3
New York, America East, 2141 – the day Jana jumped

'You made a hell of a mess, Dora,' said Jana as she wincingly rifled through the blood-soaked pockets of a dead man.

'No more than they would have, if I hadn't got here in time,' replied Dora, sorting through the pocket lint of a second corpse. 'Only it would be you lying here in pieces, not these three.'

'Me too, don't forget,' said Kaz, who was rummaging in the pockets of the third.

'Can we please hurry?' said Quil, who stood guard at the door that led on to the skyscraper roof. 'In the last ten minutes there's been an awful lot of commotion on this roof, somebody's bound to have noticed.'

Jana glanced up at the windows of the skytowns that loomed over them and wondered if she was right. This city could be incredibly myopic when it wanted to be. She wasn't sure that, even though it was so comprehensively overlooked, the flashes of time travel and slaughter that had occurred here had attracted any attention at all.

It had only been a few minutes since her younger self had

burst on to this roof, fleeing the three mysterious men who'd attempted to drag her off the street as she'd played hooky from school. Now their bodies lay in various states of dismemberment, victims of Dora's sword. A head lay to her right, an arm to her left. And behind her, she knew, was a puddle of blood that she had left as she bled out, slumped against the lip of the roof, stabbed by the mad version of Quil they'd met back in the seventeenth century.

'Got something,' said Kaz, holding up a wallet and pulling it open. He rummaged inside and pulled out an ID card.

'Me too,' said Jana, feeling her fingers brushing a hard plastic edge in the pocket she was gingerly exploring.

'This guy's clean,' said Dora, shaking her head and wiping the blood off her hands on the small patch of unsoaked clothing the corpse had to offer.

The group congregated by the door and examined their finds. Dora slotted the first card into a reader.

'Red hair is Ron McKenzie, twenty-three, no job listed, but I've got an address out of town, in the favelas like you suspected, Jana.'

She popped the card out and inserted the second.

'Shorty is Abdul Dulabh, nineteen, also no job, from the same building in the favelas.'

'Tells us nothing,' Jana cursed. 'Street kids. It's the leader who interests me.' She turned back to indicate the remains of the tall, thin-lipped man who had been in charge of this little kill party.

'I don't think it's a coincidence he had no ID,' said Dora. 'My guess is that he recruited these two punks for muscle. I would bet he was the one who took the commission from Quil.' She stopped and flashed a glance of awkward apology at Quil. 'I mean the other one. The mad one.'

57

'Should we just call her Mad Quil?' said Kaz.

'Do you have to? Makes me sound like an angry porcupine,' said Quil, stone-faced.

It took a moment for Jana to realise Quil had made a joke, and she laughed more out of surprise than amusement.

'He may even have been a professional,' continued Dora. 'At the very least, a connected criminal.'

'So he's the one we need to track, but he's the one we know least about,' said Kaz, shaking his head.

'I can fix that, but you'll need to give me a minute,' said Dora, walking back towards the corpse. As Jana watched, Dora picked up the leader's severed head by the hair and jumped away into time.

'What, um . . . what do we think she's going to do with that, exactly?' asked Kaz, wincing.

A moment later Dora burned back into existence and dropped the head back where she'd found it. She walked back to them, reading from a tablet.

'Vladimir Alkaev,' she read, 'twenty-nine, known member of organised Russian gang, suspected in multiple beatings and murders, never convicted.'

'How did you do that?' asked Jana, both impressed and kind of grossed out.

'His DNA was on record with the police,' said Dora briskly.

'And you, what, turned up there with his head and asked them to run it through the system?' asked Kaz, open-mouthed.

'Something like that,' said Dora with a grin, before turning to Jana and asking 'So now we know who they were, what next?'

'Now we get the hell out of here,' she replied, hearing footsteps clattering up the stairs to the roof.

New York, America East, 2141 – two days before Jana jumped

'I still don't get why we are following this line of enquiry,' said Quil, her voice tinny through the earpiece. 'I thought we were trying to understand the reasons for my creation.'

'We are, Quil, I promise,' said Jana, swerving to avoid a mother who was chasing after a runaway toddler. She kept her eyes firmly fixed on the back of Alkaev, who was making quick progress through the busy Manhattan crowds.

'But all you are doing is seeking evidence that the other version of me tried to have you killed,' protested Quil. 'This is something we already know. At the end of this wild goose chase you will find her or her husband and we will be none the wiser about the real mystery here.'

'Trust me, please,' said Jana. 'I have a hunch about something.'

'We don't have time for this,' muttered Quil.

Jana didn't bother to refute such an absurd complaint.

Dora had fought hard to be the one to follow Alkaev. 'I am highly skilled in such things, and there is no chance that he will recognise my face,' she had argued.

'I can wear a chameleon shroud,' Jana had countered. 'And you can advise me as we go. We can stay in contact.'

'Jana, this is my skill set—'

'But it's my mystery to solve,' Jana had replied firmly, and Dora had gracefully conceded. Dora had been pretty quiet during the pursuit so far, though. The main voice in her ear had been Quil's, moaning about the pointlessness of this exercise.

She was so distracted by the nagging in her ear that Jana momentarily lost track of Alkaev in the crowd. She cursed under her breath and panicked slightly until she picked him out again, ducking off the street into a diner. She followed him inside. It was breakfast time and the diner was busy, a bustling mass of customers lining up for coffee and bagels, while waitresses cut through them bringing eggs and hash browns to the people seated in the booths that lined the long wall. Alkaev made a beeline for a booth and took a seat opposite a woman, of whom Jana could only see the back of a head.

Alkaev was smart; the seat he'd taken was in the farthest corner of the room, allowing him to survey the entire diner. Jana had no choice but to join the line for coffee and try not to make her observation too obvious. A waitress attended Alkaev and his mysterious fellow diner almost immediately. She stood with her back to Jana, who assumed she was taking their orders, but instead the woman paid the waitress and rose to her feet, as did Alkaev. The Russian headed for the door to the street and the woman he had met walked calmly through the back door, into the kitchens. She never once turned around, so Jana could not get a look at her face, and there was no way she could follow her through there without revealing herself.

Jana wanted to run outside and try to find a way to the rear of the building, but she couldn't do so until Alkaev had passed her, otherwise he'd recognise her instantly. The few seconds as he walked towards her felt like an eternity, but just as he drew level with her and Jana prepared to turn and follow him outside, she caught her breath in surprise. The waitress who had been attending their booth had turned around and winked at her.

'Dora!' muttered Jana under her breath. 'I told you to leave this to me!'

Jana saw Dora the waitress's lips move as she replied, 'And as I said, this is what I do best.'

So saying, Dora the waitress vanished through the kitchen door in pursuit of Alkaev's contact.

Jana turned and left the diner, resuming her pursuit of Alkaev. As she passed into the crowd she pressed a button on her watch and the chameleon shroud blurred and snapped into an image of a different person. There was a chance she could have been spotted otherwise and, confident she remained unnoticed, Jana continued to follow her quarry.

'Was it Quil?' she asked.

'No,' replied Dora in her earpiece. 'Late middle age, white, smart suit, perfect hair. This was someone well-to-do and, I'd guess, from this time period.'

Jana felt a sinking feeling in her stomach as she absorbed Dora's description. She did not recognise the woman from it, but just the fact that it wasn't Quil was enough to make her more certain than ever that she was right in her suspicions.

'That just means Mad Me or Sweetclover are using a proxy,' said Quil through the earpiece. 'What does that prove?'

'Dora, did you hear anything they said?' asked Kaz, chiming in.

'No,' came Dora's disembodied voice. 'But she passed him a photograph of Jana, with something written on the back.'

'A photograph?' said Kaz, audibly surprised.

'No data trail that way,' replied Dora.

'So whoever this woman is, she's definitely the one who commissioned my kidnap and decapitation,' said Jana.

'It would appear so,' said Dora. 'You can probably let the Russian go, Jana. We know where he's going. And he'll be dead soon, anyway.'

Jana agreed and stopped dead in the street, letting Alkaev be swallowed by the crowds. 'Don't lose the woman, Dora, whatever you do,' said Kaz. 'She's the key to this.'

'Relax,' replied Dora. 'Meet me back at the hotel.'

Jana heard a soft click as Dora deactivated her comms.

New York, America East, 2141 - eight weeks before Jana jumped

The screen flickered and an image appeared. Sharp, good colour – not the kind of image Jana would expect from a tiny, hideable surveillance camera.

With its square and simple steel and glass furniture, the room was instantly familiar to her. She closed her eyes and took a deep breath to steady herself.

On the screen, her mother, Abhilasha Patel, was pacing, restless and angry. This was her mother as Jana remembered her – a slim, elegant woman in her early forties, with creases around her eyes that spoke of tension, not laughter.

'And these polls are correct? You're sure of it?' she said.

On the second screen, showing the feed from the other camera in her mother's office, Jana could see a man sitting on the couch against the far wall. Elegantly dressed and immaculately groomed, he nonetheless slouched across the corner of the couch, at ease in a way that Jana found oddly threatening.

'No question,' he said, his voice deep and warm. 'We've

got the finest data money can buy, and it all says the same thing. You just don't have the backing of the white middle-class vote, and without it, you can't beat Kotawela. You're neck and neck in all constituencies except the white middle class. He consistently has better numbers there than you do.'

'But why?' said Jana's mother, still pacing, her voice raised in frustration. 'His policies will hurt them even more than mine.'

'Since when has anyone cared about policies?' scoffed the man. 'The optics are better. *Way* better. Family man, beautiful wife, photogenic kids doing well in private school. That stuff always plays well with the conservative vote.'

'I'm supposed to compete with a photo shoot?'

The man shook his head and smiled. 'You're not this stupid,' he said. 'You know how this works. Your marriage is a train wreck. Your kid is a train wreck that's crashed into a plane wreck. And you're on the podium on your own, a woman without visible support who does not – forgive me – exactly radiate warmth. If you can't keep your family together, how are you going to keep what's left of the union together? Plus, he's a businessman, you're a lawyer. Nobody likes lawyers. People think they're smug.'

She stopped pacing and stood looking down at the man, who seemed glibly unintimidated.

'So, what, you think I've gone as far as I can?' she asked angrily. 'Have I topped out? Is this it? Local government? Six months ago *Vanity Fair* pegged me for the White House!'

The man shrugged. 'Six months is a lifetime in politics.'

Abhilasha sat carefully at the opposite end of the long sofa, leaned forward, hands folded in her lap, and asked, 'What can we do to turn it around?'

The man sighed and looked thoughtful. 'I really don't know if you can,' he said, shaking his head.

But Abhilasha was not going to take no for an answer. 'What would it take?' she said, steely and determined.

The man appraised her, biting his lip. 'You'd have to be a different person. You'd have to completely change the narrative of your personal life. You'd need to show some warmth, some weakness even. You need to find a human story, something relatable. You've come this far on steely resolve, fiscal management, law and order – all the good stuff. People will vote for that for mayor or even senator. But for president . . .' He shook his head. 'For president they vote for a person. It's more about gut feeling than it is about policy. Do you seem nice, decent, like them, somebody they want to have a drink with. And you . . . you just don't seem that approachable. If you want to keep climbing the greasy pole, you need a new strategy, a new persona.'

Jana's mother regarded him appraisingly. 'You don't think I could pull that off, do you?'

The man paused a moment before shaking his head. 'Not as you are, no.'

'What does that mean?'

The man sat up and leaned forward too, finally seeming to become properly engaged in the conversation, abandoning his relaxed attitude. Jana realised he'd been building to this – he was going to make a pitch.

'External factors,' he said.

'Explain.'

'Nothing humanises a person like tragedy,' he said, eyes twinkling. 'We need to hit you with something nasty. Knock you down a peg. Give you a chance to show some vulnerability.'

He left off there, allowing the idea time to sink in. Jana

could see her mother considering his words, the realisation of what he was suggesting dawning on her face and giving way to calculation and appraisal. Any normal person would have dismissed the implication out of hand, but she was actually thinking about it.

'Say, a bereavement of some kind?' he said eventually, picking his words with exaggerated care. Jana could tell that he was slightly nervous, taking a risk on proposing something so radical, not completely certain he had judged his audience correctly.

Abhilasha held the man's stare for a long time. Jana felt butterflies in her stomach, certain she knew what she was about to say.

'Such as my husband's?' said her mother, causing Jana to squeal in alarm. That was not what she had been expecting.

The man smiled, relieved to find that he had assessed the conversation correctly.

'That kind of thing, certainly,' he replied, obviously excited by the direction he'd managed to steer the conversation in. 'But in itself, that wouldn't be enough. The kind of strength a person shows after a family member dies is, well, it's commonplace. Ordinary. Admirable but not exactly unusual. You'd need to create a scenario where a loss like that would provide you with a platform to show your nurturing side. A scenario that allows you to show the world what kind of woman – what kind of *mother* – you really are.'

Abhilasha laughed bitterly. 'I'm not a mother at all,' she said. 'Not any more.'

'Let's see what we can do about that, shall we?'

They both fell silent. Jana could see her mother struggling with the enormity of what she was about to do. The man waited patiently, knowing he had her on the hook.

'Draw up scenarios,' she said, almost whispering. 'I want to know my options.'

Jana tried to hold it in but she couldn't help it. She turned and flung open the door of the van and vomited onto the street.

'The woman we saw meeting Alkaev in the cafe is a fixer for this man,' said Dora, gesturing to the screen, which revealed a picture of the man Jana had just witnessed her mother conspiring with. 'His name is Amos Hope, he's a political operator. He *arranges* things.'

'When she becomes president,' added Quil, 'he will be her chief of staff.'

Jana still felt queasy. They had driven away, returning to the hotel suite they had made their base in this time. She sat in the suite now, cradling a mug of coffee still too hot to sip away the taste of vomit at the back of her throat.

Kaz sat to her left, Quil to her right, and Dora sat across from them, talking them through her investigation.

'Hope and your mother hatched a plan to reshape your mother's public image, as you saw. The plan was as simple as it was ruthless. First, they commissioned a second clone of Yojana Patel. The memories she would be given were carefully shaped to produce a young woman perfect for your mother's needs. She would be given happy memories of healthy relationships with her parents, which would make her more compliant, more obedient. This clone – you, Quil – was prepared and ready to go before the attempt was made on Jana's life. The idea was for you to come online immediately after Jana died. A seamless transition.'

'Why behead me?' asked Jana, feeling her gorge rise again.

Dora hesitated, and suddenly couldn't meet Jana's eye.

'Proof,' she said eventually. 'The body was going to be incinerated, the head given to your mother.'

'So it wasn't about the chip?'

'Oh it was,' said Dora, nodding. 'Hope was going to keep it as insurance. Proof of your mother's guilt. Handy to have something like that on a potential president.'

Dora continued. 'At the same time you were being switched, your father was supposed to meet with an unfortunate accident while driving home from work.'

'I told you she is a monster,' said Quil, sadly. Jana was at least grateful that she had the good grace not to take too much satisfaction in being proven right. 'She arranges her husband's tragic early demise and then ensures she will have a sweet, obedient daughter who she can pretend to raise alone. Great narrative. Great struggle. Tons of sympathy. Grieving widow, devoted mom. All the material she needed to convince the electorate that she had a heart. All her image problems gone in a single day. And all it would take was two lives.'

Jana felt Kaz squeeze her leg tightly. She turned and smiled sadly at him, then took a sip of her coffee.

'What went wrong?' she asked.

'You did,' said Dora.

Jana felt a sinking feeling and a sudden twinge of nausea. 'Oh no,' she said softly. 'I jumped.'

Dora nodded.

'You jumped. You vanished. And your mother panicked. Called off the hit on your father. Put you in storage, Quil, in case you could still be useful. And organised a private army of investigators and fixers to find you, Jana.'

Jana slapped her forehead. 'But they couldn't, because I was in 1645.'

'Exactly. Your mother assumed you'd run away, but couldn't

be sure you wouldn't pop up again at any moment. Hard to explain away Quil if you did, so after a couple of months' fruitless searching, she ordered the clone destroyed.'

'And my father?'

New York, America East, 2141 – six weeks after Jana jumped

Jana sat at the foot of her father's single bed and tried to keep her tears at bay.

The room was spartan. A chair, a desk, some books on a shelf. He could have afforded more, much more, but when he had taken up the professorship and moved across the country, he had chosen to live in a small set of rooms on the university campus. Jana wondered if maybe he had been punishing himself.

There was a single photograph in the room – a framed picture of Yojana, aged six, on his desk. Jana wondered how he could bear to have it there.

A wardrobe held a few suits and a couple of pairs of old shoes.

There was a tattered paperback of an old thriller on the bedside cabinet. There was still a bookmark in it. He'd never finished it.

The empty bottle of pills sat beside the book. The empty bottle of vodka sat beside it.

'Did he leave a note?' Jana asked.

Dora, standing in the doorway, shook her head.

Jana surveyed the small room, the tiny collection of belongings, the abandoned clothes, and she couldn't help herself. Her tears came in great, racking sobs as she buried her face in her hands and wept.

'Did I do this?' she cried. 'Did I just abandon him?'

She felt arms encircling her from both sides, and she leaned into them, letting Kaz and Dora hold her steady.

'Not you,' whispered Kaz.

'He killed himself, Jana,' said Dora.

'If he did kill himself as a result of your disappearance, out of some mixture of unresolved guilt about Yojana's death and his failure to look after you, then you can't blame yourself,' came Quil's voice, hard and angry. 'It was our progenitor's mother. She didn't pour the pills down his throat, but this was her just the same. She was the one who caused you to jump off that roof. And let's not forget that even if you hadn't jumped, he was marked for death anyway. This poor bastard was doomed, no matter what.'

Jana looked up to see her clone standing looking down at her, her face a crumpled mixture of sadness and fury.

'This is what she does, Jana. Everything she touches dies.'

Quil held out her hands to them.

'Let me show you.'

4

'I was born in a skip, buried in corpses.'

Quil paused for a moment, to let that sink in.

'How do you think you'd deal with that?' she continued. It was not a rhetorical question.

Jana thought for a moment. 'Scream the house down, I guess.'

'You'd think that, wouldn't you. But in fact you'd be too scared to scream. Too disoriented. You'd go into shock pretty much instantly. Hyperventilating. Scratching and scrabbling your way towards daylight, pushing through the limbs and torsos, slipping and oozing over the cold flesh of lifeless strangers.'

Jana tried not to let her disgust show too obviously on her face.

'I wasn't birthed from a womb,' said Quil. 'Although I'm pretty sure I slipped into sunlight from between someone's legs.'

Jana smiled, humourlessly. 'You've told that story before,' she said, recognising a carefully turned phrase, refined through the telling for maximum shock value. Quil was mining her tale for black humour. Jana respected the impulse; it was exactly what she would do in the circumstances.

Obviously.

'First things first,' said Jana, looking at Quil. 'Let's visit your birthday.'

'Don't need to,' replied Quil, tapping the back of her head. 'I've got it all in here, if you're ready to experience it.'

Jana was not at all sure that she was.

'When you woke up, for the first time, you thought you were me,' she said.

'Kind of. Your memories, and Yojana's, were the template for my simulacra, but don't forget they had been edited. I was a revised version of you.'

'A version that didn't know I was a clone, that had no memory of Yojana's death, and who thought my childhood had been the happiest ever.'

'Yes. And who fancied boys.'

'I'm not sure I want to know what that's like,' said Jana, pulling a face.

Quil said nothing for such a long time that it amounted to saying a whole lot.

'Yeah, OK, hit me,' said Jana eventually, shamed by her reluctance. 'Wait! When you stream your memories into my ENL chip, I'll experience it in real time, so how long are you going to keep me under?'

'Long enough to know what happened,' said Quil. 'And what it felt like.'

Jana squeezed her fists tight. She was lying on a bed in the hotel suite in New York, in 2141. Quil sat at her bedside while Dora and Kaz hovered nervously at the door.

'Are you sure about this, Jana?' asked Kaz.

'Well unless you're going to do it for me . . .?'

Kaz shook his head. He had steadfastly refused to be chipped, saying the whole idea gave him 'the screaming heebie jeebies'. Dora, who had embraced technological enhancements to her eyes and hearing, had also not been chipped. Although she had not entirely ruled it out, she felt the idea of a live stream of data flowing from her mind into cloud servers at all times was 'the kind of security risk Garcia would have had me shot for even considering'.

'Well then,' said Jana. 'Stop hanging around and go do something useful while I walk a mile in Quil's shoes.'

'I was born naked.'

'Nobody likes a smartarse.'

The panic was instant. She couldn't see a thing, could hear only vague muffled sounds, felt naked and slick with some-thing, and ohmygodohmygodohmygod was that a hand on her face?

Jana began kicking and fighting, writhing and hyperventi-lating, sliding and slipping over cold flesh in darkness, her mouth parroting silent screams as she tried to claw her way upwards.

(But it isn't me, thought Jana, experiencing and observing at the same time, sitting at one remove within the body of the clone who would call herself Quil but right now still thought she was Jana. It was like living through a memory of something she'd forgotten. Jana imagined this must be how dreaming felt. She tried to relax her consciousness and go along for the ride, more passenger than spectator, but it felt so strange . . .)

It was hard to tell how long it took to make her way to the surface, but it felt like an eternity.

(Ten seconds, thought Jana.)

Jana *(I need to think of her as Quil)* Quil burst upwards out of whatever weird pit she was in and scrambled across the surface – don't think about the bodies, don't think about the blood, don't think, don't think at all – until she reached the lip of the container and slid awkwardly over the edge. As she fell into space she had just enough presence of mind to realise she had no idea how high she was, but it was not as if she could be any more panicked, so she fell like a stone for another eternity.

(A half second at most.)

She hit a hard, cold surface with her right shoulder and yelled in pain. She rose to her feet and looked around. She was in a large room lit by only the red glow of an exit sign above a pair of fire doors. She turned and saw the container she had struggled out of. It was smaller than she expected; shallower too. It had felt like she was climbing out of the depths of hell, but the lid was only just up to her chin. She must have been at the very bottom. She looked away quickly, not willing to let her mind process the horror of the container's contents.

(So many corpses! Jana had to wonder at the efficiency of a cloning facility that produced so much . . . waste.)

Quil was naked, cold, covered in a foul-smelling stew of fluids leaked from the things in the container.

Where the hell was she? How had she gotten here?

The last thing she remembered was kissing her mom goodbye and leaving for school with her guards. She had been in the car one moment, and the next she had woken up here.

Had she been kidnapped? Why didn't she remember?

(Jana wondered too. What had been their mother's plan? Obviously they would have needed to implant some memory to explain the time loss, but it would have to be something innocuous, less traumatic than a serious accident lest they risk this clone working out her provenance as she had done. Whatever their plan had been, they must have discarded Quil before they'd entirely finished sculpting her memories.)

As Quil walked away from the container, there was a soft click and the lighting came on. The room was a featureless concrete cube and at first she thought it was empty apart from the container. But then she realised that the container sat at the end of a conveyor belt that would, when operational, carry it through a screen of hanging plastic in the far wall.

Quil knew she didn't want to be in a room with a box full of bodies, and she wasn't going to risk the fire doors in case they were alarmed, so she hurried to the thick plastic strips and pushed through into the next chamber.

The conveyor belt led to a flat platform with two hydraulic pumps on each side. There was a chute beyond it with a sign above that read 'Furnace'. The whole sickening process was obvious. The bodies were placed in the container until it was full, then it slid through here and the contents were tipped down the chute to be incinerated.

Quil realised this had been her intended fate – burned to powder like so much garbage.

It was at this moment that she tried to throw up. She fell to her knees retching and heaving, but all that emerged was thin bile. She regained enough presence of mind to wonder why her stomach was so empty. She'd had a full breakfast before leaving the house – how much time had passed since then?

(Good thinking, but it's because you've never eaten so much as a mouthful of food.)

When the nausea had abated, Quil regained her footing and tried to focus her thoughts, to bury the panic and concentrate on getting out of here.

There were no doors in the furnace chute room, and she had no idea where the doors in the other room led, so even if she got lucky and they weren't alarmed, she could be walking right back into the hands of the people who'd done this to her, whatever *this* was.

She had one thing on her side – she thought it unlikely they would inventory the bodies before incinerating them, so no one would be looking for an escapee. If she could remain undetected, she would not be hunted.

Her first priority had to be getting out of this room. She felt a dreadful sinking feeling when she realised there was only one safe route out.

She walked to the edge of the furnace chute and peered down into the darkness below. There was no uprush of hot air, so it was a safe bet the furnace was not currently burning. And there had to be doors on it, to scrape out the ash. So if the fall wasn't too great, there was a better than even chance that this way out of her current predicament would be unalarmed and unmanned.

(Quil had gone beyond panic into the kind of fear that leaves you numb but functional, like a sleepwalker. Jana recognised the mental state well.)

Quil clambered on to the lip of the chute, dangled her legs into the abyss, closed her eyes, crossed her arms and slid down into darkness. The chute was not smooth and it tore a hundred different scratches into her back and buttocks before she slid off it. Another eternal fall.

(Three seconds.)

Quil landed softly in a deep cushion of ash that billowed around her and clogged her mouth, nose and lungs. Repulsed by the mountain of human dust, heaving and writhing as she clambered to her feet and tried to see through the murk to find a door, trying hard not to think what the occasional hard things buried within the ash might be, Quil stumbled into a metal wall. She felt her way around it, past one corner, then another, until finally she found a hatch that – merciful heaven, thank you – swung outwards when she pushed.

She tumbled out in a cloud of ash. She spent the next few minutes heaving, spitting out ash, blowing it out of her nose, scraping it from her ears, trying to claw it off every inch of her skin – but it had stuck to the slime she had been covered in and hardened into a kind of carapace; peeling it off hurt more than leaving it in place.

She was armoured in corpses.

Quil rubbed her eyes until she could see. She was in a service area, a basement room lined with insulated pipes. She could see doors, and these did not have fire bars on them, so she pushed them open slightly and surveyed the corridor beyond. Bland, half lit, it was quiet and deserted. She had a sense that it was night-time, although she had no evidence beyond the eerie quiet.

She crept out the door and along the corridor. Emboldened by the silence, Quil began checking the doors that led off the corridor until she found a small washroom with a shower and metal cabinet that contained grey overalls. Too scared and exhausted to feel delight, Quil listened for ten minutes before feeling confident enough to turn the shower on. After five minutes of waiting, she accepted that there would be no hot water and stepped underneath the freezing torrent anyway, grateful for even that mercy as she rinsed the ash and slime off her.

Shivering, but clean, she stepped from the shower a few minutes later, towelled herself off with one set of overalls, then stepped into another, rolling the legs and sleeves up so she vaguely fitted into it. She was clean, clothed and basically unharmed. The shower, and the attendant rituals of cleanliness, had helped her calm herself. She was still scared, but she felt a little more in control.

She found a staircase leading up into the main building. The door at the top had a glass panel in it that allowed Quil to see into a huge lobby, marble-floored and glass-walled. This was not what she had been expecting. She could see through the glass walls and it was indeed night; a few lights twinkled in the distance, but she was disheartened to realise it was going to be a long walk to any kind of civilisation. The main doors were closed, and there was a glowing keypad beside them with a red light shining on top, indicating that they were locked.

She began to feel the panic rising again; she couldn't see a means of escape. Then she caught a glimpse of movement through the window and stepped back from it as a security guard strolled through the lobby.

(No way!)

The guard stopped and stared at the door she cowered behind, and she felt sure he would see her through the window, but after a moment he turned away.

(Oh my fricking God!)

The guard walked to the front door and swiped a card across the reader. The light turned green and he pushed through the doors and walked outside. Quil watched as he lit a cigarette and walked away from the door, with his back to it. And he just kept walking until he vanished around the side of the building.

(Jana wanted to scream the house down. How the hell could she get out of this simulation? She needed to talk to Quil NOW. Quil needed to know what she'd missed. But Jana was powerless, still locked into the experiences of her clone, and so she forced herself to focus back on the memories she was experiencing. She would be out of here and back to her own life soon enough, she could tell Quil then. But her mind raced with the implications of what she'd seen . . .)

Quil hovered at the top of the staircase trying to decide what to do.

(Run for it, you idiot!)

There was a large part of her that felt crawling into the cellar, finding the darkest corner and settling in for a long cry was the best course of action. But she thought of her mother, how much she loved her, how they spent so much time talking and shopping and just hanging out, how devastated she'd be by her loss . . .

(Really? Wow!)

. . . and she somehow found the strength to push the door open and make a dash for the front door, her bare feet slapping loudly on the cold marble floor. The door swung open and she scanned for the security guard, but there was no sign of him. Reasoning that he must be doing an external circuit of the ground floor, and would probably circle back around any moment, Quil didn't hesitate. She ran as fast as she could down the driveway that lay before her.

The night air was cold but dry, and a half-moon hung above her in a cloudless sky. She did not know where she was, but the stars were so bright she knew she must be some distance from a city. The driveway carried on in a straight line into the darkness, and Quil ran until she felt sure she was no longer visible in the penumbra of light that shone from the glass walls of the building she was fleeing. She stopped and looked back. It was three storeys tall, all white panels and glass fronting. It looked cold and efficient; less office block, more research centre, she thought. That was borne out by the company name emblazoned across the top of the building.

(Oh come on! Are you serious?)

She still struggled to make any sense of what had happened to her, why she was here or how, but she was free, no one was chasing her, and she knew the name of the organisation responsible. All she had to do was find a way to civilisation, and she would be able to bring the police back here and get to the bottom of it.

She turned away again and ran – straight into a chain-link gate that she had missed in the darkness.

Lights snapped on to her left and right, automatically coming to life and zeroing in on the source of the disturbance. She yelped in alarm, and then an actual alarm drowned her out, its plangent whine echoing across the now brightly lit lawns.

The gate that stood before her was locked tight. Feeling that she had no choice, she slipped her right foot into a hole in the gate and began to climb. The metal was cold and sharp, and her feet and hands hurt as she forced herself to climb. A few steps upwards and the alarm cut out. She did not think that was a good sign, so she forced herself to climb faster. Hand over hand, foot over foot, ignore the pain, just climb.

There came a shout from somewhere behind her, and then the sound of boots on tarmac, coming closer.

Quil's hand reached the top of the gate and she hauled herself up until she was bent over the top on her stomach.

'Get down from there,' said a man's voice from below. He didn't even bother to shout, and he sounded more amused than angry. Somehow that made him even scarier.

Quil glanced back over her shoulder and saw two security guards, both armed but neither bringing their weapons to bear. Neither of them were the guard she'd seen earlier.

(Of course not, he's long gone, I reckon.)

Quil lifted her right leg up until it rested on the top of the gate and moved to swing herself over to the other side.

'You do know we can just shoot you through the gate, right?' said one of the guards, laughing.

'Leave me alone!' yelled Quil, crying in fear and desperation.

'No,' said a guard, succinctly. 'Now come down, or we shoot.'

Quil lay, sprawled across the top of the gate, crying at the futility of any action. If she climbed down to the guards, she knew she'd only end up back in their furnace. At least if she made a break for it the guards might miss. It was no choice at all, but even in her fearful state she knew to take the tiny chance of survival over the certainty of death.

'Screw you!' she yelled, and swung herself over to the other side of the gate.

She was facing the guards now, looking down at them through the chain-link as she started to climb down.

She was not surprised when the one who had said no raised his gun. But she was very surprised when he pulled the trigger.

If she had been expecting anything it all it was a loud bang and a bullet in the chest. But instead the gun slowly spat a cloud of flame and smoke from which emerged, ever so slowly, a whirling metal bullet that came towards her at a snail's pace. Time slowed; Quil felt as if she were moving through molasses – the bullet was slow but so was she, there was no way she could avoid it hitting her. Her fingers lost their grip in her panic, and she felt herself toppling backwards, away from the gate, a hollow feeling in her stomach.

Time snapped back into place; the bullet vanished to be replaced by a sharp stinging on her forehead and a deafening crack. And then . . .

. . . Freefall.

Jana snapped back to reality with a jarring yell of alarm and disorientation. She screwed her eyes shut and took a few deep breaths, holding tight to the bed until she was totally certain that reality had reasserted itself sufficiently to withstand interaction.

She opened her eyes and saw Quil, still sitting beside the bed.

'So,' she said. 'Now you can see how—'

'GUYS!' yelled Jana at the top of her lungs. 'GUYS GUYS GUYS! GET IN HERE NOW!'

Quil stopped, wide-eyed in shock at being so rudely interrupted and ignored. Before she could voice an objection, Kaz and Dora burst into the room, he with a gun raised, she with her sword drawn.

Jana sat up in bed excitedly.

'Guys, you are not going to believe what I just saw!' babbled Jana.

Kaz and Dora looked at Quil, who shrugged.

'The facility where you were cloned, the one you were escaping from . . .'

'Yes?'

'Tell them what it was called.'

Quil turned to Kaz and Dora, confused, and said, 'Io Scientific. It's some kind of—'

'No fricking way,' said Kaz, open-mouthed.

'Seriously?' said Dora.

'Way! Seriously!' said Jana.

'So?' asked Quil, exasperated at being interrupted a second time. 'I checked them out, they're just a biotech company. Nothing special about that.'

Jana shook her head vigorously. 'Quite the opposite. That building wasn't the one we went to, it wasn't in Cornwall, but this was definitely the HQ of the same company in your time. Probably in America.'

'You encountered this company in the past?' asked Quil, intrigued.

'Did we ever,' said Kaz.

'Quil,' said Jana, thrilled to be dropping such a juicy piece of explanation. 'It's *your* company. You started it. Future you, the you that we encountered in the past.'

Jana was thrilled beyond words to see Quil wrong-footed again. She'd been so smug when she'd proposed sharing her memories with Jana, confident that she'd be able to surprise Jana with revelations akin to the one she had experienced when she saw young Yojana die. But instead Jana was at it again – conjuring revelations out of seemingly thin air. Jana could see she had annoyed her clone, and she was secretly quite pleased about that.

'So do you think . . . oh man.'

'Yeah, I do think,' said Jana. 'I think she probably created the company in the past, focused her research on cloning and did everything she could to create the exact circumstances necessary for her – your – creation!'

'Woah,' said Kaz.

'Yeah,' said Dora.

'And that's not all!' said Jana, even more excited by the next titbit that she couldn't wait to drop in their laps. 'There was a security guard in the building. I saw him – I mean, she saw him.'

'One of the two at the gate, or the one who accidentally left the door open and let me outside?' asked Quil.

'Yeah, that one, the inside one who wandered off for a smoke.'

'What about him?'

'Didn't you think it was a bit odd the way he looked at the window? That he oh-so-conveniently left the door open for you so you could escape?'

'Um, not really,' said Quil. 'Why?'

'I'll tell you why,' said Jana, stretching out the moment,

enjoying keeping Quil on tenterhooks. 'Because I recognised him.'

'What?' said Dora.

'Yup,' said Jana, gleefully wondering how long she could draw this out for. 'He saw you through that window. Or even if he didn't, he knew you were there. And as for accidentally leaving the door open, don't make me laugh. He let you escape. He wanted you to escape.'

'So who was he?' asked Kaz.

'Can't you guess?' replied Jana, bouncing on the bed in excitement.

'Argh, spit it out!' barked Quil.

'It. Was. Steve!' said Jana. Then she sat back and enjoyed the gobsmacked looks on Dora and Kaz's faces.

'Who the hell is Steve?' said Quil, through gritted teeth.

'The guy who rescued us from Io Scientific in 2014,' said Kaz. 'We know he's from the future, but we don't who he is. Or even if he is a he. He, they, was, were in disguise.'

'Dora knows who he is,' said Jana pointedly. 'But she's keeping it to herself. Because reasons.'

All eyes turned to Dora, who said nothing. Jana could see she was as surprised by this revelation as Kaz was.

'Are you sure?' Dora said eventually.

'One hundred per cent.'

'That's . . . unexpected. But not entirely surprising, I suppose. It makes sense, if you think about it.'

'It would, if you would only tell us who she, he or it is,' groaned Kaz.

Dora just smiled, turned and left the room.

'Are you really going to hold me to my promise to not hurt your friends?' said Quil, looking after Dora. 'Because right now . . .'

'Go for it,' said Jana. 'But seriously, she'd dismantle you.'

'So let me get this straight,' said Quil. 'The place where I was made was a company created by myself, kind of. And there was someone from our future inside the facility who helped me escape.'

'Yup,' said Jana. 'And I'll tell you what else.'

Quil looked at her wearily. 'Go on.'

'Well, did it never occur to you to wonder why you woke up at all? I mean, you were in a giant trash can full of corpses. None of them got up and made a break for it. You'd been thrown into a pile of biological waste. Why weren't you dead?'

Quil held Jana's gaze. 'So you think this person, this Steve, might have intervened before leaving the door open?'

'Seems likely,' said Jana. 'Maybe he switched out a vial so you didn't get a lethal injection, or perhaps he was the one tasked with terminating you and he just didn't and said he did. I dunno. But it seems like a good bet.'

'Why?' asked Kaz.

Jana shrugged and looked over at Quil.

'Don't ask me,' she said. 'I've never met the guy.'

'Or perhaps you have!' said Jana, dramatically.

Quil bestowed a withering look upon Jana and stalked out of the room.

'You enjoyed that a little bit too much,' said Kaz.

'Squee!' replied Jana, and she gave another little bounce.

5

Jana *(Not Jana)* Quil allowed herself to be led by the arm. She did not enjoy having this strange person's hand wrapped around her forearm, but she supposed far worse methods of persuasion could have been used. As she walked she tested the rise and fall of her footsteps, certain that something was wrong with her legs. Maybe she'd hurt them in some odd, non-painful way when she'd fallen from the gate. They were harder to raise than normal.

(Jana observed from within Quil's memories and marvelled at how slow her clone was to catch on. At least she'd been allowed to skip all the tedious waking up in a strange room bit – Jana had done that herself enough times, no need to rehash it all again through Quil's memories, thank you very much.)

The person leading her was short and stocky, unusually so, but he was by no means the strangest thing about this odd place. She was pretty sure she had not been brought back into the building from which she'd escaped. That had been modern, gleaming. The hangar through which she was now being led was dismal, metallic, industrial, all oil and fumes and dimly lit heavy machinery. So they had moved her. She had passed out when she fell, grazed by the bullet, and then . . . what?

She suspected they had sedated her and shipped her to this

place, wherever it was. She didn't understand why they hadn't just thrown her into the incinerator and been done with her like they'd originally planned, but she was grateful, sort of.

The man pulling her reached out and pushed a heavy door, which swung open with a metallic screech that made Quil wince. He stood to one side and, still holding on to her arm, pushed her inside. Then he let go and walked away, kicking the door with his heel as he did so, causing it to screech shut in her face.

'Drink?'

She spun, surprised as much by the pleasant tone of the question as by the unexpected woman who'd asked it. The woman was short and squat also, like the man had been. She wore old, stained denim overalls and was holding out a plastic bottle filled with a cloudy, colourless liquid. Quil eyed it suspiciously.

The woman smiled and took a sip, then wiped the top clean (with her filthy overalls) and proffered it again. Quil reached out and took the bottle, taking a gulp. It was completely tasteless. Even water had a taste, but this was the absence of taste. It was like drinking air.

'It's best not to think about how many times it's been recycled,' said the woman.

Quil paused, unsure what this meant but suddenly unwilling to drink any more of it. She placed the bottle on the low workbench in front of her, pushing aside piles of mechanical parts to clear a small space for it.

'Where am I?' asked Quil, trying to sound brave.

The woman eyed her curiously. 'Don't you know?'

'Would I ask if I did?' retorted Quil.

The woman inclined her head, acknowledging the point.

'You're aboard the mining ship *Texarcana*, ten days out from port. We're just about to turn around and head for home.'

Quil boggled.

(Jana boggled.)

She wanted to argue, say that what was happening was impossible, but the weight of evidence provided by her environment, and the realisation that her difficulty walking was the result of artificial gravity, told her that it would be pointless.

After everything she had been through, being on a spaceship was a step too far for her to comprehend. She couldn't muster anger, surprise or fear – she was just too confused. She stared at the woman blankly, uncomprehending. She moved her mouth, trying to formulate a sentence, but no words came out. Finally she shrugged.

'OK,' she said, and she sat on a stool that stood beside her, rested her elbows on the workbench and buried her face in her hands.

If the woman was thrown by Quil's unusual response, she did not seem it. 'What is your name?' she asked, not unkindly.

'Jana Patel.'

'And how old are you?'

'Seventeen.'

'And can you tell me how you got here?'

Quil looked up, quizzical. 'Can't you?'

The woman's eyes narrowed, assessing. 'What's the last thing you remember?'

Seeing no reason not to, Quil told her everything – how she'd left for a normal school day, that there was a gap in her memory before she'd woken up in a trash can full of corpses, escaped, been shot and woken up in the cabin on this ship.

When Quil had finished her tale, the woman did not reply. Instead she gestured in the air above the workbench and a holoscreen appeared between them.

'Replay footage from loading bay,' she said. 'Timestamp

July twenty-second, twenty-one hundred hours and five minutes.'

Quil noted the date, realised that at least eight months had elapsed since she'd left home for school, and then noted that her ability to be surprised seemed to have vanished.

The screen flickered and grainy security camera footage began to play, without audio. The camera was at a high angle, looking down into a cavernous hangar, similar to the one she'd walked through moments earlier. The far doors of the hangar were open and through them Quil could see rocks tumbling past. She realised she was looking out into space. A huge robot arm with a massive claw at the end of it was anchored in the centre of the hangar, stretching out through the doors. In its three-fingered grasp was a large rock, which the arm was in the process of retrieving.

'This is what you mine?'

Through the screen Quil saw the woman nod. 'We're in the Kuiper Belt,' she responded. 'We scan the rocks for minerals, retrieve the ones that offer the best yields, refine them on ship, then return to port when our holds are full. But this rock is different. Watch.'

The arm retracted into the hold and the hangar doors swung shut. The rock was deposited on the ground and the arm pulled away.

'This rock was special,' said the woman. 'We received instructions a week ago to come to exactly these coordinates, find this rock – the exact dimensions and properties of which were included in our orders – bring it aboard and fly straight home. A whole mission for a single rock.'

Before Quil could ask why, the screen glowed. The rock was surrounded by a coruscating aurora of red sparks. And then, out of nowhere, a figure popped into existence a few feet above the rock, and fell backwards on to it. The person seemed lifeless; they slipped off the rock and fell to the floor, hard, face first.

Quil reached up and felt the large bruise around her right eye and gasped.

The figure on the screen was her.

'That, Jana Patel, is how you arrived aboard my ship. Is there anything you want to tell me?'

'That's the asteroid in the warhead of the timebomb, isn't it?' asked Jana as soon as she exited Quil's memories.

Quil nodded.

Jana had not expected much from her trip back through Quil's timeline – a bit of psychological insight perhaps, some backstory. Instead, she was finding patterns throughout Quil's life that surprised her. Io Scientific, the timebomb . . . it was all connected.

Mars had been a predestination paradox, they knew that now. By travelling back to prevent the disaster they had inadvertently caused it to happen.

But what if it that had been a smaller paradox nested within a larger one? What if their entire lives were some kind of feedback loop? Jana was increasingly worried about what she was finding in Quil's past. Her initial pleasure at taking Quil by surprise was fading into fear at all the coincidences that obviously weren't coincidences at all.

She didn't know what it all meant yet, but, much as she had on Mars, Jana was beginning to get a sense that time was playing with them, that they were helpless in the face of it. And she was afraid of where the relentless tide of events might be taking them.

'You'd travelled into the future,' Jana said. 'You were shot at Io Scientific, knocked unconscious and fell through time to this time and place.'

'I worked that out later, but yes.'

'How much time had elapsed?'

'You left for school on the twenty-third of September 2141, I arrived on the *Texarcana* on the eighteenth of July 2142, and my "birth" was at some point between those two dates. The time jump was quite small, but I can't be exact.'

Jana pondered.

'You're going to ask me who issued the orders for the *Texarcana* to go collect the rock,' said Quil. 'How they knew where it was, what it would turn out to be.'

That was exactly what Jana wanted, and also kind of didn't want, to know. 'Yes,' she answered.

Quil shrugged. 'I don't know. The *Texarcana* was an IMC ship, but when my army raided their offices, years later, they found no trace of any orders relating to her. It was like the ship didn't exist. Off the books. Completely.'

'Huh,' said Jana, adding another mystery to the pile. 'OK, so you arrive on this ship. You still think you're me. What next?'

'I couldn't send a message to Earth even if I wanted to.'

Quil paced restlessly around the workbench, unhappy with this response.

(Jana recognised the setting – Quil was back in the room where she had first met the woman who was talking to her now. Some time had elapsed, because she could feel her stomach was full and her head was less achy and confused – since the last memory Quil had lived at least a day, had a full meal and caught a solid night's sleep.)

'Why not?'

'We're under a communications blackout for the duration

of this mission,' explained the woman. (*Jana found new knowledge in Quil's mind – this was the captain of the ship, and her name was Arihi.*)

'Then break the blackout, please, I'm begging you,' pleaded Quil.

'You misunderstand,' replied the captain. 'They ripped out all the comms equipment before we left.'

Quil was taken aback.

'Is that normal?' she asked.

Arihi shook her head. 'Nothing about this mission is normal,' she said, exasperated. 'We're completely unable to make contact with anyone until we get back to port. But as soon as we do, I promise you, we'll contact your home.'

Quil slumped back on to the stool, defeated. 'My mom will be losing her mind with worry.'

(HA!)

Arihi came and stood beside Quil, resting her hand on her shoulder and giving it a comforting squeeze.

'Tell me about her,' she asked.

'Oh she's wonderful. She so clever, and she works very hard, but she always makes time for family. *(As if)* She's very loving, helps me with my homework. *(Gag)* She's always there for me. *(Retch).*'

(*Jana could feel the prepared phrases bubbling up inside Quil. There were no memories attached to them, just feelings and clichés that had been fed into her simulacra. She believed what she was telling Arihi, but if you'd asked her to give examples of those times spent doing homework or whatever, she'd be unable to do anything but say 'Oh, all the time' in a vague kind of way. As an outsider, it was obvious that it was artificial, but from inside that moment, Quil had no idea she was spouting such nonsense.*)

'And your father?'

'He died.'

(So they'd programmed knowledge of her father's death into her head in advance of his actual murder. Wow, that was cold.)

'How?'

Quil paused. 'That's odd, I . . . I can't quite . . .'

(She couldn't remember. So the memories weren't fully implanted. They'd dumped Quil when she was still a work in progress. Interesting.)

'You can't quite remember?'

'Hey what is this?' said Quil angrily, rounding on Arihi as a way of deflecting from the yawning empty fear that was opening up inside her as she examined her memories. Had she been damaged by the gunshot and the fall? Or by whatever happened to her at the facility? Or by whatever it was that had transported her here?

Arihi stepped away, hands wide, non-threatening. 'Just interested, that's all,' she said calmly. 'You're a puzzle. Trying to work you out.'

'I'm not a puzzle, I'm a girl. A girl who's been kidnapped and shot at and sent into space somehow. But just a girl.'

Arihi shook her head slowly, her face sorrowful. 'You believe that, don't you?'

Quil felt a hard spike of panic. 'What does that mean?'

The captain bit her lip and regarded Quil curiously, with a fair amount of pity in her eyes.

'When you appeared in the cargo hold, just dropped in on us out of thin air, you were unconscious. You had a bad wound to your head, plenty of bruising. So we took you to the sick bay, got the doctor to look you over, clean you up, stabilise you.'

'Stabilise?'

'You were very dehydrated. You'd not eaten. You needed all sorts of drips and injections to get your body in some kind of balance.'

'What does that mean? You were sticking needles in me while I was asleep?'

'We were just looking after you, I promise.'

Quil was angry and scared. She had made a decision to trust Arihi, but she was beginning to question it now.

'But Quil, there's something you have to know. Something we found out when we examined you.'

Quil felt sick.

'Oh god, was I raped? In that place, after I was taken, did someone rape me?'

Arihi shook her head vigorously. 'No no, nothing like that. You're . . . perfect. Too perfect. That's the problem.'

'What do you mean?' said Quil, rising off the stool, gripping it hard, digging her fingernails into the plastic.

'Jana, you're a clone.'

Quil stood, bewildered, for the longest time just staring at Arihi, mouth open, blinking. Then she laughed.

'That's ridiculous,' she scoffed. 'I'm Jana Patel, my parents are Abhilasha and Prabal. I live in New York. I was born seventeen years ago.'

Arihi was shaking her head. 'No. You were born about three days ago, is our best guess. In a facility far away from here.'

Quil began to back away from Arihi. She could feel herself starting to shake. She'd made the mistake of trusting this person, this stranger, and now she was paying the price. This was all some sick joke. Some kind of test. The footage of her materialising out of thin air must have been faked. What was this? A psychological experiment? Some kind of sick game?

Was she still in the lab? Was she being watched by people who were taking notes somewhere?

Arihi stepped towards Quil.

'Get away from me!' she screamed, grabbing a wrench from the workbench and brandishing it.

'Jana, listen to me carefully,' said Arihi, staying still, keeping her hands wide and unthreatening. 'I don't know who made you, or why, or where. I don't know how you got here. I don't know why we were sent to get this rock, or why we're in comms blackout. All I have is questions. I'm not your enemy. I swear to you. But if you let me, I'll do everything I can to help you. I think you're the key to this, somehow. The reason for this mission, the comms blackout. I think someone sent us out here to get you as well as the rock. Don't ask me who, I don't know. Whoever they are, whatever they're doing, we can get to the bottom of it together. But first you have to know the truth. And the truth is, you are a brand new, freshly minted clone.'

'I have memories!'

'So did I, when I was born.'

'What?'

'I'm a clone too. Everyone on this ship is a manufactured person, designed and mass produced to work out here in deep space. But you, you're different. You're a custom build. Our memories are generic. We're born knowing how to operate machinery, how to move in different strengths of gravity, that kind of thing. They don't bother giving us personal memories – no families or any of that stuff. We know we're clones when we're born. But you . . . someone did a lot of hard work creating your memories, your DNA is almost perfect, you'd pass for natural-born everywhere. Our doctor only spotted it because, well, all he works on are clones. He knows the signs.

And once he tested your DNA he found markup in there, labelling you the creation of some outfit called Io Scientific.'

Quil dropped the wrench not because she believed Arihi, but because her hands were shaking so badly she couldn't grip it any more.

'Think back, Jana. Think of some injury you received. Something trivial. A graze or a cut that left a tiny scar, some slight change in skin tone, something only you know about, something completely insignificant, one of the many small facts that make you you. Think.'

Quil's breathing was out of control; she was seeing spots at the edge of her vision. She felt light-headed and weightless. But she thought, and she remembered.

'My wrist,' she gasped.

'Left or right?'

'Right. I burned it taking a cake out of the oven. You wouldn't know it had ever happened, but I can see it, the outline of the scar.'

'Then look.'

Quil stood frozen with fear. Unable to move her head, staring at Arihi in terror.

'Look at your wrist, Jana. Tell me if you see it.'

Quil forced herself to move her head and look down at the upturned wrist, the soft brown underside of her arm, so tender, so painful when it had brushed the metal cake tin.

She just had time to register the absence of the outline before she felt her head swimming and the world fading out of focus . . .

(There was a jumpcut in Jana's mind. She was grateful Quil wasn't making her live through all the memories in real time, but it was disorienting and weird when she encountered one of Quil's edits and suddenly found herself in the midst of another

memory. She knew immediately that four days had passed since the last memory. Quil's body felt stronger still, and her emotions were very different. The confusion was still there, but now there was a hard core of rage burning at the heart of it. And, Jana fancied, a nub of loss, fear and loneliness within that.)

Quil was in the hangar, standing on a platform looking down at the rock that had been salvaged just before she came aboard. Arihi was standing next to her.

'We've analysed it as much as we are able,' said the captain. 'There's nothing in that rock that we recognise. Not a single mineral or element. It's stone, we think it has a granite base, but it's been infused with . . . stuff.'

Quil laughed. 'Stuff? Is that a technical term?'

'Whatever it is, it's not naturally occurring. This is a made thing.'

'Made by who?'

Arihi shrugged. 'Aliens?'

'Come on,' scoffed Quil.

'If you've got a better idea, I'd love to hear it, because I don't.'

Quil considered the rock. 'Is it radioactive?'

'It's not emitting any kind of particle we can detect.'

'And the only time it's done anything is when I arrived?'

Arihi nodded. 'Just before you appeared, it started to glow. And you and it both sparked like crazy when you materialised. It's been quiet since.'

'And you want me to touch it?' Quil sounded about as keen as she felt.

'Just to see if it causes a reaction. It's harmless, look.'

Arihi stepped down off the platform, walked across to the rock and placed her hand on it. Nothing happened.

Quil shrugged and followed suit. But as she approached

the rock she felt a strange tingling in her extremities. She looked down and saw red sparks hovering around her finger-tips. It reminded her of the bonfires they had at home each winter, when they burned the autumn leaves and sparks would dance in the updraughts.

She corrected herself. She didn't remember that, not really.

(Jana felt the sharp stab of pain as Quil rejected the memory, and empathised – she knew that feeling.)

Her pain at the memory distracted Quil from her fear, and when she had returned her attention to the sparks it was with wonder, not terror. She waggled her fingers and they followed, like fireflies.

She stepped closer to the rock and the sparks grew brighter.

'Are they hot?' asked Arihi, stepping backwards in alarm.

Quil shook her head and took another step. Her whole body began to glow and the sparks haloed her entirely.

Quil began to laugh.

'This is amazing!' she said, fully forgetting her anger, loss and pain for the first time since her creation.

She reached forward and touched the rock. It hummed through her bones, making her body vibrate with power. She laughed again, joyful at the thrill of it. She felt a lurch in her stomach and turned to look at Arihi . . .

. . . And then Quil was falling through time again.

'You do this deliberately don't you?'

'Do what?'

'Pull me out of your memories at the most interesting moments.'

Quil did not smile. She was not in the mood for banter. 'This isn't entertainment, Jana,' she said witheringly. 'This is my life.'

'Yeah, but edited, curated, sorted into a compelling order for my consumption, with all the boring bits left out.'

'Jana . . .' warned Quil through gritted teeth.

But Jana wasn't listening. She'd had enough for one day, and wanted the opportunity to share what she'd learned with Dora and Kaz, to get their take on things. She was already halfway out the door.

She found Dora in one of the workout rooms in the hotel's basement gym. She stood at the door watching Dora through the glass window as she did t'ai chi, slow and elegant. She did not want to disturb her friend's meditations, and so she waited patiently, content to watch until Dora had finished. When she did, she looked up, noticed Jana's face at the window and smiled. She beckoned her inside.

'How long have you been there?' she asked.

'Only a moment,' lied Jana. 'You're very graceful.'

Dora grimaced. 'I feel lumpy,' she said. 'Ever since Mars. The changes in gravity during our journey there and our time on the planet were uncomfortable. I have not regained my equilibrium.'

'Try spending your time in somebody else's head. My *brain* feels lumpy.'

Dora sat cross-legged on the mat and gestured for Jana to sit with her. She did so.

'I cannot imagine what it must be like to experience the world through somebody else's eyes.'

'Not just eyes – all the senses. And you can't control anything, you can't move, you're just a passenger. You can think independently – which is weird, because you've got two sets of thoughts and emotions fighting it out – but that's all. I don't like it.'

'But is it teaching you about Quil? Anything useful?'

Jana considered. 'It's hard to say. I've lived through the edited highlights of the first few weeks of her life, and she's such a mess. She doesn't know what to think, how to feel. She's this big mix-up of anger and fear and confusion. It was awful for her. When I realised I was a clone, I'd been alive seven years. I reacted badly, of course. I withdrew, stopped engaging with the world or with people properly. I suppose I was in shock. But for her it was so much worse. She found out much sooner than I did, but only after the most awful birth. She's having so many feelings at once, it's like she hasn't been able to decide how she's reacting yet.'

'We know how she'll choose to react in the end,' pointed out Dora.

'By going to war with the whole solar system, yeah. But I still can't find the thread between the girl she is at this early point, and the woman she became. I think there must be some other big trigger moment waiting for me, for her I mean, and I'm kind of nervous about it, if I'm honest.'

'Is there anything we can use, though? Any detail or weakness or fact we can exploit against her if she does travel back in time and become the Quil we met in 1645?'

Jana shrugged. 'Not yet. I'm finding it hard to think about her in that way any more. I suppose that'll happen, if you share somebody's worst moments – you start to sympathise with them.'

'That is understandable. And she is not the Quil we met in the past – if we get this right, that Quil will never exist. This is the real her, and she is partly you. It is only natural that you should feel a strong connection.'

'I suppose,' conceded Jana. 'I just wish I had been there. Not just in a memory, but in real life. She's kind of like my sister. I feel bad that I couldn't help her. And yes, I know how irrational that is, but I can't help it. I want to protect her.'

Dora laid her hand on Jana's and squeezed reassuringly. 'You are helping her. We all are, Jana. She knows we aren't the bad guys. Now we know she isn't either. We came on this trip so we could understand each other, and I think it's worked. All we need to do is finish up here, head back and set up the quantum bubble, ensure our personal timelines stay on track and then we've done it. History changes. She won't go back in time, all that madness in Pendarn and Beirut will vanish from history. We'll be free, and Quil can do whatever she wants.'

'But I don't think that can be right, Dora,' said Jana, finally voicing the fear that had been building in her ever since she experienced Quil's birth. 'Because we know that Io Scientific created Quil. And if she doesn't travel back in time and start the company, she'll cancel herself out of existence.'

Dora exhaled sharply. 'I hadn't thought of that.'

'The paradoxes are getting so complicated, I'm losing track,' said Jana. 'What'll happen to us? To our memories, if we change time like that, if Quil gets completely unwritten?'

Dora shook her head. 'I have no idea.'

'It could mean you and I never meet. Never met. Won't meet. Oh dammit, you know what I mean.'

'It could.'

'I wouldn't like that.'

'Neither would I, but . . .'

'Hey, what's up?'

Jana snatched her hand away as Kaz walked into the room. 'Nothing,' she replied. 'Just taking a break from the Quil show.'

She rose to her feet and walked past Kaz. 'Better get back to it,' she said, heading for the elevator.

6

'I needed some kind of purpose, so I decided to become a physicist,' explained Quil. 'It was the rock. Too many mysteries and questions. I needed to study it, find out how and why it had affected me.'

'You didn't go home, not even once, just to look at it?'

'It wasn't my home, I realised that. What would I go there for, anyway? To confront her? To reclaim a life I never owned in the first place? No. There was no point. I needed to find a purpose and a life of my own. After I left the mining ship I arrived back on Earth, in 2132, in Cornwall, not far from here.'

'The warhead, drawing you back.'

'I know that now, but at the time I was just confused. It seemed so random. I couldn't control my time jumps.'

'So, scientist.'

Quil nodded. 'I wanted to get out to Neso and talk to Professor Kairos, but I was still a teenager, totally alone. I had to be careful.'

'So you're on Earth, nine years before you were even born. No ID, no name, nothing. How do you start?'

Quil considered Jana appraisingly. 'Someone helped me,' she said.

'Who?'

'At first I assumed it was my future self, but now I think it might have been you guys,' she said after a long pause.

'No way,' said Kaz, folding his arms and scowling.

'But—'

'No,' he said again firmly.

Jana took a deep breath. 'I'm not asking permission, Kaz.' She turned to Dora. 'Well?'

Dora pursed her lips. 'I'm not sure.'

'Dora, it has your fingerprints all over it,' said Jana, trying not to plead. 'Who else could create a fake identity like that? It must have been you.'

'It could have been Steve,' countered Kaz.

'It was just lying there?' asked Dora.

'At her feet, when she arrived in Cornwall in 2131. Without it, she'd have been completely screwed.'

'A complete set of ID, a bank account, everything she needed?'

'A life in a box, put there by someone who knew where and when she was going to arrive, and what she would need to survive when she did. It had to be a time traveller. It had to be us.'

'And if we don't do it, then maybe we stop all of this before it even begins,' said Kaz. 'Maybe this is our moment to stop.'

'But we've won, surely?' argued Jana. 'Quil isn't going to become our enemy now. I think we've already changed history. It's in our interest to make sure this timeline remains intact. So we have to help her get to this point.'

Dora shook her head. 'We *think* we've stopped her going back in time and becoming our enemy,' she said. 'But we haven't stopped the slaughter on Mars. If we don't help her in 2131, we might be saving countless lives. Who knows what would happen to her, if she didn't have that ID? She'd be completely helpless. I don't think she'd last a week.'

'Or she could jump off into time again, end up somewhere else and turn out far, far worse,' countered Jana.

'So your argument is basically better the devil you know?' said Kaz.

Jana nodded. 'Reckon so.'

Dora thought for a moment and then nodded once, decisively. 'OK, let's do it.'

Kaz shook his head. 'This is a mistake.'

'You're outvoted,' said Jana firmly.

Quil provided them with the exact details of the fake identity she had found ready and waiting for her. Dora made note of it all, and then jumped away to prepare everything necessary. So when young Quil – only a week or so old – had been thrown across time after touching the asteroid aboard the mining ship, she materialised in Cornwall with a box at her feet containing everything she would need to become Anita Lonkhar, including full ID, a generously stocked bank account and an offer of a place at Moscow University to study physics.

She thought about it for only a second before deciding to take the gift at face value and use it to pursue the course she had already set her heart on. She did not wonder who had provided it for her – as far as she knew, she was the only person able to travel through time, and so she assumed her older self had left it for her.

'I took it as a sign that I was in control and on track,' she explained to Jana. 'So I threw myself into my studies. I found I had a talent not just for physics, but for biology also. I took parallel degrees in both sciences. And then medicine.'

'Wow,' said Jana. 'I guess Mom really did modify the template for you, huh.'

Quil smiled. 'You do not think yourself capable of simultaneously studying for three PhDs?'

Jana shook her head, and sighed. 'I've been told I have a high opinion of myself, but even my vanity has limits.'

'I lived a normal life for seven years. I didn't travel in time at all during that period. I just studied – cloning, genetic modification and temporal theory. And watched our progenitor's mother, of course, rising up the greasy pole of American politics. I felt as if I were preparing for something, but I never really knew what. I had a sense of – it sounds silly to say it out loud to you – but I had a sense of destiny. That there were things I needed to accomplish. I knew, all the time I was studying, that I was preparing myself for a great task. I just didn't know what it was.'

Jana bit her tongue to prevent herself from saying 'So you were a megalomaniac at a very early age?'

'When I graduated, it was 2138,' continued Quil. 'I figured I would take some time to travel.'

'Wait a minute, though,' said Jana, brooking the narrative flow. 'You were in grad school for seven years. You weren't alone there. There were other students. Classmates, housemates, professors. You must have made friends, had relationships. Formed some kind of family.'

Quil paused and bit her lip. She looked uncertain, hesitant. It was the first time Jana had ever seen Quil look truly vulnerable, as well as a little bit confused. Confused by herself.

'Not really,' she said. 'I studied. All the time.'

Jana was incredulous. 'No boyfriends? Not even a drinking buddy or two?'

Quil shook her head. 'I had lovers. Sometimes. But I couldn't let them get too close, if I did they might have gotten in the way of my studies. No distractions. I had things to do.'

'Your destiny.'

'Exactly.'

'So where did you travel to?'

'I circled the Earth, visited Mars. Saw all the great wonders.'

'Alone.'

'Yes.'

'What about your great destiny?'

Quil looked at her feet, again seeming vulnerable. 'I . . . I was running away from it. I knew there was something I needed to do, but I didn't want to do it. So I turned my back on it all for a while. Now, I think it was just cowardice.'

But Jana didn't think Quil sounded angry at her younger self; she just sounded sad.

'You see, I was always very conscious of my nature,' continued Quil. 'I am a clone. I was manufactured to serve a purpose. I didn't know, not then, what that purpose was – that our progenitor's mother wanted a human prop for her political ambitions. I just knew I'd been created because somebody, somewhere, felt they required me, and that I had been thrown away before being used. That sense that I'd been made for a reason sits very deep in me. Maybe it was built in, I don't know. But I needed to find a purpose of my own, and something told me I would find it out there, in space. Among my people. Eventually, I couldn't put it off any longer . . .'

Quil stood *(and Jana stood inside her memories)* somewhere near the back of a huge hall, rapt. *(She was Anita at the moment, and Jana was curious to see the moment Quil changed her name, took up her crusade. It was close now. Jana could feel the fire of righteous anger in Quil's breast and knew that the spark had been lit.)*

'The campaign is a simple one,' said the man at the podium, far away across a sea of heads. 'It is a campaign for basic human rights. Rights that were won generations ago, rights we enjoy every day – the right to free love, to free speech, to free movement – but which are now being denied to a portion of the human race.'

The event was one of many being run across the world on a day of action convened by a crusading organisation called All Humans. Jana knew that her father had advised this group when they put together a legal challenge in 2139, the thrust of which was that the universal bill of rights, implemented worldwide in 2122, should be applied outside Earth's atmosphere. Jana knew they would lose the case, but that hadn't happened yet. In this room, on this day, hope was still alive.

'There are clones among us,' said the man, warming to his theme. 'We know that private individuals with the right cash and connections have been able to commission the creation of bespoke people for decades. It is illegal, but it happens. We all know that. We have no idea how many clones there are walking the Earth, what lives they lead. But we do know that there are thousands, possibly even tens of thousands, of cloned humans living and working out in space, mining the minerals that keep our planet alive. And we know that they are slaves!'

A yell of agreement from the crowd, a thrill of excitement in Quil's breast.

'We know that they are denied their freedom!'

A yell of anger from the crowd.

'We know that they . . .' the speaker pointed to the policeman who stood at the exits, protecting the event – or protecting the rest of the city from the event – ' . . .will work tirelessly to maintain the status quo that favours their masters and mistresses, to prevent us rocking the boat, weakening share prices, damaging the bottom line. But we are a democracy, and our rights are protected.'

(By the very police you're shouting at, thought Jana wryly.)

The speech went on for a while after that. Quil was lapping up every word, but Jana got bored, and although she couldn't control Quil's head or shift her viewpoint, she could still study the crowd, most of whom had risen from their seats to cheer and applaud the speaker, and hurl abuse at the police, who remained unengaged and stony-faced. They were young and vocal but they didn't seem to her like the kind of people who could effect actual change. She could feel that Quil had the same response, a kind of indulgent impatience – liking the passion and the crowd, but knowing they would all go back to their safe, quiet lives when the event ended, resenting them for that and feeling deep down that more direct action was needed, and that she should be the one to take that action.

Cut to . . .

(Jana hated it when she jumped over one of Quil's memory edits. It was disorientating and made her head spin. The environment she had been edited into could not have been more different to the one she had just been experiencing. The air was thick and cloying, full of steam and the tang of metal and dust. She felt light, and moved clumsily. Her feet clanged on a metal walkway and there was a handrail in her right hand that she was using to keep herself upright as she hurried down a dimly lit corridor, following a hunched figure ahead of her. Jana knew, because Quil knew, that she was on a mining station in deep space, somewhere beyond Neptune. A honeycomb of tunnels permeated this asteroid; it was almost

large enough to be a planet or at the very least a moon, if it had fallen into the orbit of some larger body rather than floating about, barely tethered to the sun, bumping into anything that crossed its huge, elliptical orbit.)

Some months had passed since All Humans Day, and Quil had volunteered for the cause. Taken on as an official observer, she had been ferried out here on an IMC ship as their guest, no expense spared, to observe how humane and enlightened their treatment of their manufactured workforce really was. Her job was to smile and nod, go through the motions of the official, sanitised tour she was being given, all the while looking for opportunities to slip away and get the real story.

She had slipped away from her escorts half an hour earlier and met up with a woman who had passed her a message the previous day. She was off-grid, and she knew there would be hell to pay when they found her, but she had to see the reality of things for herself. She had to bear witness.

'This way!' called the figure ahead. 'And keep your head down.'

That last advice came a split second too late as Quil's forehead bounced off a low metal beam. Problem with being the tallest person on a ship built for a crew of uniformly shorter height – she had a growing collection of bumps and bruises on her head.

The corridor opened out into a small rock antechamber, and a large entrance ahead of them opened into a much larger chamber still. The figure ahead of Quil turned *(and for a moment Jana thought it was Arihi, but it was in fact another clone, whose name she was surprised to find Quil did not know).*

'You said you wanted to see the things they wouldn't show you,' said the clone. 'Then see.' She gestured for Quil to pass through into the larger chamber and she did so, her stomach full of butterflies.

The cavern was not, as she had expected, a factory floor or mining processing plant. She had presumed the worst she would see would be the working conditions. But in fact, the cavern formed the mining base's living quarters. And it was squalid beyond belief.

The stench of effluent and body odour was overpowering, and Quil's eyes watered as she stepped inside. She had been shown cabins before – small, admittedly, but clean and tidy. Washing facilities had been communal, but similarly functional. The cleverness of the deception had been its ordinariness – they had not tried to convince her that the clones lived in luxury, just that they were treated humanely. She had already written an angry piece about the 'official' living conditions, but she had known, even as she wrote it, that it wasn't going to change anything. But the awful shanty town that lay before her now confirmed all her worst fears.

Boxes and crates, packing cases of all shapes and sizes were scattered across the cavern floor in a rough grid pattern, forming narrow streets. Each container was being used as an abode by one or more workers, who slept on hard metal or rock. A stream of effluent ran down the middle of the street ahead of her.

'This is how we live,' said the woman. 'If you can call it living.'

'Why?' was all Quil could manage to ask.

'Keeps costs down. Conditions are much nicer on the work floor at the processing plant. They incentivise us to work longer hours by making our off-duty time as squalid as possible. And if there's a high suicide rate, who cares? We're quick and cheap to replace.'

'Disease?'

The woman shrugged. 'Not so much any more. Herd immunity sets in after the first few outbreaks.'

The lack of light was oppressive, the heat was intense, the smell overpowering. This was no kind of life at all, and Quil's disgust shaded into fury as she walked down the 'street'. Nearly everybody was asleep. Quil could understand that working was preferable to spending leisure time in such a hellhole.

'You need to record this,' said Quil's guide. 'Show the people of Earth how we live.'

Quil tapped the side of her head. 'ENL chip and eye-mods – I can just export my memories. Everyone will know, trust me.'

'Good, now follow me.'

She led Quil past a group of sleeping women, huddled around an open fire under old blankets, and up to a container that sat nearly flush with the cavern wall. There was a narrow gap behind it and the woman squeezed in and vanished from sight. Nervously, Quil followed, holding in her breath and pushing herself in between the rock and the metal, inching sideways after her guide. The sharp jagged surface of the rock scraped her back, and the rusty metal grated her forehead, but after a few sideways steps she felt a void behind her and she backed into it and, ducking her head, she shuffled until she was facing into a low tunnel that stretched away on a downward slope. There were no lights here, so her guide pulled out a torch and led the way.

'Where are you taking me?' asked Quil as they walked, crouched down, her lower back aching, her knees bent and her head a mass of cuts. At least the smell of the living quarters had dissipated; that was something.

'There are some people who want to meet you,' was all her guide would say.

They shuffled along for ten minutes or more *(Jana sighed inwardly – this would be a good point for an edit, she thought)* before the tunnel opened up into a cavern that was small but, thankfully, high enough for Quil to stand upright. Her spine cracked as she did so and she groaned in pained relief.

The air was muggy and foetid. Quil felt light-headed, as if the oxygen mix was slightly wrong. The chamber was lit by a string of electric lights hung from a wire that snaked around the wall in a circle, but the power was low, so the room was half in shadow.

'This her?' asked an old clone who rose awkwardly to his feet when he saw Quil and her guide enter.

'Who else would it be?' replied the guide.

The man grunted. He had been sitting on a box behind a makeshift desk constructed of packing case legs and a sheet of jagged metal on which sat a row of ancient computer terminals. Two other clones, a man and a woman almost as old as the man now standing, sat on either side of him; they looked up, their interest briefly kindled by the new arrivals, then, after casting withering glances at Quil, they returned to their work, whatever it was.

The old clone stepped around the desk and shuffled towards Quil until he was standing in front of her. He looked her up and down from within a pungent miasma of sweat and urine.

'What do you want?' he asked with a sneer. His few remaining teeth were black and his breath made her wince.

Quil didn't know how to respond, but she felt threatened and vulnerable. She had a feeling that the wrong answer would result in her vanishing from the face of the universe. She considered for a moment how best to play the situation, knowing that she was completely at the mercy of this mysterious gang.

'For you to take a bath,' she said, 'and a trip to the dentist.'

The old clone's face froze, his eyes widened and his face

reddened. He took a sharp breath and opened his mouth, but before he could offer a stinging rejoinder he was brought up short by the sound of the female clone at the desk behind him audibly stifling a giggle.

'You and me both, sweetheart,' said the old man who sat beside her.

'Oh, I like her,' said the giggling old woman.

The man in front of Quil scowled. He could perhaps have recovered his authority and dignity in the face of her abuse, but the moment his friends joined in he was a busted flush. And he knew it.

'Well I'd like a pony and a castle,' he wheezed, with a hint of a smile, 'but you can't always get what you want, can you?'

'Look,' said Quil, trying to disguise her relief at passing the first test. 'You brought me down here. I reckon you're the ones who want something.'

The man inclined his head, acknowledging her point.

'First, reassurance,' he said, leering as he looked her up and down. 'Why are you here, hmm? Beautiful young woman like you, travelling out to the middle of nowhere. Bored little do-gooder come to look after us poor forgotten slaves. Going to save the world, are you? Until your trust fund runs out, anyway. Then it'll be home to Mummy and Daddy, squeeze out a few brats and tell stories about your crusading youth and your adventures in the asteroid belt at dinner parties. We've seen your type before, lovely. Sent out here on fact-finding missions. Take the tour, buy the official line, hurry back to Earth feeling all virtuous, and telling everybody that we're just fine up here, safe in the bosom of our kind corporate masters.

'But Liko has been watching you' – he indicated Quil's guide – 'and she thinks you're different. Vouches for you. Says we should give you a chance, let you see behind the curtain. So here you are.'

He folded his arms and looked up at her, chin jutting out defiantly.

It took Quil a moment to realise his monologue was over. She decided to match his verbosity with brevity.

'I'm here because I'm like you,' she said. 'I'm a clone. A reject, a mistake. I don't have a mommy and daddy to crawl back to. No trust fund. Just me. But I have contacts, and money, and skills that would surprise you. So stop posturing and tell me who you are, what you're doing hiding down here and how I can help.'

By the time she'd finished, all four pairs of eyes were fixed on her in astonishment.

'You're a clone?' said Liko, aghast. She reached out almost involuntarily, and touched Quil's bare arm as if to check that she was real.

'Baked and birthed,' she replied. 'And more besides.'

'Huh,' breathed the old clone, emitting a gust of blistering halitosis and holding out his hand. 'In that case, welcome to QUIL.'

Quil took his hand and smiled.

'They were it?'

Quil nodded, amused at Jana's incredulity. 'The whole resistance, in that room. Three ancient old techies, one young woman. And me. The three oldies – Qiomars, Ululani, Inoki – and the young woman, Liko, had taken advantage of an explosion a few years previous. Another industrial accident, three hundred dead due to lack of safety controls. They were on the fringes of the blast and let the company believe they'd been destroyed. They went underground and started to collect evidence. But they were old, ill, had no medical support or rations – they had to live off the grid on what they could scrounge. They were heroes, truly.'

Jana leaned forward in her armchair and sipped her coffee. 'And the name?'

'An acronym, he'd made it up by taking their first initials. He thought "the Resistance" was corny. Wanted a cool handle.'

Jana shook her head and laughed, mildly annoyed she hadn't worked that out. 'Ridiculous. So let me guess, they were using those old computers to hack into the base's systems and copy evidence of mistreatment.'

'They had so much,' explained Quil. 'Video of beatings, executions, one massacre when a riot broke out a few years earlier. Documents, spreadsheets, secret briefings. Everything we needed to show Earth exactly what was going on – how they were abusing the clones.'

'And you were their courier, getting the information into the media, onto the net.'

'Yes. I rejoined the tour, returned to Earth, circulated the material and started a crusade. I had to do it anonymously, of course. So all the leaks were signed QUIL. The press thought it was the name of the leaker, and eventually I came to adopt it as my pseudonym. But back then I was naive. I thought that the leak would be enough. That the evidence alone would force change. I was stupid. Nobody cared, not really. There were debates, and articles, online outrage. But no legislation, no political intervention. Just lots of backhanders and threats from vested interests. I think there was maybe one honest politician involved, but he died in a very convenient accident. The more we leaked, the more the status quo was enforced. Nothing changed except the rhetoric coming from the author- ities. A propaganda campaign began, dedicated to spreading all sorts of grotesque falsehoods about clones. They – the politicians, the wealthy, everyone we were fighting – created fear and suspicion in ordinary people, cut the legs of popular support out from under us.'

Jana sighed. 'I'm sorry,' she said, and she meant it. The old saw about walking a mile in somebody's else's shoes had never seemed more appropriate. She'd literally lived through the formative moments of Quil's life and although she'd questioned herself ruthlessly, worried that she might be experiencing some variation of Stockholm Syndrome – becoming sympathetic to her enemy through prolonged exposure – she knew now that what she was feeling was simpler and more straightforward than that.

Jana was certain that, in Quil's place, she would have done exactly the same things, taken the same steps, walked the same path. She might not have Quil's intelligence, or her sexual identity – she was clear that she and Quil were different, by design – but the fundamental essence of her – of *their* – personality remained the same. She understood and agreed with Quil's actions as she had experienced them.

It was clear to Jana that the poison Quil had been given on Mars – poison created by their 'mother' specifically to drive her 'daughter' insane – combined with the trauma of being blown back in time and suffering such horrible injuries, had created a monstrous perversion of the crusading rights activist Quil really had been. But Jana was certain, now, that this history had been avoided.

She was curious about what kind of person Quil would become when her war was over. Jana found that she was looking forward to finding out.

'Everybody was sorry,' said Quil, unable to disguise the bitterness in her voice. 'But nobody did anything. Not really.

The corporations fought back. Cracked down. They found QUIL and executed them, but by then I had other support. Other plans. I had accrued an army of sorts on an abandoned outpost that we reclaimed and refitted. It was me who sent Arihi to collect the asteroid. Hacked the mainframe, sent out fake orders and had her bring it to my lab, where I began studying it in the hope of answers. In my frustration at its impossibility, and the intransigence of the Earth regime, I decided to make it into a weapon. I only ever intended it as a deterrent, but that was self-delusion, wasn't it. Mankind never made a weapon that wasn't used, if only once. I knew that it would take something spectacular to shake people out of their complacency. Something life-changing, something nobody could ignore.'

'An attack?'

Quil shook her head. 'For a moment, maybe, I considered using the timebomb. When I was at my most despairing and angry. But I'm not a terrorist, no matter what the Earth Government would have you believe. Sure, I could have gone down the same path as every other freedom fighter in history. Sacrificed some innocents, caused an atrocity, generated outrage and death.'

'But that's not your style, is it?'

Quil laid her hand on Jana's. 'It makes me glad that you know that. No, bloodshed wasn't the answer. I needed to change hearts and minds. I put the timebomb on our flagship, and leaked its existence to the enemy, but it was only ever for show.'

'So what did you do? How did the war start? If it wasn't a terrorist attack, what was it?'

Quil smiled a grim smile. 'Something much more creative,' she said.

7
27 May 2155 –
the day the war begins

'This is how it begins?'

'Of course it is, this is how it always begins: with a knock on the door in the night.'

Sudden panic. Disorientation. Confusion. A tightness in your head. Gummy eyes, stale mouth. Heart pounding hard enough to hear.

You've been woken violently. By what? A noise, you think. Your head is jerking left and right as you try to identify possible threats. You're still acting on instinct, not properly conscious. It's dark, but not pitch black. You can make out the familiar landscape of your bedroom in the soft blue glow of the nightlight. You're snug and warm in your bed, gripped tight by fight or flight.

You get your bearings. There's nobody in here but you.

You hold teddy tightly, and try not to cry.

You jump involuntarily as a sharp, loud banging sounds

from downstairs. Someone is hammering really hard on the front door.

You snuggle down deeper into the bed and pull the covers up over your head. Maybe if you're really quiet . . .

You hear the door to your bedroom burst open and you yelp in alarm. Light floods into the room, momentarily blinding you. You screw your eyes shut and tears squeeze out and trickle down your cheeks. You hadn't realised you were already crying.

The covers are pulled back violently and strong hands grab your arms and begin to lift you from your bed. You kick and scream, until your vision clears and you realise it's your papa carrying you, and you begin to cry audibly, nuzzling into his shoulder.

He shushes you as he hurries out of your room on to the landing. The banging from the front door is louder out here and it makes you wince. You look down into the entrance hall and see the front door bulge and crack with each bang. You realise someone is breaking it down and you cry louder.

Papa shushes you as he turns right and runs down the corridor to the back staircase. You do not understand why he is not taking you to the panic room he once showed you. Steel-plated, as secure as a bank, he told you. With cameras and screens, its own air and water. You could stay safe in there until the police arrived. But you get into the panic room through Mama and Papa's bedroom, not down the back stairs. Why is he carrying you away from safety?

'What's happ'ning?' you cry. 'Where's Mama?' But Papa shushes you again as he takes the back stairs two at a time. He reaches the ground floor and pushes through the swing doors into the kitchen.

The back door is right ahead of you but Papa skids to a

halt when you both see a tall, dark figure through the glass, raising something and bringing it smashing through.

You scream and cling on tighter as Papa turns and runs back into the house.

You feel a warmth spreading between your legs and realise in shame that you have wet yourself, your hot pee-pee soaking into Papa's pyjamas. Papa turns left and runs along the corridor that leads to the laundry room. There is another door here that leads into the garage.

But this way, too, is blocked. The internal door opens before you reach it and another tall, dark figure steps through into your house. They're in the house! Why is this happening?

Papa stops and turns again as the man behind you cries 'Halt!'

Papa ignores him and runs back to the foot of the back staircase. There is the sound of crunching glass from the kitchen, and a huge final smash from the front door as it gives way and crashes to the floor.

There is a lot of shouting, loud and angry. You can't hear what they're saying, the noise is too much, everyone shouting over each other.

'Halt or I fire!'

'Armed police!'

'Get on the ground!'

'Armed police!'

'Do not move!'

'Surrender the child!'

'Get on the ground!'

Papa stops running and you bury your face deeper into his shoulder. Maybe if you don't look at all the angry men with guns, this will all go away.

You hear boots, lots of boots, stomping towards you as the shouting gets louder.

Papa doesn't say a thing, but he holds you tighter than ever, so tight it almost hurts. You hug him back, paralysed with terror.

The stomping stops and the shouting dies away. You open your eyes and see that you are surrounded by police officers in black armour, all with guns aimed at you.

You are too scared to scream. You stop crying too, as if frozen solid by terror.

'Put down the child,' says one officer firmly, not shouting any more.

'He's my son,' says Papa. 'You can't have him.'

The officer steps forward, breaking the circle, his gun pointed at Papa's head. 'If you do not surrender the child, I am authorised to use all necessary force.'

Papa does not reply. The officer stays where he is.

'He's my son,' says Papa softly and you feel his chest heave. You realise that Papa is crying. You have never seen him cry. It is even scarier than the men with guns.

'We both know that's not true,' replies the officer, which confuses you.

There is a long silence and then you jump involuntarily, as you hear a loud scream echo down the corridor from the entrance hall. Even though you have only ever heard her talk softly and with love, you recognise your mama's voice. Then there is a loud bang, followed by a thud, and then another loud bang, and another.

The circle of police breaks as they turn their weapons and point them back down the corridor.

'What the hell?' says one of them. 'Report!'

Papa begins to lower you to the ground while the police are looking away, but you fight him, trying to hold on tighter. He prises your fingers off him and places your feet on the floor.

He looks down at you. His face is streaked with tears.

'Run,' he whispers, but you cannot move.

Between the legs of the police you see Mama come running into the corridor. She is waving a gun, firing bullets at the policemen, her hair is wild, her face red and angry, she is screaming.

There is a deafening thunderclap of noise as the police open fire on her. You see her twitch and jerk, red splashes the walls, stains her clothes, she falls forwards, blood arcing out behind her.

You turn and run, pushing your way through the legs of the police, your size working to your advantage. You clasp teddy tightly. All conscious thought has ended. You are now just a frightened creature composed only of fear and the instinct to survive.

Behind you, you hear more shooting and screaming. Papa's voice in among more shouted orders. More gunshots, more thuds. You run towards the kitchen door, your bare feet sliced by the glass from its shattered window.

Then someone punches you in the back and you are flying forwards. You hit the ground face first, feeling the glass slicing your cheek. You skid on the glass until you stop, then you try to climb to your feet. But nothing works. Your eyes can't move, but they can still see your reflection in the glass of the oven door as you realise you can't feel anything. No pain, no fear.

You look into the oven glass and see yourself, a small, terrified boy, no more than five years old, clutching a teddy bear on the floor in a spreading pool of dark liquid.

You hear crunching glass and see two legs appear behind you.

'Dammit,' says a voice far away, as if heard through

water. 'We were supposed to bring the Godless freak in alive.'

Then the voice fades away and all that is left is your eyes, staring into their own reflection.

Then that fades away too and there is only darkness.

Jana snapped back to reality, scared and confused.

'It's OK, relax, take a deep breath, it wasn't real,' she heard Quil say. 'Not for you.'

She was shaking, breathing raggedly and . . . oh God, her crotch was wet.

'Drink this.' A cup was held to her lips and Jana sipped coffee and whiskey. She blinked away the sun-blindness caused by the sudden transition from indoor night-time to outdoors on a fresh spring day and focused in on Dora, Kaz and Quil. They were sitting on a wooden bench in Washington Square, Philadelphia. The sun was high, the air was heavy with the scent of flowers, but Jana's crotch was cooling rapidly.

She shifted, uncomfortable and embarrassed, willing herself to stop shaking.

'Don't be ashamed,' said Quil. 'Everybody who received the transmission wet themselves too.' She pulled a clean pair of jeans and underwear, and some wet wipes, from a bag and handed them to Jana. She indicated some nearby bushes. Jana took them and stood up, wobbling on unsteady legs.

'Let me help you,' said Dora. Unhappy at needing help but grateful nonetheless, Jana let Dora take her arm and walk her behind a big bush.

'I'll be fine now, thanks,' said Jana, waving Dora away. She stood with her hands on her knees, taking deep breaths, for a minute or two until the worst of the shaking had subsided, then she set about cleaning herself up. Her senses were unusually heightened after her experience. The red of the rhododendron was dazzlingly vibrant. The grass was greener, the sky bluer and the birdsong – loud as it was to compete with the hum of city traffic – was more melodious.

Nothing like dying to make you appreciate living. Jana thought she'd have learned that by now, but a person can't live with the constant apprehension of death. It would drive you mad. She had not suppressed the memories she had of young Yojana's death, but neither did she dwell on them. And the fact that she did not dream was probably a blessing, because she felt certain she'd have endured years of nightmares if she could. This boy's death had been worse, though. Yojana had just been confused. She hadn't really had time to be afraid for more than a few seconds. This boy had experienced such fear. It was . . . there wasn't a word for it.

When she was presentable again, she paused and took a moment, reorientating herself, closing her eyes and giving thanks for the sunlight on her skin.

By the time she returned to her friends, she had regained some semblance of control. The park was not crowded. This was siesta time and most of the people in the park had been napping under trees or on blankets laid out on the cool grass. Quil had explained that the demographic here was such that only about thirty per cent of the local population had the kind of neural interface chip that Jana had, but even so, the effects of the broadcast could be seen and heard.

Somewhere distant a woman was screaming hysterically, unstoppable. There was a cacophony of car horns and sirens. Jana saw three people walking shakily towards the exits, wet stains on their trousers, faraway looks in their eyes. A shaken father tried to comfort his son, their football kickabout derailed.

'What exactly did you do?' Kaz asked Quil as Jana rejoined them.

She had brought them here but had refused to tell them why, or to warn Jana of what she was about to experience. As the only one of the group who had a chip, only Jana had received the transmission.

'You hacked the chip network,' said Jana, half horrified, half impressed. 'Not you personally, though. One of your agents here on Earth.'

Quil nodded.

'Did everybody experience that? Everyone with a chip?'

'Forty-seven per cent of the world's total population just shared the moment of Stefan Seavers' death,' said Quil.

'When you say shared . . .?' asked Dora.

'The chips store memories and experiences,' explained Quil. 'High-end models stream them straight to a server for storage in real time. We hacked into the server, copied the last five minutes of Stefan's life, then streamed it direct into the brains of everyone with a chip.'

Dora whistled, obviously impressed. 'You just made, what, four billion people wet themselves. Wow.'

'But why?' asked Kaz.

'I'll show you,' said Quil. She rose to her feet and began walking. Kaz, Jana and Dora exchanged puzzled glances, shrugged and followed. She led them out of the park and into Walnut Street, where chaos reigned. Traffic was at a standstill, with many cars having been abandoned. People were milling around, half of them traumatised, half confused. There were many individual arguments going on as people who had not received the transmission berated those who had for holding up traffic, and a couple of those confrontations were beginning to attract other people on either side.

'At the moment the population is divided,' said Quil as they walked past a man who was literally red in the face with fury, standing beside a car with a slight dent in the bumper, yelling at a young couple who lay on the pavement beside a moped with a bent front wheel. The young man who had been driving lay against the kerb, shaking uncontrollably, unhurt but in shock, while his girlfriend tried to comfort him and ignore their abuser.

'Those who experienced Stefan's death are struggling to come to terms with what just happened, the rest are either furious or confused. But there's a change coming.' So saying, Quil pointed to a scene happening at a nearby intersection where a group of people were crowded around a woman in distress. She was lying on the road beside her car while a man performed CPR and a group of bystanders tried to hold back a distraught man and two teenagers; Jana presumed they were the woman's family. All had the dark stains on their trousers that indicated they had shared the transmission. Meanwhile a couple of police officers who were trying to calm the milling crowd and get to the woman to render assistance were encountering anger and resistance. Confused as to why so many people were trying to prevent them helping a sick woman, the police looked at first alarmed and then angry at the way the crowd was shouting at them to leave.

'All of a sudden, a large percentage of the population see the forces of state authority in a very different light indeed,' Quil said.

One of the police officers, a young woman who was surrounded by normal citizens shouting in her face, drew her weapon when a man poked her in the chest. But the crowd was too large and too angry, and she didn't have time to bring it to bear before she vanished in a sea of shouting citizens.

'Nothing like being murdered by the police to make you question authority,' said Quil, obviously pleased by what she was seeing.

'This is sick,' said Kaz.

Quil rounded on him, calm but forceful. 'No. Standing by doing nothing while the forces of state security murder children in the name of protecting you from imaginary monsters, that's sick. This' – she indicated the growing chaos around them – 'is the reassertion of sanity. You can't bury your head in the sand and pretend nothing's happening when it's your door they knock on in the middle of the night. And now all the smug, complacent, self-satisfied sheep who've been propping this government up, voting them into office, looking the other way when their neighbours and friends vanish, are starting to realise it.'

'I'm missing the wider context,' said Jana. 'What's the government – what's our mother been doing?'

By way of answer Quil stopped walking and pointed to a billboard on the side of a bus shelter.

The display showed a cowering woman, on her knees, hands raised in fear. In front of her, standing tall, protecting her, stood a square-jawed police officer, weapon raised and aimed at a threateningly tall man who loomed over him, features misshapen, hands like talons, teeth bared and pointed, feral, menacing, monstrous.

'Beware the enemy among us,' the slogan read. 'Report your suspicions to the police. Help us to help you.'

Jana didn't need an explanation, and she could see that Kaz didn't either, but Dora still seemed confused. Quil noticed this too, so she explained, directing her words to the young woman from the seventeenth century.

'When our mother's plan to win the populace over by

humanising herself was derailed,' said Quil, 'she hit on an alternative strategy. An old strategy, tried and tested over and over again in the darkest periods of history.'

'Fear,' said Kaz.

Quil nodded. 'Clones were the perfect bogeyman. They look like you, they sound like you, they live among you. They might be anyone – but they're different too. Stories were spread about mutations, monsters who lived among the populace. Clones who could control minds or change their faces, or become invisible, or move objects using telekinesis.'

Dora scoffed. 'Seriously?'

'Monsters created by rogue science,' said Quil. 'People who looked as normal as you or me, but who had special abilities that gave them an advantage. A secret network of super-powered clones, working to undermine society for their own evil ends, breeding more of themselves in underground labs, placing agents at all levels of society. An enemy within.'

'And people fell for it?' asked Dora, surprised at how unsurprised Kaz and Jana were by Quil's words.

'Oh Dora,' said Jana. 'People have been falling for it for centuries. You should know better than any of us; you were the one who was almost hanged as a witch, remember?'

'Are there really clones with abilities like that?' asked Kaz.

'Don't be stupid,' said Quil. 'It's theoretically possible, but no one would ever do it. Although, I suppose if I did, the war would have been over a hell of a lot quicker than it was.'

A burst of gunfire echoed across the intersection from nearby.

'We should get out of here,' said Kaz.

Quil shook her head. 'No, there's something else I want you to see first.' She kept walking, leading them past the confusion and violence and turning left on to South 6th Street.

'Hard to believe a whole country fell for this,' said Kaz as they walked past more billboards, more distraught people, more confused, scared police.

'America isn't a whole country,' said Jana. 'Not any more. After the assassination of President Trump and the second civil war that followed, it split in three. Pacifica, Texarcana and America East, which became known as the New World. The population was already afraid – of spies, of another war. I left about ten years before this, but it's not honestly very surprising to me that things have gotten this bad.'

'Our mother played on that, too,' she said. 'Claimed that Pacifica and Texarcana both had advanced programmes creating weaponised clone infiltrators. Worked like a charm. She won a landslide victory in the New World by promising new legislation, crackdowns, mandatory testing. Security theatre. When the war began, she was the obvious choice to be the first president of Earth.'

'But why do all this?' asked Jana. 'She was always ambitious but this . . . I don't understand it. She was cold, distant, controlling. But this is proper mad stuff. Dictatorship, oppression. I just . . . as bad as she was to me, to us, Quil, I wouldn't have thought her capable of this. Where did this come from?'

Quil shrugged. 'I don't know. I don't really care. Maybe Grandad abused her, maybe she resented Granny making her do the washing-up, maybe she's genuinely, properly unhinged. Maybe she just really, really likes power. It makes no odds, in the end, *why* she did this. Understanding her motives won't help me stop her. It's irrelevant information as far as I'm concerned.'

Jana did not think it was irrelevant at all. Surely understanding an enemy was the key to defeating them. But there was something defensive about Quil's dismissal of their mother's motivations that made Jana wonder about her motives. How much of her war was driven by her sense of injustice, and how much by a personal vendetta against the woman who created her and then threw her away like so much garbage? The single-minded determination that drove their mother to seize power by any means necessary wasn't a million miles away from the single-minded determination needed to create and lead an army in a war across the solar system. Maybe that was why Quil didn't want to delve too deeply into her opponent's psychology – she was worried what it might reveal about her own, how much of a mirror it might hold up. This version of Quil wasn't quite the monster that the scarred and poisoned version they had met in the past was, but she had just made nearly half the population of Earth experience the death of a child. It took a special kind of ruthless certainty to do something like that.

Jana wondered how much of the drive that led these two women – her mother and her kind-of sister – to become monsters was part of her own make-up.

The quartet reached the intersection with Chestnut Street and found their way blocked by a line of jittery-looking police officers facing away from them, their guns drawn. Beyond them, Jana could see a crowd of people, all dressed in black, all wearing very familiar plain, white masks. The crowd was just standing, facing Independence Hall, chanting 'We are not monsters!'

'This way,' said Quil.

She led them into the lobby of an office building and took them up in the elevator to the top floor. The office was in chaos and nobody challenged them as they walked into a large office, the glass wall of which looked down on to the square. Quil locked the door and pressed a button that tinted the internal windows, masking them from view.

'Welcome to the Philadelphia massacre, everybody,' said Quil. 'Take your seats; the show is about to begin.'

Jana and Kaz exchanged worried glances, then stood at the window beside Dora and Quil.

'Let me give you the play by play,' said Quil. 'Below us are about a thousand protestors. All clones. They are staging a protest here because the president is in there.' She pointed to Independence Hall.

'Surrounding them is a spontaneous demonstration by ordinary citizens. They've just experienced the reality of the policies they've voted for and they don't like it. It's probably too early for them to feel shame at their own complicity, although that will come, later. Right now they just want answers. They're not completely rational, not thinking clearly. Dying will do that to a person. They've ceased to be individuals, they're just a mob. A large, angry mob threatening the local seat of power. There are mobs like this gathering all over the New World, and variations of this scene are going to be played out all day. But this is the worst. The mayor here is a close political ally of our mother. He has his eye on the Senate in the next election, and she's here to show her support by inaugurating him personally. He wants to curry favour with her, and he knows that only the most hard-line operators win a place in her inner circle. He's chipped, so he experienced Stefan's death, but unlike everybody else he saw it only as an opportunity. In about five minutes he's going to give the order to open fire. He hopes it will secure his political future.'

Jana felt a sick anticipation. She didn't want to see what was about to happen.

'If there's a massacre here,' said Dora, 'then it's as much

your fault as his. You created the conditions for what happens.'

'I know,' said Quil quietly, and Jana realised that Quil truly understood the seriousness of her actions.

'But you can't make an omelette without breaking some eggs, right?' said Kaz, contemptuously.

Quil did not respond.

'I don't need to see this,' said Jana quietly. 'I know what point you're trying to prove, Quil, but in the last few weeks I've seen enough bloodshed to last me a lifetime. Enough. I'm leaving.'

Cursing the fact that she was still unable to travel through time solo, she held out her hands. Dora and Kaz stepped forward and took them without hesitation. Quil looked at them, surprised and disappointed.

'I didn't bring you here for entertainment,' she said, seemingly frustrated at their inability to grasp her motives. '*This* is the reality of what I'm fighting. This massacre, people like this doing things like this – this is what I'm trying to stop. You need to see it, the reality of it, to understand. It's not some abstract history lesson. These are real people, ordinary people. Stupid and gullible and complicit but not evil. Not really. I've shown them a glimpse of the reality they profit by and they're questioning it. What happens next is a distillation of everything I'm trying to stop. It's not numbers of dead or pictures of the aftermath. It's real blood and bone and murder.'

For the first time since they'd embarked on this excursion into Quil's timeline, her sarcasm and smugness had dropped away, and Jana could see that Quil actually *cared*. Jana pulled her right hand free and stepped forward, reaching out.

'I get it,' she said softly. 'We get it. But you've got to understand that we've seen massacres already. In the past, in Pendarn. Unarmed men kneeling, helpless, while soldiers created by another version of you slit their throats, stabbed them and shot them as they begged for mercy. A whole army wiped out in an instant by technology they couldn't understand. And on Mars, innocent civilians slaughtered just to create useful optics for the evening news. We get the point you're trying to make. We're just saying that you don't need to make it. Not to us, not any more. We get it, Quil. We know the human cost of the struggle. We don't need to see it again.'

Quil stood staring at Jana for a long time, then nodded once, slowly. 'OK,' she said softly. 'Fair enough.'

A single laser beam shot up from the crowd in the square and began slicing down towards Independence Hall.

There was a cacophony of gunfire and screaming.

Quil reached out and took Jana's hand.

'Let's get the hell out of here,' she said.

As the office faded around them, Jana saw Quil look back over her shoulder, out of the window, down at the violence unfolding below. She wondered what she would see if she could look into Quil's eyes at that moment. Would Quil be happy or haunted by what she saw? It worried Jana that she still didn't really know the answer to that question.

Interlude 1:
Neso Campus, Neptune
University, June 16 2204

'It was a form of synaesthesia. You are familiar with the term?'

Professor Yasunori Kairos talks as we walk the short distance from the lecture theatre to the laboratories. The artificial suns are high in the milky sky above, their heat tangible through the diamond dome that encloses the campus.

Biology and the quirks of the human brain are not my specialty – I am a physicist – but I am familiar with the term.

'Synaesthesia is when the brain routes signal incorrectly, leading to a confusion of the senses,' I replied.

'Exactly. A person who suffers from synaesthesia – although suffers is the wrong word, it's not a disease is it, let us say a person who experiences it – may be able to see sounds, or hear colours. The connections in their brain are badly wired, the input from one sense is accidentally sent to the receptor for another. It is an effect we can all experience now, using the cerebral input chips to share the experiences of synesthetic. It was all the craze a decade ago. Have you tried it?'

I shake my head, realise that he is not looking at me and so say, 'No.'

'You should. It's a fascinating experience. Anyway, the ability to travel in time was a form of synesthesia.'

Everything I have learned about the quantum universe and the relationship between time and space, rejects this idea. The ability to travel in time is dependent upon speed or space-time warping. The idea that it can be a biological process is laughable.

I was warned, when I was offered the job as Professor Kairos's lab assistant, that I was venturing off the beaten path and into the thickets of fringe science, but I had not expected anything as outré as the theory the professor is expounding as he greets me for my first day on the job. I begin to worry that I have damaged my career by hitching my wagon to his train.

'Surely not,' I say, trying not to sound too dismayed or dismissive.

'Time is quantum, so time is a product of perception,' he explains. 'Hours, minutes, seconds – these are human creations that have no objective reality. Animals do not measure time in days or weeks, they have no conception of past or future, they live in a constant now. And so did our distant ancestors, our animal forebears on the African plains.

'Because time is quantum, and because it was unobserved, we have no idea what kind of superposition it adopted. How did time behave before we became conscious of its passing? Did it flow backwards, did it skip randomly from one moment to next week and then back to yesterday? Did it flow sideways in some fashion?

'We can never know.

'All we can know is that one day a neuron sparked in an

ape brain, the ape stepped out of the endless now and thought 'I'll do it later'. At that instant, time was *observed*, the superposition collapsed and it began to flow in a linear fashion. One moment began to follow another in a nice, orderly procession. Of course, one could argue that the effect is retrospective, that when we observed the background radiation of the big bang we forced the superposition to collapse all the way back to the moment of creation, but that is a side note.'

I feel patronised. The professor is explaining rudimentary quantum physics to me as if I am a freshman. I try not to let my indignation show.

'I know this,' I say, forcing good humour into my voice.

'Of course you do.' He waves his hand dismissively and I am reassured. 'But imagine – what if a synesthetic person observed a quantum effect?'

I stop dead in my tracks at the unexpected question. It has never occurred to me to consider such a proposition, and the implications of that simple question cascade through my brain. In a moment, I am properly excited.

The professor does not notice, and continues his walk and talk. I hurry to catch up to him.

'We know that the act of observation can affect the state or behaviour of a thing,' he is saying, 'but all those observations are made using the same senses – the same eyesight, the same hearing, the same sense of smell.

'But what if the nature of the observation changed? What if we observed a quantum effect with a sixth or seventh sense? Would that, perhaps, change the behaviour of the thing observed in an entirely different manner?

'You could posit that if one were to be observe time using a theoretical psychic sense, telepathy say, that it might flow slightly faster or slower, or even backwards. Do you see? It is not only the act of observation that forces quantum states to collapse, it is the means of observation that dictates the kind of collapse that is witnessed.'

'Yes,' I say. 'Yes, I see.' And I do, somewhat. I can feel equations bubbling up from the back of my mind as the implications of Kairos's theory percolate. My heart rate is up.

'My scans demonstrated that the mineral the time travellers were exposed to had subtly altered their brains, parts of which lit up in the most extraordinary ways. I believe they developed an entirely new sense. The boy, Kazik, once told me that he could feel the mathematics of the universe. Literally feel it.

'Everything is numbers, we know that. At its deepest level, everything is mathematics. It is the language of the universe, and the time travellers could read it.'

He pauses. 'No, read is the wrong word – they could sense it, feel equations in their minds. They perceived time using a new sense, observed it in a different way, and when they did so it behaved in a different way for them. It flowed forward or backwards around them. I would posit that they were actually perceiving the mathematical reality of imaginary time, which . . .?'

It takes me a moment to realise he is asking me a question. Eventually I parrot the standard definition, 'Which sits at right angles to linear time in the same way that breadth sits perpendicular to length.'

He looks askance at me and nods.

'Yes, well. The source of the mineral that affected the time travellers was an asteroid recovered from the Kuiper Belt about seventy years ago. The properties of it confounded me. It was, I think, a manufactured thing, but its origin remains a mystery. Whatever its provenance, it sat just slightly out of sync with time. It had mass and duration, it was not instantaneous, but some part of it existed within imaginary time, and it bestowed the ability to perceive that reality upon the time travellers, do you see?'

'How?' I ask.

'I never discovered how they came by their abilities. Dora, the girl from the seventeenth century, had a theory that she shared with me the last time I saw her. The implications of it were . . . unsettling. But it is of no matter, I was never able to prove or disprove it either way.'

I wait for him to share Dora's theory, but he does not. I prompt him.

'Is that your area of current research?'

He shakes his head emphatically. 'No, my efforts are expended in a very different direction. A more practical one. Come, see.'

We have reached the door to the laboratories, which he opens and holds for me, ushering me inside. I have butterflies in my stomach as I cross the threshold. I have heard stories of the work that goes on here. Some of the discoveries these labs have produced are legendary. I have no idea what work I am going to be assisting the professor with, but I have a sense that this is a turning point in my life. A moment I will look back on in the future with . . . what? Pride? Regret?

The corridors and staircases are a blur but I know we descend many many levels below the surface. I ask why we do not use the elevator, but he tells me there is none.

'My work has some unexpected gravitational side effects that could possibly pose a serious risk to an elevator's occupants,' he says.

Finally, we reach the bottom of the staircase. I look up and the stairs reach to the vanishing point. I am exhausted, but the professor has not broken a sweat. He notices me noticing that and smiles.

'I climb these stairs twice a day,' he says with a smile. 'I have never been fitter!'

In front of us is a pair of heavy metal doors, like the kind you would find on a bank vault. The professor presents his eyes and palm to the biometric reader, and the door slowly swings open to admit us.

Inside is an enormous room, round like the inside of a football, with white painted walls. It is a cavern carved out of deep rock with great precision. The doorway opens onto a walkway several metres wide which in turn leads to a room with solid, metal, windowless walls. A box, really. A metal cube inside a stone sphere.

It is a measure of how enormous the sphere is that the cube is the largest enclosed space I have ever entered (second to the sphere, I suppose), and I have visited the old cathedrals on Earth.

The professor leads me down an aisle way to a series of huge, screens – actual screens, not floating holo-displays. Before them are sat a group of seven people, checking read-outs, turning dials and pressing buttons on massive metals consoles. It is all very old school – hardware is practically obsolete these days.

I hypothesise that the same gravimetric disturbances that preclude elevators also interfere with the holographic displays and motion sensors that would more usually be deployed for this type of work.

But of course, I do not know what this type of work is, yet.

The professor introduces me to the scientists but their names and faces are a blur to me. I have locked onto the display on one of the screens and it fills me with excitement.

'Is that . . . is that what I think it is?' I ask.

'That depends what you think it is,' responds the professor. I note that, given long enough exposure, I may come to find him insufferable.

'I think it's an anti-matter generator hooked up to some kind of dwarf star alloy injector,' I say.

'Then yes,' says the professor. 'It is exactly what you think it is. Come.'

He gestures for me to follow him past the screens to the far wall of the metal box cathedral. He presses a button and a screen withdraws revealing a single window, about a metre square. The glass is so thick that I can tell it is distorting the image, but I can make out an enormous apparatus hanging from the topmost point of the sphere like a spider hanging from a line. It has massive red metal legs, articulated in two places, pointing down towards the absolute centre of the sphere. There sits an enormous chunk of rock, suspended by cables from above and below.

And as I see this, I realise what he is doing.

'You're recreating it,' I whisper in awe.

'Yes I am,' he whispers back, gleefully. 'You see, I analysed the asteroid that granted the power of time travel. I was at close quarters to it for a long time and I scanned it to the last micron. The base was unexceptional – a V-type carbonaceous asteroid, probably from somewhere out near Jupiter or Uranus.

'But there were seams within it. Well, seams is too strong a word, maybe threads would be better. Tendrils, tiny almost infinitesimal lines of exotic matter unlike anything I had ever seen before, not in reality, not even theorised. These tendrils were composed of incredibly dense matter. So dense that if the asteroid had been composed entirely of the same substance, its mass would have equalled that of the Earth. The substance warped space-time around the rock, and through it. I cannot say what its origins were, but I believe it was formed by the interaction of anti-matter and heavy metals somewhere near the event horizon of a black hole.'

I look at the apparatus that hangs before me. My mind swirling with wonder at the scale of the professor's ambition.

'You've done the equations?' I ask. Then I shake my head, annoyed at myself. 'Of course you have.'

I can barely conceive of the mathematics involved, but the translation of that mathematics into a real-world machine capable of creating the threads of exotic matter and threading them through a suitable chunk of rock in order to recreate the asteroid that was destroyed so many years ago – that leaves me breathless.

'I am so close,' he says. Then he claps a hand on my shoulder. 'We are so close.'

He presses the button, the screen closes. He turns me around and walks me back to the screens and the rest of his team.

'Today is the first attempt,' he says as we walk. 'We are going to try and place one single thread, a micron thick, through the centre of the rock.'

I feel a momentary thrill of fear. The forces he is describing, the power that will be summoned in the sphere surrounding this suddenly flimsy-feeling metal cage, are elemental. I can see so many things that could go wrong, so many ways that this experiment could end in disaster.

'I presume we will prepare the system and then retreat to the surface to monitor the experiment?' I say, trying to sound matter of fact, worried about embarrassing myself as I puff my way heavily back up the stairs.

'No no, we need to remain here. Were something to go

awry – and I assure you that will not happen, the equations and engineering have been checked and rechecked many many times – the adjustments needed to restore balance would need to be made very quickly. Even the tiny time lag created by remotely operating the instruments from the surface could be disastrous. Also, as I have explained, the gravimetric disturbances caused by the process would hinder our remote control. No, we must be close, for safety's sake.'

I do not think safety is much on his mind, but I do not say so. It is not a good idea to start your first day by questioning the wisdom of your mentor's pet project. Instead I ask the question I've been wanting to ask since I received the professor's summons.

'Why am I here?'

'A long time ago a young woman asked me to explain how quantum effects interact with large amounts of temporally unstable materials. My whole life since that moment has been spent trying to answer her question. I think you might be able to help me.

'Your work on the interactions between gravity and spacetime in quantum foam intrigue me. I believe they may have an application to the work I am overseeing here. I think you could help me understand the effects we are about to witness.'

My pride and ego are flattered. I know my work is good, but to have such a compliment paid to me by a giant in the field is more than I ever dared hope for.

'I will do my best,' I say, humbly.

'That is all I ask,' says the professor, smiling. 'Now, I want you to be here to be a witness to this first attempt. It is the data from this event that you will be helping me to analyse, so it is only proper that you see it happen.'

He shows me to a seat.

'Sit and watch, then afterwards we shall talk some more.'

So I take a seat and watch. My specialty, as he has mentioned, is theoretical quantum physics. Practical experimentation is rare in my field, my work exists as equations, so the experiment I am about to witness is thrilling. If the professor succeeds at creating the material he describes, and threads it through the rock as a means of stabilising and preserving it, we will be able to measure time fluctuations in a way never before possible.

The professor joins his team and they have a huddle, a final discussion before go. I cannot make out what they are saying, but there is one dissenting voice – a woman of about the professor's age seems to be challenging him about something. He waves aside her objections, smiling, but she is not mollified. The rest of the group look at their feet, or stare down the woman, either staying out of it or taking the professor's side.

Eventually she concedes, and her argument is either abandoned or overruled. She does not, however, look happy as she returns to her instruments.

I find my thoughts returning to the concerns I had before the professor flattered me. My fears have not entirely been quelled, and seeing the discussion just now makes me even more nervous. But it is too late to say anything. I can hear the winding up of colossal engines, and the metal floor of the box-lab begins to hum with vibration.

The screens are a jumble of images. There are no live camera feeds – I guess because the cameras wouldn't survive out there – but there are lots of monitors and sensors taking readings. I can see the power flowing through the metal apparatus, the raw materials being fed in through lines to a kind of crucible where the incredible forces required to transform them are being conjured. Then the output is filtered down the arms and stored, ready for deployment.

The preparation process takes ten maybe fifteen minutes. I do not measure the passing of time because I am mesmerised by the impossible power of what I am witnessing.

'Are we ready?' The professor has to shout to be heard above the noise.

One by one his team affirm that they are. The woman is pale as she shouts her agreement.

The professor steps forward and presses a big red button.

And the screens shut down.

The consoles lose power.

The hum stops.

The lights go out.

We are plunged into total lightless silence.

I think I hear someone moving past me quietly, away from the instruments. Just a rustle of silk in the darkness. I must be imagining it.

Everyone starts shouting. I can't make out the words, but there's panic in all the voices.

Instinctively I stand, but once I have stepped away from the chair I lose all my bearings. I have never experienced such complete darkness.

Somebody pulls a phone out and switches on the torch. Others follow suit.

They begin trying to get the equipment working again, but nothing is responsive. I keep quiet and stay out of their way.

A minute passes, and the panic lessens. But then the humming begins, softly at first, I feel it through the soles of my feet.

The instruments burst back to life in a blaze of colours and sounds.

I immediately see that something is terribly wrong. The material is flooding down the lines, the crucible is burning, the deployment arms are weaving the material through the rock deftly but continuously. The machinery is completely out of control.

'Shut it down,' cries the professor, over and over again, but nothing anybody does makes the slightest difference.

I notice a glow coming from the far end of the metal box lab, at the wall where the window is. Starting in the centre of the wall, a red haze is spreading outwards. It sparks and fizzes.

'Look!' I shout. The professor follows my pointing finger and sees the encroaching sparks. He gasps as I skid to a halt beside him.

'What is it?' I ask.

The professor is transfixed by the glow. 'Time,' he says sadly. 'It is time. Catching up with me.'

He turns to me and the rest of his team.

'I am so sorry,' he says. 'Please forgive me. I have been so stupid.'

The glow is spreading along the right and left walls now, rushing towards us.

'I should have known,' he says. 'She warned me.'

'Known what? Who warned you?' I shout, looking around for the woman he argued with moments before. She is nowhere to be seen.

The professor does not answer me. He just stares at the glow as it rushes towards us.

Light and time seem to bend around me as the sparks engulf us. I am screaming as they do.

And then I am cold and weightless and floating in the empty nothingness of space. I see, even as my eyeballs freeze, the professor and his team tumbling away from me in the void.

And there before us, glowing red but seeming to cool, is a huge rock, floating free of us into space.

I watch it tumble and fade until there is nothing left of me.

Interlude 2:
Poland, 16 September, 2015

Kaz walked down the dusty country lane, enjoying the fresh, crisp autumn air. It had been dark when he had caught the first train from Kielce, so even though he had been travelling for three hours, the morning mist was still burning off the landscape as he made his way from the small local station, through the sleepy village and out into the farmland that surrounded it. Every joint in his body ached, and his head throbbed as he walked, the pain a reminder that he had somehow survived being at the epicentre of the most devastating explosion in history. The doctor in Kinshasa had warned him that it might take months to fully recuperate from his physical injuries, and Jana had made it plain that his psychological ones might take even longer. He had promised them both that he would take some time to heal, and so here he was, seeking temporary sanctuary in the land of his birth.

He paused for a moment and checked his phone, which was buzzing insistently in his pocket. According to the GPS, he had arrived at his destination. He looked around, spinning through 360 degrees, looking for a landmark. Off to his left, emerging from the mist, he saw an old farmhouse standing on the edge of a dark wood. Three storeys tall, painted white, it looked well-kept and inviting. There was a paddock to one side where Kaz could see a horse nibbling the grass. Kaz limped towards it, feeling nervous and uncertain. A low brick wall, pitted and old, marked the edges of the garden. Kaz pushed open the wooden gate and stepped on to the path that led to the light blue front door. As he closed the gate behind him, Kaz saw one of the downstairs lights come on, and a figure passed before the window. Kaz stopped, looking through the window into what appeared to be the kitchen, craning for a glimpse of the man inside.

Kaz had last seen his father, Zbigniew, when he had returned him to this own time and place – Kielce, Poland, 2014. It had been a sombre parting, both of them riven with guilt over the fate of Kaz's mother, Peyvand, lost in time after Quil had intervened in their attempt to save her from a car bomb explosion. A year had passed for Zbigniew since then, but Kaz had been expecting to find his father in the same flat, so he had been surprised when the door was opened by a young man he had never seen before. However, Zbigniew had warned the flat's new occupant to expect Kaz, and had left his new address.

Taking a deep breath, Kaz walked up to the front door and knocked firmly.

Kaz swallowed the vodka down in one gulp, trying not to wince as he did so. It was cold and sharp, fresh from the freezer, and it both burned and froze as it slipped down his throat. He placed the small glass carefully on the kitchen counter and shook his head once to decline his father's offer of a refill.

'I don't think,' said Kaz, 'that finishing a long walk with a drink is part of any fitness programme I've ever heard of.'

'It will do you good,' said Zbigniew. 'You are old enough now that you should learn how to hold your drink. Your metabolism is running hot after the walk, and if your limp is anything to go by, you have some injuries to heal. The vodka will loosen your muscles and stop them feeling so stiff tomorrow.'

Kaz was pretty certain this was complete nonsense, but he shook his head and smiled indulgently.

'If you say so, Dad.'

'I say so,' said Zbigniew with a smile that made Kaz pretty certain his father was just messing with him.

Kaz sat at the large wooden table while his father returned the vodka bottle to the freezer and busied himself making coffee. The kitchen was large and warm, with a terracotta tile floor and simple wooden furniture – table, dresser, cupboards. It felt homely and well used and about as far from the kitchen of a retired soldier and widower as Kaz could have imagined. His father had never been much for cooking, but now there were jars of flour, a well-stocked spice rack, an apron hanging from a hook on the door. These weren't the only things about his father's new house that had surprised Kaz when he had arrived here the day before; there was a line of family photos on the mantelpiece in the living room, pictures of Kaz and his mother, Peyvand, in happier times, and there were paintings, posters and prints hanging in hallways and rooms around the house. The flat Kaz and his dad had shared in the years after Beirut had been spartan and functional, the quarters of a soldier who did not want to feel comfortable. There had been no hint of personality, let alone luxury, in their living space. This house felt entirely different.

'I didn't think I'd ever see you again,' said Zbigniew, his back to Kaz as he spooned grounds into the filter. 'I figured that if you found your mother, you'd come straight back and let me know what had happened. It's been a year. I assumed . . .'

There had been no hint of this in the greeting Zbigniew had given Kaz when he had opened the front door minutes earlier. There had been no tears, no hug, no visible relief. But then his father had always been a soldier, and he had never been demonstrative.

'I thought I'd give you some time,' said Kaz, haltingly. Truth be told, he wasn't entirely sure why he had travelled to 2015 rather than 2014. It would have been easy for him to arrive moments after he had left and end his father's suspense. 'To grieve.'

Kaz's father placed the filter in the coffee maker and leaned over to fill the jug from the tap.

'So,' he said as he did this. 'She is dead.'

There was no emotion in his voice, no shaking shoulders, no shock or disbelief.

'Yes,' said Kaz.

Zbigniew turned off the tap and poured the water into the coffee maker. 'How?' he asked as he did this.

'Quil.'

Kaz saw his father nod, just once, as he closed the coffee-maker lid and flipped the on switch. Only then did he turn to face his son.

'I had assumed as much,' he said. 'All those years raising you on my own, letting you believe your mother had died in the explosion . . . if she had been alive, you would have found a way to let me know. I knew she was dead right away. So you mustn't think my reaction callous. I don't know how long you have been grieving – but for me it has been five years.'

Kaz nodded, feeling a lump in his throat and a wobble in

his lower lip. He refused to cry in front of his father, so he bit it back and took a deep breath, staring at the tabletop to steady himself.

He felt a hand on his shoulder and looked up to see his father looking down at him.

'No, don't do that,' said Zbigniew, with a kind, sad smile.

So Kaz held on to his father for dear life, and wept.

24 September, 2015

It took a few days for Kaz to feel properly comfortable in his father's new house, but by the end of the first week it began to feel familiar. His father devised a punishing fitness regime for him, and Kaz spent the best part of each day walking, swimming in the nearby lake, chopping wood and tending the garden. He was feeling stronger and more sure of his body every day; his bones ached less, his strength was returning.

He and his father spent many hours talking, sitting by the fire in the evening. Zbigniew told Kaz he had taken his pension and decided to settle once and for all. After years travelling the world as a peacekeeper, he felt like staying in one place, close to his old home, and putting down roots. Kaz was forced to reassess his father, who he had thought constitutionally incapable of this kind of settled contentment. Zbigniew told Kaz stories of his time in the army, most of which Kaz had never heard before. Kaz knew his father was hoping he would respond with stories of his own, and Kaz had obliged him with some tales of his days as a pirate, and his exploits in the seamy underbelly of Barrettown on Mars. So far he had avoided discussing the real crux of the matter, and his father did not pry.

Now, kneeling on the ground with the afternoon sun warm on his skin, Kaz was gathering vegetables for dinner; his father was making a stew.

'I have a choice to make,' said Kaz as he pulled another carrot from the earth and dropped it into the basket.

'Uh huh,' responded his father, who stood beside him pulling peas off the vine.

'It's not much of a choice, really. I mean, I know what I have to do, but . . .'

'Tell me.'

Kaz put his hands on his knees and paused. 'It's Jana. She wants to travel forward in time again, to the war. She thinks it's her duty to stop Quil and her mother. And she wants me to go with her.'

'Do you think you should?'

'Yes,' said Kaz firmly. 'She's my friend, and I owe her that. She and Dora have a better chance if I'm there. But . . .'

'But?'

'But I want to kill her, Dad. Quil, I mean. I really, really want to kill her.'

'And you're worried what that says about you.'

'Yes.'

'You've killed before. I was there, remember.'

Kaz remembered the guard he had shot beneath Sweetclover Hall when they had rescued Quil, moments before the time-bomb had exploded.

'Yes, but that was in self-defence. This would be different. I'd be deliberately hunting someone down for revenge.'

Zbigniew sighed and sat down on the earth beside his son.

'You know the hardest part of being a peacekeeper?' he asked. 'Breaking the cycle. You get dropped into places where the most horrific things have been done. Terrible, unforgivable crimes. And often there's no functioning justice system in place, so the only form of justice for the survivors and the families of the victims is revenge. So the victims of the crimes commit their own atrocities, seeking to balance the scales, thinking that will bring them some measure of peace. And then the victims of their justice retaliate and it never, ever ends.'

'So how do you break the cycle?'

Zbigniew shrugged. 'Sometimes you can't. Sometimes all you can do is put yourself between the two parties and keep them separated. But sometimes, if you're very lucky, and if one or both of the parties has a leader with an ounce of humanity left in them, you can broker a peace, find some justice in persuading everyone to accept responsibility for what they've done. It's hard, but I've seen it done.'

Kaz looked across at his father, whose face held such compassion and strength. All his life Kaz had wanted to be more like his mother. Her adventurous spirit, her determination to ferret out truth and stories. His father had seemed distant and mysterious. Not cold, nor aloof, just never entirely present, and certainly not the kind of role model he had ever aspired to emulate. He wondered now how he could have failed to appreciate how much he had to learn from him, too.

'It would be very dangerous,' said Zbigniew. 'I know you've seen combat, but from what you've told me they were skirmishes at best. You're talking about walking into a full-blown war. Surviving that kind of situation is as much about luck as training or skill. If you're going to risk your life, you need to be certain, absolutely certain, that you know why you're doing it and what your objective is. So what would your primary objective be, son? Killing your enemy, or protecting your friends?'

By way of explanation, Kaz finally told Zbigniew the exact circumstances of Peyvand's death.

30 September, 2015

The sun was setting over the woods, casting long shadows across the house and field. Kaz stood at the edge of the trees, took a deep breath of the clean country air and closed his eyes. This was a good place. He could understand why his father was happy here.

'This could be your home now,' said Zbigniew, who stood beside him. 'If you wanted it to be.'

'I know,' said Kaz. 'We'll see.'

'I understand.'

They stood there in companionable silence for a few minutes. Kaz felt fit and ready, in body and mind, for the ordeal ahead. He knew what he had to do, and why he had to do it, and he was prepared for the possibility that he wouldn't survive. His father was too. Benefits of being a soldier's son, thought Kaz – having a father who respected the decision to go to war.

'If I'm not back by morning, I'm not coming back,' said Kaz eventually. 'I won't make you wait this time.'

'OK.'

'And when I do come back, I want you to introduce me to your girlfriend.'

Zbigniew didn't reply.

'Oh come on, Dad. Cooking? You? With an apron? Pictures on the walls? Flowers in the vase on the piano? What, did you think I wouldn't notice?'

After a long silence, Zbigniew spoke, sounding uncertain for the first time Kaz could recall. 'You must understand, son, it's been five years for me since—'

'I know,' Kaz interrupted, letting him off the hook. Nervous Zbigniew made him uncomfortable. 'You don't have to explain or apologise. What's her name?'

'Um, Malgosha. She's a photographer.'

Kaz smiled. 'Of course she is. Good for you. I look forward to meeting her.'

'I'd like that.'

Kaz turned and pulled his father into a hard embrace.

'Love you, Dad.'

'Love you, son. Good luck.'

They broke apart, Kaz stepped backwards, then closed his eyes and flung himself away from 2015, into the future, towards whatever destiny was waiting for him.

Part Three

Contact with the enemy

8
Kinshasa, Democratic Republic of Congo, 2 June 2120 – 38 years to timebomb impact

Jana felt like a spare part.

Dora was off in the future, gathering intelligence, making plans, laying in the supplies they would need. Kaz was in the past, spending time with his father, getting his head together, dealing with the death of his mother. But they could both travel through time solo, and Jana couldn't yet. So she was stuck here in Kinshasa, kicking her heels.

She walked around the garden of the clinic, building her strength for the coming battle, sifting through the events that had brought her here.

Their plan had been so simple. They had rescued Quil from the timebomb, administered the antidote to the poison that had made her mad, then travelled back through their lives, learning about each other. Quil had learned the truth about Jana's origins and upbringing; Jana had learned the truth about Quil's. She had come to understand and empathise with her clone sister, even to think of her as family, of a kind. When they had returned to the quantum bubble, they had thought their mission a success. Now that Quil knew who she was, she would not travel back in time to 1640, wouldn't meet and marry Sweetclover, wouldn't pursue them through time fuelled by a paranoid vendetta for the slaughter of Barrettown on Mars. During the brief moment when they thought they had successfully changed history, Jana had considered her options and had decided, to her surprise, that she wanted to travel to the future with Quil and finish the war she had started. Two sisters, fighting together to overthrow their mother and make the solar system a better place for their kind.

But time had played a cruel trick on them.

When Professor Kairos had realised that a quirk of quantum mechanics had created two Quils – the one she had come to think of as her friend, and the mad one who was her implacable enemy – all their plans had crumbled. They hadn't changed time at all; they were as trapped by it as they had ever been. They'd created their enemy by initialising the quantum bubble and splitting her in two in the first place.

When the mad version of Quil had arrived in the quantum bubble, the superposition that had split her in two had collapsed, and the version of Quil that Jana had befriended had been extinguished in a blink of an eye. Now there was only the mad one left, the one who had killed Kaz's mother, the one they had to stop.

'Penny for them.'

Jana skidded to a halt, startled out of her reverie. Kaz stood before her on the path, smiling. She ran forward, flung her arms around him and squeezed for all she was worth. He laughed and squeezed back.

'Missed you. Feeling better?' she asked after she released him.

'Much. You?'

Jana gave a shrug. 'Kind of. When you left I could shuffle. Now I can walk. Give me another week and I should be able to manage a scurry.'

She looked him up and down, appraising. His posture was much better than when he had left, and his skin looked pink and healthy.

'You look better,' she said.

'Yeah, Dad took good care of me.'

'How is he?'

'Retired to the country, and kind of loved up, I think.'

'Really?' said Jana, incredulous.

'I know, that was my reaction. Where's Dora?'

'In the future. Plotting plots and scheming schemes, like she does. She should be back soon, said she'd aim for tonight, so we'll see what happens then.'

They walked together through the garden, swapping gossip until they reached the clinic's entrance.

Jana gasped in shock when the doors opened to reveal Henry Sweetclover, sitting patiently in the lobby, waiting for them.

'What?' she said.

Sweetclover rose to his feet and stepped forward. 'I know you probably wish to kill me, but I beg you to hear me out. I have great need of your assistance.'

Jana and Kaz exchanged an amazed glance, then Kaz punched Sweetclover in the face.

Jana winced as she heard his nose break.

* * *

'Explain the superposition to me again?' said Sweetclover, his voice muffled.

Jana, Kaz and the freshly returned Dora sat in a semicircle facing the chair to which Henry Sweetclover was chained. Their patient explanation of events was proving difficult for the seventeenth-century aristocrat to grasp.

Jana sighed. 'Look, all you need to know is that when we created the quantum bubble we kind of cut Quil in half, made two versions of her. One that went back to the past and met you – the mad one – and one that stayed in the bubble with us – the good one. When they both ended up back in the bubble at the same time one of them was cancelled out. Ours. The nice one.'

'And my wife is poisoned, you say?'

'Yes,' said Jana. 'By her – our – mother, the Earth president. It's a toxin designed to induce paranoia, aggression, irrational behaviour. Our Quil got the cure, yours hasn't.'

'That would certainly explain a lot,' muttered Henry. 'But it has been much worse since she returned to her own time.'

'Worse for you, maybe,' said Dora coldly. 'I do not think we would see much difference.'

'I reckon she's just got more things to be paranoid and irrational about, now that she's back in the middle of her war,' said Jana. 'She is literally under attack, right?'

'Perhaps that is it,' acknowledged Henry.

'Now you,' said Kaz.

Henry shifted uncomfortably in his seat. 'Would you be so kind as to undo these restraints?' he asked.

Kaz rose to his feet, stepped forward and punched Sweetclover in the face again.

'Jeez, Kaz, come on,' said Jana, but he silenced her protest with a glance.

Blood trickled down Sweetclover's chin from a fresh split in his lip.

'I came here to help,' he said, spitting blood.

'So you say,' said Jana. 'But we haven't seen any evidence of that yet. Tell us why you're here. What happened after you and Quil jumped away from the bubble? What changed to make you willing to betray her?'

Henry shook his head. 'Not betray. Save. Rescue. From herself. She is out of control. I thought, maybe, you would be able to help me . . . restrain her. But if what you say about the poison is true—'

'It is.'

'Then all you need to do is give me the antidote so that I can travel back to the future and administer it.'

'Sorry, doesn't work like that,' said Jana. 'The warhead of the timebomb acted as a lodestone – it pulled us back to Earth every time we jumped. But after the detonation, after the destruction of Sweetclover Hall, the warhead was destroyed too. You can't jump forward any further than the second before the timebomb exploded.'

Sweetclover groaned. 'I had forgotten. How could I have been so stupid?'

'That was your plan – to jump back to the instant you left? Why? What was happening? Where were you?'

'It's a long story,' was all Henry could mutter. He looked horrified and crestfallen.

'Then tell it,' said Kaz. 'We've got *plenty* of time.

9
Cornwall, England,
7 April 2158, 8:43 A.M.

Henry Sweetclover looked into his wife's eyes and felt a chill in his veins as he realised she was enjoying herself.

'What's their response time?' she asked again.

The man kneeling at her feet – a security guard who had been guarding the perimeter of the Sweetclover estate and who had escaped the blast of the timebomb, but not the attentions of Quil's genetically engineered soldiers – clenched his jaw and looked up at her defiantly.

Quil sighed and nodded to the soldier standing beside the man. The soldier reached down and twisted the man's head violently, snapping his neck. The guard flopped to the ground and lay there twitching for a few moments while Quil turned her attention to the other guard, who knelt beside the corpse.

'I'll ask again,' said Quil. 'What's their response time?'

The woman did not hesitate to answer. 'It depends on whether they come by sea or air,' she said, her voice trembling. 'Air, it takes seventeen minutes, so they'd have been here by now. By sea, thirty-six minutes from scramble. Which gives

166

you about twenty minutes before the army arrives and wipes you out.'

'Such a shame you won't live to see that,' said Quil, nodding to the soldier again and turning away, uninterested in the death of another enemy.

Henry stood and watched her leave, a sick feeling deep in his stomach.

'Kill everything,' had been her order, and the monstrous creatures that had emerged from the ruins of his former home had obeyed without question. Everyone in the Hall at the moment of impact, and most of those in the grounds, had been vaporised by the timebomb, but the guards patrolling the perimeter had survived. Their bodies now formed an obscene pile on the edge of the impact crater.

He had initially imagined Quil's horde of monstrous warriors swooping down on Pendarn and slaughtering the civilian inhabitants. In fact, Pendarn was underwater, submerged beneath the rising tides of a warming world. The land that had once formed the Sweetclover estate, on the uprise of rock overlooking the town, now formed an island in a long archipelago that was all that remained of Cornwall. He could see why it had been a good site for a secret detention centre. Isolated, sea-bound, it was far from prying eyes and offered no chance of escape.

Henry was repulsed by the soldiers Quil commanded. They came in two forms. The majority were men selected from various points in history by Quil, captured and stored in suspended animation in the cave beneath the hall. Quil had genetically enhanced their strength and endurance, while at the same time reducing their capacity for individual thought. They were huge, hulking men, all muscle and malice.

The smaller number, the shock troops, were something else

again. Although they were clones based on a human template, they had been made whole in the Io Scientific labs using technology that should not have been in existence at that time. Standing eight feet tall, they were physically imposing, like massive mountains.

'Isn't he beefy,' Quil had said with relish, grinning, when she showed him the first of these clone warriors back in 2013. 'Viking template. A man named Brynjar. It means armoured warrior. Appropriate, no? I found him raiding a village in 836. The most perfect physical specimen I've ever seen.'

These new Vikings, which numbered only a hundred, were indistinguishable from one another. Their skin was hard and chalk-white, like porcelain, and it made a grinding sound when they moved. Their eyes were slitted, like a cat's, and they had sharp, pointed teeth. Quil had designed them to be the perfect warriors; animalistic and unnatural.

'They said clones were monsters,' she had explained with relish. 'They said we were the stuff of nightmares, they conjured bogeymen to scare the populace into submission. Now I'm going to give them their nightmare. I want to see the president's face when I march into the White House at the head of an army of monsters.'

He rejoined Quil by a group of her soldiers who were operating a bundle of electrical equipment they had brought up from the cave. She was talking into a radio urgently.

' . . . survived, obviously,' she was saying. 'Look, Arihi, firing the weapon at the detention centre was a stroke of genius. I assume your plan was to give me a chance to escape rather than reduce me to my component atoms?'

There was a pause, then a female voice crackled from the speaker. 'Either or.'

Quil snorted a laugh. 'Fine. Look, I need extraction, and I

have a lot of people here who need airlifting. How quickly can you get to me?'

'We'll have a drop-ship with you in half an hour.'

'Make it ten drop-ships.'

'Ten?'

'Lots of people. You'll see.'

'Will you be safe until we arrive?'

'We have incoming, but I'm pretty sure we can handle them. See you soon. Out.'

Quil passed the radio to one of her soldiers and turned to Henry.

'That was my second-in-command, Arihi,' she explained. 'She's in orbit on the flagship of our fleet.'

Henry did not think the woman had sounded like anybody's subordinate. He might not have served in the army, but Henry knew how a soldier was supposed to speak to a superior officer, and there had been none of the appropriate deference in the clone's tone. Henry glanced sideways at his wife, wondering.

Quil strode off towards her elite force and Henry fell in alongside her.

'She fired the bomb at you. Tried to kill you. Are you wise to trust her?'

'She made a judgement call. Either the bomb would kill me and prevent me being tortured for access codes, strategies and the like, or it would give me a chance to escape. She knows I have travelled in time. She's the only person up there who does. And she knows I couldn't control it, not at the time of my capture, not like I can now. She and I had discussed the possibility that I might interact with a temporal explosion in a different way to anybody else. So she was gambling that the explosion would destroy the detention centre and throw me through time to safety. And she was right, kind of. If your maidservant and her friends hadn't intervened, I might even have avoided being burned to a crisp in the process.'

They reached the phalanx of porcelain-white monsters – and Quil began giving orders. They listened intently, focused on her words, still and silent; then, when ordered to move, they ground into life, rumbling away to take up defensive positions around the perimeter of the estate.

'They only have to hold off the Earth forces for ten minutes, and then the drop-ships will be here and we can evacuate,' she said by way of explanation. 'I doubt they've sent a big force anyway. Probably think everyone here is dead. Come on, we can survey the area from the ridge. I want to see them in action.'

So saying, Quil took off again, striding eagerly up the incline that led to the high ridge that looked down on to the crater. Her excitement at finally being able to watch her creations in combat was palpable. Henry found her enthusiasm disquieting.

When they reached a good vantage point – the same spot where they had stood to watch the timebomb's fiery descent – Quil stopped and turned to survey the area. Henry did the same. The crater dominated the landscape, a huge earthen bowl where his home had been, with a chasm at the bottom leading down into the cave below. Around the lip of the crater, Quil's army of genetically modified soldiers were standing in ranks. They didn't move or fidget, didn't look around at their fellows or their surroundings. They just stood, motionless, awaiting orders. They wore heavy armour and carried guns – projectile weapons, and lasers – and they made a fearsome sight.

The shock troops were taking up their positions in the

gulleys and pathways that led through the landscape up to the fence that marked the perimeter of the estate. There were three main approaches to the fence – one west, one south east, one north – and all were guarded by concealed creatures.

Henry pitied the soldiers who were about to come walking up those pathways.

They waited for five minutes, surveying the still, silent landscape until the soft, distant burr of engines was carried to them on the wind.

'Here they come,' said Quil, excited.

Henry spotted the first group of ten soldiers in the distance, advancing slowly up a narrow gulley from the north, about half a mile away. He pointed them out to Quil.

'There!'

'And there,' replied Quil, pointing west, where another group were approaching cautiously, weapons raised, up a path through the woods.

'Wait for it . . .' she said, holding Henry's hand, squeezing it tightly in thrilled anticipation.

The soldiers in the gulley were attacked first. The shock troop monsters fell upon them from above, a silent, white blur. Not a single shot was fired, not a noise was heard. The soldiers were dead before they knew they were even under attack.

To the north, the creatures emerged from the forest like ghosts, teeth bared. They brandished no weapons, made no sound. These soldiers did have time to register their attackers, but no shouts of alarm were heard, and no shots were fired. The creatures tore into the soldiers, literally ripping them asunder with their arms, tearing soft, exposed flesh with their obscene teeth. The slaughter was over in seconds.

'Perfect,' breathed Quil in awed delight.

Henry disentangled his fingers from hers and walked down the hill alone.

The drop-ships descended upon the island in a storm of noise and dirt, blowing up loose earth from the crater and whipping up dust storms.

Solid and inelegant, the ships were large – each as big as an entire wing of his vanished home, reckoned Henry – and they settled on to the grass beside the crater where Quil's army had cleared space for them.

Huge bay doors dropped down and slammed into the earth to reveal the ships' holds, lit by red flashing lights. Each hold was crewed by two of the Godless army that waited for Quil in orbit, and Henry was struck by the obvious similarities between the women and the men, and the way they wore masks similar to that worn by Quil during her recuperation in the seventeenth century. Unlike her, however, these Godless warriors had decorated their masks with patterns, shapes and colours to assert their individuality.

Quil directed the soldiers into the holds, and broke her shock troops into ten groups, dividing them equally between the ships.

'In case we lose any,' she said.

The hulking stone-skinned monstrosities marched into the holds in unison. Henry tried and failed to mask his disgust at the blood that soaked their uniforms and their faces, red on white. They looked like they'd been . . . *eating*.

Although their faces gave nothing away, Henry could tell by their body language that the masked Godless clones were confused and disturbed by their obscene cargo.

'Henry, with me,' barked Quil. He followed her into the hold of the nearest drop-ship. She nimbly scaled a ladder at the end of the hold and led Henry through a short corridor into the cockpit.

The windows were ringed with screens, and there was also a HUD display beamed on to the windows themselves. In front of all this information sat two pilots, awaiting orders. Quil strapped herself into a seat behind the pilot on the left. Henry tried to strap himself into the seat behind the other pilot, but the complexity of the latch defeated him and his wife undid herself, leaned across and fastened him in with an indulgent kiss. Once she was reseated she gave the order to take off.

'Hang on, Henry,' said Quil, smiling broadly at him.

The ship lurched, the engines roared, and Henry felt a jolt in his stomach as the horizon visible from the window shifted and the ship lifted off the ground.

He heard Quil laugh, but did not risk turning to look at her.

'You're as green as grass, my love,' she giggled. 'Here.'

He felt a paper bag being pushed into his hands and without hesitating, he opened it and buried his face in it. He had flown on planes, which had been bad enough, but the thought of leaving the atmosphere behind filled him with terror. He closed his eyes, focused on his breathing and tried with all his might not to throw up.

He managed it, too . . . right up to the moment the engines stopped and he realised that the limbs that were moments ago too heavy to lift were now floating of their own accord.

'Ew,' said Quil. 'Did you have to wait till we hit zero-g?'

Henry stepped from the shower feeling refreshed, but still not entirely sure he was one hundred percent in control of any of his bodily functions. The gravity in the flagship, created by the spinning central wheel, was half of that on Earth, and the porthole that showed the planet spinning madly around kept reminding him of the unnaturalness of his position. He draped a towel over the porthole, which helped. He sat on the bed, glad to have washed the vomit from his hair and the stink of fear from his body, but he still felt a dizzying mixture of shame at his weakness, disgust at the carnage he had witnessed and fear at how he would be accepted aboard this ship.

He was a man, natural, Godly if you like, on a ship of people (and monsters) who despised, with good cause, everything he was. No matter how much Quil assured him that he was safe and welcome among her people, he did not share her certainty. He worried that his presence might weaken Quil's position among her own kind. She had married a womb-born. Might some of her fellow clones not consider that an act of treachery?

The room he was in was small and boxy, with a low ceiling that meant he had to walk with a stoop. This had been the same in the corridors he had been led down after his arrival on board. All of the Godless – with the exception of Quil – had been bred short and squat; powerful and muscled, they were anything but elegant, and the aesthetic of the ship reflected that. Every space he entered felt slightly too small for him. This lack of space combined with the light gravity to render Henry clumsy and awkward.

He dressed himself in the clothes that had been laid out on the bunk – simple black combat fatigues – and only managed to bang his head on the ceiling once, his elbow on the porthole and his knee on the edge of the bunk. Not bad, really. Taking a deep breath, he opened the door. The woman who had escorted him here was still standing patiently outside. Her mask was decorated with black and white etchings of the

Fibonacci spiral, which made Henry think of her as cold and mathematical even though he had no other evidence of her personality beside her quiet solicitude when he arrived, and her polite invitation to follow her to the bridge now.

She led him through the ship. Now that he was able to appreciate his surroundings, he was surprised to find that the interior was a riot of colour. He realised he had been expecting bland conformity and functional inelegance even before he'd seen his poky cabin. The ship was crewed by copies of humans, and he was ashamed to find that he had expected them to be lacking in something, some fundamental spark of humanity. His wife had the memories of a real person; she had been designed bespoke, individual, a copy of a real person, not like the factory-farmed photocopies that made up the army she led.

The vibrant creativity evident on every wall belied his shameful prejudice. Landscapes, portraits, murals of all kinds, colour and shape and form – life! – sang from every wall and door. It was chaotic, unordered and seemingly random, but it was the very opposite of the grey conformity he had been expecting. He knew that each clone was based on one of two templates – a single male and a single female. As he walked through their living art gallery, Henry wondered what this revealed about the personalities and talents of those original templates. Somehow, even though he knew it was wrong, he felt even worse for the clones when he considered the possibility that they might all be copies of people with deep-seated artistic needs. How much worse to be forced to live your life in the dark interior of an asteroid mine when your overriding desire was to express the beauty of the universe in art.

He cursed both the prejudice that had led him to be surprised, and that which had replaced it, causing him to categorise humans as more or less touched by God, more or less deserving of liberty, depending upon whether or not they had art in their soul.

By the time he reached the bridge he felt sick and ashamed, and humility made him doubt himself. He had never felt more keenly the difference between the Henry Sweetclover who now joined his wife at the head of her army, and the man he had been when he had first encountered her. So much had changed, within and without. He had so few verities left that he clung to the central certainty of his life more tightly than ever – his love for his wife, and hers for him.

The bridge was a loud, busy space full of bustle and activity. Masked men and woman sat at consoles ringing the circular room, while the centre was dominated by a large table above which floated a dazzling array of holograms. As he approached it he tried to decipher its complexity, but beyond identifying Earth and a cluster of dots that he took to be the Godless fleet, the rest of the lines and arcs, spirals and scrolling lists of figures made his head swim.

It took him a moment to realise that Quil was standing at the table staring deeply into the web of light, arms folded. He had not picked her out of the crowd immediately because she was wearing a plain porcelain mask, undecorated, of the kind she had used to hide her burns during the first years of their marriage. Now the only way he could tell her apart from her fellow clones was her height. He supposed it made sense for her to reassume the aspect she had presented when she had commanded this fleet, so many years ago in her personal timeline yet only days ago for the people who crowded on to the bridge now. Standing around her was a jostling mass of Godless – all her officers, come to witness her miraculous return and help brief her on the current state of affairs.

This was a council of war.

Not wishing to draw attention to himself, Henry stayed on the fringes of the room. Nonetheless, many of the masked faces turned towards him when he entered – and many stayed fixed in his direction as his presence evoked . . . what, he wondered? Fear? Hatred? Jealousy? He tried to ignore their scrutiny and fixed his eyes on the hologrammatic display, waiting, as was everybody else, for Quil to give her assessment.

'You have done well, Arihi,' she said eventually. She reached out and squeezed the upper arm of the woman who stood next to her. Arihi's mask unsettled Henry. Painted on to it was a plain face, artificially aged to make it look like a mediaeval artwork, ringed with gold like an ancient icon of Christ. Henry found the effect sacrilegious, and immediately distrusted the woman who had chosen to make such a statement.

'I just followed your game plan,' Arihi replied. Henry was surprised that she did not conclude with 'Sir' or 'Ma'am', as seemed proper when speaking to a superior. Quil did not seem offended by her lack of deference, so Henry assumed that was the way she liked it.

'Well, apart from the whole shooting a giant asteroid at me,' said Quil, her tone neutral and lacking in menace, which made it seem even more menacing to Henry.

Arihi paused, gathering her thoughts, then responded. 'The defences around the detention centre were formidable. Once our spies had established your location, we spent a day assessing our options. A ground assault was out of the question. Neither drop-ships nor conventional missiles would have made it through. The timebomb was our only option. At least that way there was a chance. It was not a decision I took lightly.'

Quil did not reply immediately, letting the silence hang.

In the first months of their acquaintance, Henry had found it difficult to read his wife's emotions. The mask she had worn had concealed so much of the unspoken information that informed conversation. So much can be communicated by a look, a glance, a slight downward turn of the lips, the clenching of a jaw. Henry had none of those cues during his courtship of her, and it had taken him a long time to conquer the unease and uncertainty this caused. Eventually he had learned to read the language of her whole body, which spoke eloquently of her feelings. The set of her shoulders, the placement of her hands, what she was doing with her fingers and feet, all gave clues to her state of mind. She had insisted on keeping her mask on even when she slept. For years he had never seen her face; it had only been revealed to him when she had completed the surgery to restore it, whereupon he had needed to learn to read her emotions anew. It was as if she had suddenly started shouting all the time; the emotions he had learned to divine from subtle clues were now obvious and instantly apparent. Her face delighted him.

Here, in this room of masked people, Henry felt all at sea again. He did not know the body language of these strangers – although he wondered if all the men and women shared their physical dialect, meaning that he would only need to learn two sets of cues – and so he was unable to get a sense of the mood. In the broadest sense, he could tell that the room was tense; the hunched shoulders and shuffling feet made that plain. Henry felt suddenly the danger of his situation. He would have much less warning than usual if one of the crew on this ship of ciphers was angered and preparing an argument or an attack.

'It was well done,' said Quil eventually. Henry studied the set of Arihi's body, looking for a slight relaxation of the shoulders, a sigh; some sign that Quil's approval caused her relief. He saw no such indication, and that concerned him. What kind of subordinate officer did not fear their leader's censure? A dangerous one, he concluded.

'Earth's forces made their last stand in the skies above Mars,' said Quil, speaking louder now, addressing the whole bridge. 'Earth itself lies undefended. But we would be foolish to think them defeated. They will make us fight for every square inch of ground that we take. Key installations are heavily defended from aerial attack, as the detention centre was. But the cities are vulnerable. We can end this war quickly, if we wish.'

'But not cleanly,' said Arihi.

Quil shook her head. 'No. If we were willing to bombard major cities from above, I expect we could force a surrender and win this war in less than a day. I know that many of you feel this to be the best course of action. That you hold human lives at little cost. And while I would be unmoved by the suffering such a strategy would inflict, I still believe it would be counterproductive.'

Henry had not realised how afraid he had been of his wife's plans until she said she was not planning on inflicting wholesale civilian casualties and he breathed a huge sigh of relief.

'As you know, I had hoped to win the war in one fell swoop, by aiming our timebomb at the White House. Such a show of strength would have quelled all political resistance. But that is no longer an option. Now we storm the White House by land.'

Quil turned to Arihi and nodded. She in turn gave a signal to a soldier who stood by the large doors at the far end of the bridge from Henry. The soldier pressed the door control and they opened to reveal one of Quil's monstrous shock troopers. There was an audible intake of breath from the assembled clones as it strode into the room, its limbs grinding like stone. People instinctively recoiled from it, clearing a path and leaving it standing in a clearing that widened gradually for over a minute. Henry didn't need to see the faces of the people in the room to feel their fear.

The impact of its height was greatened by the relative shortness of the clones. The effect might have been comical if not for the streaks of gore that garnished the monster's face.

It looked to Henry like a wolf standing among sheep.

'For years, they've been telling the world that there are monsters in it,' said Quil. 'Let's prove them right.'

She reached out and stroked the creature's face with the back of her hand, gently, like a mother caressing a child. Then she withdrew her hand and clicked her fingers once.

The creature turned, reached out, grabbed Arihi by the arms and, before she could utter a cry of alarm or surprise, it ripped out her throat with its teeth. As her blood spurted over the creature's black uniform, her iconographic mask slipped sideways and fell to the floor with a sharp clang. She was older than Henry had expected, her face lined and weary. Her eyes were wide in horrified surprise and her mouth worked silently, trying to make sounds through vocal cords that were no longer there.

Eventually her head lolled back, lifeless, and the monster dropped her, letting her fall to the floor with a wet crunch.

'So perish traitors,' said Quil, calm and matter-of-fact. 'If anybody else feels like trying to kill me, by all means have at it.' She spread her arms wide, inviting attack, spinning slowly to present her undefended chest to the entire bridge.

Nobody made a sound, nobody moved.

'No one?' She stopped spinning and stood firm, bestriding the corpse of her once second-in-command.

'Arihi was just the latest in a long line of people who thought they could kill me,' she said, her voice harder and colder than Henry had ever heard it. 'If anyone here harbours doubts about my cause, is considering betraying me to the enemy, believes for one second that I am vulnerable in any way, know this – you will fail, like all the others failed. You will die like all the others have died.'

Quil paused to let her words sink in. Henry watched, stunned by the sudden change in her. Had she planned this? Was this carefully considered theatre, a performance and an example designed to instil fear and obedience? Or was it instability, a moment of madness? Had she really just switched from calm to murderous in an instant? For the first time he allowed himself to voice the fear that he knew had been growing inside him for some years.

Was his wife mad?

10
8 April 2158, 12:02 P.M.

She'd told him he didn't have to come.

As Henry felt his stomach lurch up towards his mouth he wished, more fervently than he had ever wished anything before, that he had agreed to stay behind on the Godless flagship and watch from the heavens. But his sense of honour and duty to his wife had compelled him to insist upon being allowed to stand by her side as she prosecuted the final battle of her great war. He had called upon every weapon in the armoury of seventeenth-century manhood to convince her of his sincerity, and she had been charmed by his old-fashioned chivalry, and agreed. So here he was, encased in lightweight but awkward body armour, in a drop-ship hurtling towards the ground at ungodly speeds. He'd thought his ascent to the flagship had been bad, but this was so much worse.

If he had been sitting in the cockpit rather than in the back with the troops, he would have been able to see the other ninety-nine drop-ships streaking hotly downwards towards Washington on the eastern seaboard of North America; but he had no wish to add terrifying visuals to the terrifying feeling in his stomach and the terrifying noise.

'Whoa!'

'Brace!'

Quil and the pilot spoke simultaneously and Henry did not have time to wonder what they were warning against before the ship gave a violent lurch, cracking his head against the bulkhead.

'What's happening?' yelled Henry, craning to look through the cockpit door and out of the window.

He swiftly wished he hadn't. Ahead and below were hundreds, maybe thousands, of red streaks blooming out of the cloud tops like the tendrils of some gargantuan behemoth reaching up to pluck them from the sky.

'Don't worry.'

Henry felt a gloved hand on his knee and he looked across the aisle at the Godless woman sitting opposite him. Her mask was painted with a grinning goat's head, slit-eyed and demonic.

'We'll be down and safe in no time, I promise,' she said, and squeezed his knee.

It was an oddly kind and unexpectedly intimate intervention, and it made Henry even more uncomfortable.

'Deploying countermeasures!' yelled the pilot.

The ship lurched violently again, and from that point until they ploughed into the ground, he lived like salt inside a shaker, waiting to be spat out of his container and scattered to the four winds.

'Coming in hard!'

The impact when they hit the ground was bone-shattering, but somehow he was still in one piece when the shuddering stopped. There was a moment of calm and then an absolute cacophony began.

'Let the shock troops go first,' said Quil, climbing out of the cockpit and into the body of the ship. 'They can take the worst of it.'

As the rear door slammed down and the monsters scraped their way out into the sunlight, and a swarm of bullets that bounced off them as if they were made of stone, Quil leaned down, lifted her mask and kissed Henry on the lips.

'Still sure you want to be here?' she asked with a wry smile.

'I belong by your side,' he said, aware of how corny it sounded, but not caring because it was true.

Quil turned to the Godless soldiers sitting opposite Henry.

'I know you were detailed to be my personal guard,' she barked. 'But I'm telling you now that you are his, not mine. You keep him safe.'

The four Godless nodded.

Quil turned back to Henry. 'It's as I briefed aboard the flagship. The shock troops go first, then the engineered from our army, then the real clones bring up the rear. We let the shock troops take the brunt of the battle, and we roll in and mop up. So stay with these soldiers, and stay behind me. Understood?'

She was talking to him like he was one of her soldiers, giving her orders and expecting him to obey without question.

Henry thought it was kind of sexy.

He nodded.

Quil walked to the rear door and poked her head out, surveying the scene. By the noises he could hear – constant gunfire, the crump of explosives, occasional screams and the whine of descending drop-ships – Henry knew it was going to be unlike anything he'd ever experienced out there. Then his wife stepped outside and vanished from view in a haze of smoke.

The genetically engineered soldiers she had created in the past followed. A moment later the Godless troops also exited the craft.

Henry looked across at the four Godless designated as his personal protectors. There was Goat-face, who had comforted him during the descent. Beside her sat a man with his mask decorated to look like some kind of helmet with a gold shield at the top, crossing red lines over black where the eyes should be, with the bottom half removed to reveal his jawline; the effect was intimidating. Beside him sat a woman with a unicorn shooting rainbows from its horn painted on each cheek. Finally there was another man, who had painted his mask yellow and decorated it with a single black curve to denote a smile, and two crosses for eyes.

'Glasses live?' asked Smiley-face.

The Godless had small screens built into the glass eye-slots of their masks, but Henry had to wear a headset that had a lens jutting from it across his right eye. He toggled it by blinking twice, as he'd been shown, and a map of the area floated in front of him, with their position and objective clearly marked. They had landed on Constitution Avenue, just inside the enormous levee that prevented the rising water levels submerging the city. To reach the White House they would have to fight their way down the avenue for a kilometre and then across the lawn in front of the house for another 500 metres. Alternatively, the map was offering them a more direct route cutting diagonally across Virginia Avenue and approaching from the west. Neither option looked appealing. Constitution Avenue and the White House lawn were heavily armed kill corridors wherein anybody on the ground was likely to be diced. The diagonal route offered more cover, but a greater chance of getting bogged down in close-quarter fighting from house to house.

Flashing dots indicated the landing sites of other drop-ships. Henry reckoned only about half of them had made it through the missiles, but even that seemed like a miracle. They were scattered in a rough grid pattern around the White House, meaning it was under attack from every side simultaneously. One drop-ship had managed to land smack in the middle of the rose garden. Quil had told him about two ships that had been aimed straight at the White House itself, both carrying only the shock troops. The idea was that they would clear the building quickly and with ease, while the conventional forces dealt with the traditional defences, securing the approaches against counter-attack. It appeared that one of those ships had been destroyed on approach, but Henry was sure that even half the number of intended monsters would be more than enough to quell any resistance.

'Coast is clear for the moment,' said Goat-face. 'We exit the ship, turn hard right and run for the first building we see. It's a lawyer's office, and it's been cleared. After that we progress along Constitution Avenue a building at a time, staying behind the fighting. I'll lead. You and you' – she indicated Unicorn and Helmet – 'cover the roofs ahead and behind us. You' – she indicated Smiley-face – 'stick with the cargo' – she indicated Henry.

'Move out,' said Goat-face, rising and leading them to the rear door. Unicorn followed hard on her heels and Henry and Smiley-face came next, with Helmet bringing up the rear.

The noise outside had not diminished. There were bangs and flashes, and bursts of bright light from lasers. The ground was shaking so much that it was impossible to distinguish the shockwaves from individual explosions. Henry did not think this qualified as a clear coast at all, but he was too scared to say so. He held his rifle tightly. He had declined the offer of a conventional laser rifle; he didn't like the way the beam cut through everything. His weapon was a modified laser that fired short sequential bursts of light, in imitation of old-fashioned projectile weapons. He felt more comfortable with it.

'Go!' yelled Goat-face, and Henry ran behind her out on to the battlefield.

Kinshasa, Democratic Republic of Congo, 2 June 2120 – 38 years to timebomb impact

'I did not want one of the laser weapons because . . . because of your mother, Kaz. Her death was a terrible accident—'

Kaz stepped forward and punched Henry in the face again.

'Shut up!' he yelled. 'You don't talk about her; you don't mention her. Ever!'

Henry nodded through bloodied tears of pain.

'Sorry,' he muttered. 'Sorry.'

There was a long pause before Jana asked: 'What happened next?'

'We ran, and we fought. People shot at us. It was very confusing. Chaotic. Loud and disorientating. We made our way up the Avenue, in the wake of the worst of the fighting. Lots of bodies. Lots of body *parts*. It was awful. But we were not in the heart of the battle. I remember I saw one of the monsters lying dead. Just one. Shot through the eye. Wreckage was strewn everywhere – vehicles, weapons, rubble and steel from the buildings that had been destroyed. Water splashed around our ankles; I think maybe the levee had been damaged.

Not destroyed, for that would have deluged us, but there was a steady flow of water into the road.'

'You made it to the White House?' asked Dora.

Henry nodded. 'I cannot say how long it took. The four Godless who guarded me were astonishing. It was as if they knew where every shot was going to come from. Neither they nor I were even wounded. Then we rounded the end of the avenue and reached the long stretch of grass that leads up to the White House itself.

'Everything was destruction and carnage. The White House was lit up within and without by explosions and laser fire. So much defensive fire was being directed from the building that it was as if it were shrouded in a curtain of light that formed an impenetrable barrier. I could make out the Godless forces mustered behind barricades and wrecked vehicles, shooting from huge holes in the earth carved out by explosions. Then there was an ear-splitting explosion from within the building, and for a moment there was an eerie silence. The defensive fire fell silent and all there was was smoke, a huge billowing cloud of it rushing towards us. It enveloped us, choking us, blinding us. It muffled all sound, but soon the firing could be heard, almost distant through the murk. Then it began to clear and the building lay before us, nothing but a shell.

'We ran towards the building, following the tide of Godless troops that poured into it. The buildings that lay to either side of the main house were ruined, also. We had a clear run into the wreckage.'

8 April 2158, 14:26 P.M.

Henry searched frantically for his wife. It seemed like days since she'd left him to lead her army in battle, but he knew it could only be hours at most. His four protectors stuck by his side, Goat-face leading him through the confusion to the ruined room where she had set up a temporary headquarters.

He saw her sitting behind a charred wooden desk with her feet up on it, receiving reports from various commanders. Although he was from the 1600s, Henry had lived in enough time periods, and seen enough films and television, to recognise the Oval Office, or at least what was left of it. Once this had been the centre of power for the whole world, but as America had splintered apart during the twenty-first century, the influence of this room's inhabitant had diminished. Only in the last couple of years, since Abhilasha Patel had been nominated to head the Unified World Government formed in response to the Godless threat, had the chair Quil was currently sitting in become once again the seat of greatest power on the planet.

Quil saw him and smiled, waving her arms to indicate her dominion.

'Whaddya reckon, Hank? Does it suit me?'

His relief that she had come through the battle safely was

tempered by his unease at her seeming enjoyment of the slaughter and the spoils it had provided.

'It's just a desk, my love,' he said soberly.

Quil pouted. 'Spoilsport.'

Henry scanned the ruined room, open to the elements on three sides and with only half a roof.

'Where is the president?' he asked.

Quil pointed to the ground and widened her eyes. 'Lurking. Hiding underground in her bunker like the cornered rat she is.'

'Trapped?' He found that hard to believe. 'Surely there are tunnels or some such contingency.'

'Of course. The duck has all sorts of secrets. It even has its own train line! But I have maps of everything, thanks to a treacherous insider with a clone fetish. We secured all the exits first. She's trapped down there in her little subterranean city. Boxed in.'

'Duck?'

'Deep Underground Command Centre. They call it the Ducc,' said Quil. 'Quack quack.'

'We're getting a global transmission,' shouted one of her adjutants. 'It's her.'

'All screens,' said Quil, sitting up and staring seemingly into space. Henry's eyeglass flickered and the map that had led him here was replaced by a woman who looked like his wife. She was roughly the same age, he thought, and considered how similar was the shape of her face, the eyes, the mouth; she could have been Quil's sister. One of the quirks of time travel, he thought – you end up the same age as your mother.

Quil's 'mother' was standing at a lectern with a picture of the White House on it. The words below the picture rather redundantly read 'White House'. Behind her was a blank concrete wall, no windows.

'Last week, the world watched in horror as Barrettown burned,' she said. 'Destroyed by a cowardly and unprovoked attack. Before this tragedy, there were many who wished to appease the Godless hordes that besiege us. They spoke of negotiation, of peace, of common ground. They believed these monsters could be reasoned with. I counselled against such weakness, but I was overruled. Representatives of your governments – good men and women, for all their naivety – travelled to Mars for peace talks. These martyrs to freedom held out the olive branch in good faith and were slaughtered for their pains. Last week, the world saw what I had seen long before – the true face of the Godless.

'And now they besiege us. Their ships circle our world, and they rain fire down on the seat of power. But I tell them this – we will fight for every inch of this planet. It is our home and you are not welcome here. The people of Earth – the natural-born heirs of the human legacy – will never surrender to you.

'This may be my last transmission, but whether I and my staff survive this day is not important. We stood firm in your defence, and we know that our loss will only strengthen your resolve.

'To the people of Earth, I say this. Report to your muster stations and prepare to defend your homeland.'

A noise came from somewhere off screen and the president glanced sideways for a second, then resumed her oration.

'The monsters are coming, but they will not find you cowed, or weak, or defenceless.'

The signal cut out abruptly.

Henry was impressed. The woman was a fine orator,

conveying strength and resolve despite her circumstances. He could imagine her rallying cry having the desired effect the world over, for all the good it would do.

'That went out on all live broadcast channels,' said Quil's new second-in-command, a male clone with a snarling green demon face painted on his mask.

'I think that deserves a riposte, don't you, Hank?' said Quil. She turned to Demon-face.

'Are we ready to transmit?' she asked.

'All ready, as ordered,' replied Demon-face, gesturing in the air. A drone camera floated into the room and hovered in front of Quil, who looked up into its lens, keeping her mask on for the broadcast, its smooth blankness offering no clue as to the feelings of the person beneath.

'Same deal as her – all broadcast channels?' asked Quil.

Demon-face nodded.

'Great. Count me in.'

Demon-face counted down from ten, with the last three digits being silent, and then indicated for Quil to speak.

'People of Earth,' she said, calmly and clearly. 'My name is Quil. I command the army of the Godless that now hangs in the skies above you, and occupies Washington. You have heard the pronouncements of your president; now hear mine.

'We have no quarrel with you as individuals. We do not wish there to be any unnecessary bloodshed. But the prosperity of your world is built on the suffering of slaves. Your lives of luxury and abundance have been purchased with the blood of countless men and women, forced to live and work in the most terrible conditions to provide the mineral wealth that supports you.

'Your leaders – your leader – tells you that all clones are monsters.

'Was Stefan Seavers a monster? A frightened child murdered as part of your obscene witch-hunt? Were any of the other men, women and children who were hunted down and slaughtered for the crime of existing? Were the peaceful protestors in Philadelphia?

'If we are monsters, we are what you made us. We are the reflection of your own monstrosity and we will not be denied. The armies that protected you are gone. The entire solar system is ours. All your colonies and outposts, mines and facilities – they belong to us.

'We could rain down fire on all your cities, as your leader put it, with ease. We could destroy your population centres, render your whole world uninhabitable. Scrub it clean of mankind. But we do not wish to.

'We wish only one thing.

'Your leader, President Abhilasha Patel. Even as I speak, she cowers in the tunnels beneath my feet, refusing to come out and take responsibility for her actions. To her – and to the people who shelter her – I say this.

'Deliver her to me, in chains, before the hour is spent. That is all we ask. If that is done, we shall turn our fleet around and leave you to your lives.

'If you do not . . . well, then the cities of your Earth shall see what monsters you have wrought.'

She gestured for the camera to be shut off and turned to Henry, removing her mask and smiling. 'How about that?' she said. 'Grandiose enough?'

'A little bit extravagant, I thought.'

She smiled. 'Well, I was going for Shakespearean.'

'Nailed it,' replied Hank.

His wife smiled. 'It'll give the evil bitch something to think about, at least.' She turned to Demon-face. 'Order all ships in orbit to prepare for bombardment of designated cities in one hour, but to hold off until I give the order.'

Demon-face relayed Quil's instructions as Henry walked over and placed his hands on his wife's shoulders.

'Do you think this is the end of the fighting?' he asked.

Reaching up to rest her hands on his, she shook her head. 'I don't think she'll surrender. We'll have to dig her out, and that's going to be harder than I'd like.'

'And you really will bombard other cities?'

'Of course,' she said. Her matter-of-factness chilled Henry as he considered the scale of the massacre she was intending to commit. 'The only way for this war to end is with Earth utterly subdued. If we can achieve that by killing the leader-ship, that's great. But if we have to resort to destroying the populations responsible for electing that leadership, then so be it. If I could just get her up here, in the open . . .'

Henry was unsure what her endgame was, but he felt a rising panic, and a responsibility. As the only other person here capable of time travel – bestowed by the transfusion he had received from Dora's blood in 2014 – he was the only person capable of taking concrete action to resolve the crisis before millions died.

'What would you do?' he asked. 'If you could get her out of her bunker and up here? How would that end things?'

'You'll see. It's just a matter of time,' she said.

That was all he could get out of her, but it would have to do.

The outline of a plan began to form in his mind.

Kinshasa, Democratic Republic of Congo, 2 June 2120 – 38 years to timebomb impact

'And that's when you jumped back in time?' asked Jana.

'I had to find an excuse to be alone for a moment – I claimed I needed to piss – and the four Godless designated to guard me proved surprisingly easy to shake off. As soon as I was alone, I jumped back to find you. It was not hard – Quil knew you would have needed a medical safe haven, and had narrowed the possibilities down considerably before she decided not to pursue you any more. I simply finished her work.'

'What was your plan?' asked Dora.

'I believed that I could alert you to the situation in the future so that you, with your skills, could infiltrate the tunnels beneath the White House in advance of our attack, and force the president to surrender herself. I would then jump back to the moment I left and return to my wife in the Oval Office to witness the end of the war. She would then be free; the world would be safe.'

'And you could retire to a desert island?' spat Kaz furiously.

'You think, after everything that you've done, that we'd let you walk off into some happy ever after?'

'I think I would have saved many lives, including perhaps my wife's, by helping to bring the war to a swift conclusion,' replied Henry firmly, unbowed by Kaz's threatening anger.

'It's not a bad plan,' said Jana.

'Not a bad plan at all,' concurred Dora.

Kaz glowered and said nothing.

'So you will help me?' asked Henry.

8 April 2158, 14:54 P.M.

Goat-face waited until Henry Sweetclover had turned the corner and was out of sight. She saw the brief red flash as he jumped back in time, then turned to Smiley-face.

'OK, you're up,' she said.

Smiley-face removed his mask and shimmered as his chameleon shroud deactivated, revealing him to be Henry Sweetclover.

'You remember what you've got to do?' asked Unicorns as she morphed into Jana.

'I remember,' said Henry.

'If you betray us,' said Kaz as his Helmet mask disguise fell away, 'I will kill you first.'

'I believe you,' said Henry. He turned to Dora as she removed her Goat-face mask. 'Good luck.'

'And to you,' replied Dora.

Henry turned and walked back towards the Oval Office.

Kaz, Dora and Jana joined hands and vanished in a flurry of red sparks, journeying back into the past.

They had one last job to do, and then all this would be over.

11

The White House, 6 January 2158 – 96 days to timebomb impact

Kaz was nervous.

He'd sailed with pirates, fought armies on the surface of another planet, travelled through time to the age of the dinosaurs.

But he'd never endured a job interview.

He'd also never attended a school with a uniform code, so was ill at ease in a suit and tie. The feel of the collar buttoned tight around his throat made him uncomfortable, and the hard soles of the shoes he was wearing felt alien after a lifetime of trainers. The polite smiles of the man on the reception desk, and the confrontational stare directed at him by the candidate sitting opposite, made him squirm.

(At least, he assumed the person sitting across from him was a rival candidate for the job, trying to psych him out with a hard stare. If not, then there was some mad guy just staring at him. Great, now he was even more uncomfortable.)

He reassured himself that he was going to be fine, that the plan they had concocted was foolproof. After safely returning Sweetclover to the day of the battle, Kaz and Dora had travelled back in time three months, to long before the ill-fated Barrettown peace conference on Mars. Their objective was to infiltrate Abhilasha Patel's White House and make preparations. When they caught up to events again three months from now, and the Godless rained down from the heavens, they would be ready.

Dora had done her job well; his references were all airtight, his CV was stellar. As long as he didn't do something crushingly stupid in the interview, he was going to get this job. And even if he did screw it up, there was a good chance Dora would be able to fix it for him anyway. The interview was a formality.

'So this is the wunderkind, is it?' The man's voice was rich and deep and full of good humour, and it fitted the tall, barrel-chested man who had entered and was now looking down at Kaz. A mop of curly grey hair topped wise eyes and a wide smile. Kaz managed to hide his disgust at being confronted with Amos Hope, White House Chief of Staff, the man who had conspired with Jana's mother to have her killed.

The rival candidate across the room flashed a look of pure, seething spite at Kaz, who responded with a quick wink before rising and offering his hand to Hope.

'I don't know about that, sir.'

Hope took his hand and shook it firmly. 'Word of advice from an old soldier. Don't be modest, kid. Keep telling people you're nothing special and they're liable to believe you.'

'Then yes, I am the wunderkind.'

'Excellent. Follow me, and close the door behind you.'

Relinquishing Kaz's hand, Hope turned and walked through

a door into a large office that boasted a big wooden desk, a series of tall leather armchairs and a sofa facing a coffee table on which sat a jug of water and three glasses. Kaz was surprised to find, however, that he and Hope were alone – he had been expecting a panel of interviewers.

Hope sat in one of the armchairs and gestured for Kaz to do the same. The informality of this gesture was Kaz's second surprise – he had expected to be grilled from behind the desk.

Hope did not beat about the bush.

'You got the job, kid. Interview's a formality, just a way of checking that you don't have any personal hygiene issues or a crazy glint in your eye that says "zealot". You're not a zealot, are you kid?'

'Um, no. Not a zealot. And I shower every day.'

Hope clapped his hands together once in satisfaction. 'Excellent,' he said again. 'Your writing is very good, the speech you sent in was the best submission by some measure. Your references were impeccable. All the paperwork is taken care of. You'll be starting as my assistant right now. Sound good?'

Kaz nodded, wide-eyed and startled. Were all job interviews like this? Had Jana just been messing with him when she'd told him all those horror stories about interviewees vomiting, accidentally swearing and, in one particularly lurid tale, wetting themselves? Actually, he wondered why he was even wondering – of *course* she'd been messing with him; it's what she *did*.

Even so, Kaz felt disorientated and unsure of himself. Here he was, infiltrating the White House using a fake ID, taking a job that required skills he didn't really have (no matter how much training he'd undergone in preparation) and all because it was the centre of a callous regime that he was intending to help overthrow. But so far he had met one member of staff and they had been brisk and avuncular. This was the centre of a government that was properly evil – he had seen the evidence of that with his own eyes – but he wasn't getting an evil vibe. He chided himself. What had he been expecting – goose-stepping Nazis in crisp, black, skull-encrusted uniforms? He had to be on his guard, because he knew what this administration – Hope and the president especially – was capable of, but the individuals within it were just people. He would have to find the line between sensible precautions and demonising the people who would be, for three months at least, his colleagues.

His task was simple – get into the White House's DUCC when the attack came. That was when his real job would begin. Until then, he just had to keep his head down, not draw the wrong kind of attention, collect intelligence and prepare for the big day. He wondered how long it would be before he got to meet the president. He knew it was unlikely he'd get more than a passing glimpse of her – she wasn't going to be mingling with the likes of him.

'The job is simple – you will be at my side at all times except when I'm in the crapper. You will be my shadow. I expect you to remember everything you think I might need to remember later. You are my ENL chip, basically. You will fetch and carry, take notes, offer reminders – *not* suggestions! – and generally be my gofer. You will be present at important meetings with important people and you will be totally silent. You will not talk, cough, sneeze, yawn, sigh, scratch, fart or in any other way draw attention to your presence when others are speaking. You are a phantom limb, *my* phantom limb. And if you don't screw it up, or annoy me, or wander into a restricted area and get yourself shot, you will have one hell of a memoir to write in fifty years' time,' said Amos. 'So I'll just—'

The door swung open sharply, causing Kaz to start a little in his seat. A tall, lean dark-skinned woman with striking black hair strode into the room, two black-suited security guards at her side.

She had Jana's eyes, her jawline, her posture. Abhilasha Patel really was the spitting image of her daughter.

Kaz gasped as he rose instinctively to his feet.

'Madam P – President,' he stuttered.

She glanced at him, startled by his presence. Even though she was the same height as Hope, she managed to communicate the strong sense that she was looking down on him. She dismissed Kaz as irrelevant without even bothering to enquire who he was.

'Amos, we have a problem,' she said briskly, then she spun on her heels and walked out, obviously expecting Hope to follow. Which, naturally, he did. After a brief pause, Kaz figured what the hell, and scurried after the group. The worst they could do was tell him to get lost. As they left the room, Amos caught Kaz's eye but he didn't signal his dismissal; his look only communicated a warning to keep his mouth shut.

Kaz did not think that would be a problem. Abhilasha set the pace, the security guards fell back and Amos matched her steps, while Kaz trailed behind.

'Ganymede has fallen,' she said calmly as she led them along a short corridor to an anteroom. They crossed this, ignoring the secretary sitting at a desk beside an internal door through which they proceeded into a crowded room.

It was, Kaz realised with a start, the Oval Office. It looked very different from the last time Kaz had been here, 97 days in the future. It still had a roof, for starters. The room was, of course, familiar to Kaz from various television programmes, but the personality of the current president was obvious in the furnishing and decorations. The two sofas that faced each other across a glass-topped coffee table were metal-framed and minimalist, and there were no other chairs in the room apart from the one behind the president's desk, a grandiose wooden beast that didn't match her tastes at all but which Kaz reckoned she probably kept as a sop to history and photographers. The artwork on the walls was what Kaz would have called 'modern', but was now over a century old. It seemed to him that the abstract geometric shapes, mostly rendered in shades of grey and blue, lacked humanity and warmth.

Abhilasha walked to the desk and leaned against it, facing towards a large crowd of people, some in military uniforms with all sorts of insignia, some in suits. This room was where the decisions were made, and these were the people who made them. No one was sitting on the sofas until Amos sat down without being asked, clearly comfortable in the room and with his position in it. A five-star general and two women followed suit. Kaz hovered just inside the door, hoping he was anonymous at the edge of the throng, lost in the crowd.

'Who is this?' snapped the president, indicating Kaz. So much for keeping a low profile. Every face in the room turned to regard him curiously. He wondered why she had dismissed him in Hope's office only moments ago, but queried his presence in the Oval Office now. He suspected she had waited until there was an audience so she could begin the meeting with a minor display of personal power, just to set the tone.

'New PA,' rumbled Hope.

'Cleared?'

'Of course.'

Abhilasha looked Kaz up and down and then, clearly deciding he was of no further interest, ignored him. Instead she waved towards the general who was sitting opposite Hope.

'Our forces set off from Ganymede two hours ago,' said the general, addressing the rest of the room rather than the president, who had obviously already been briefed. 'Their intent was to engage the Godless fleet at the demarcation line of Jupiter jurisdiction. But they never got there. The Godless outflanked us, and attacked from behind Calista as our ships took off. The flotilla was completely destroyed.'

There were gasps and curses.

'Quiet,' snapped the president. The room fell instantly silent. 'It seems they disabled our early warning system and snuck into Jupiter space thirty-six hours ago. We don't know how they achieved this, but it doesn't really matter right now. What matters is what we do next.'

She looked around the room.

'I'm open to suggestions,' she snapped, after a long silence.

Kaz could see that the people in the room were eyeing each other nervously. He got the sense that there was something they all wanted to say, but that none of them could pluck up the courage to get it out. Eventually Amos Hope spoke.

'We sue for peace,' he said.

All the eyes in the room went wide. 'Oh crap,' all the faces said wordlessly, 'he said it.'

Abhilasha stared down at her simple black shoes, her whole body rigid. Kaz saw her knuckles turning white as she grasped the edge of the desk. Nobody else moved, not a cough or a shuffle was heard, and Kaz was pretty sure they were all holding their breath. The powerful men and women in this room were all terribly afraid of the president, Kaz realised. He wondered how she engendered such fear. Was it through force of personality, violent retribution or more subtle means – disappearances perhaps, or blackmail?

He had been expecting an explosion of temper – and he was sure the rest of the room had been expecting it too – but the president did not shout or rage. She held her stiff, contained posture for a minute or so, then her knuckles relaxed, her shoulders straightened and she raised her head. Her smile was enough to chill the blood as she looked at Amos Hope and said, 'Amos is right.'

The mood in the room didn't change. The people here didn't quite trust this unexpected reasonableness.

'This fighting has gone too far,' she said, her voice supernaturally, eerily calm. 'We need a plan to end this conflict once and for all. If that means holding peace talks, then that is what we must do.'

Kaz knew full well what she meant, because he had seen the outcome of her plan. She didn't mean real peace talks – she meant a perfect trap to cut the head off the opposing army. She meant poison and treachery, and the sacrifice of many of the lives in this room in a last desperate gamble that he knew would ultimately fail.

He almost opened his mouth to speak out, but what could he possibly say that wouldn't sound either insane or traitorous? He was an observer here, for the time being. He had to bide his time.

'Amos, draw up a statement inviting the leaders of the Godless army to talks. Somewhere neutral. Mars. Barrettown.'

The security team in the White House were sloppy, thought Dora as she stood outside the door to the Oval Office wondering what was going on inside.

Not the team outside – the guards patrolling the perimeter, the checkpoint team at the gate, the snipers on the roof – they were the best in the world. You'd need to be some kind of time-travelling superspy to get past them, thought Dora, smugly. But that was precisely why the team inside the White House itself was so slack – there was no threat. In fact, there hadn't been a credible threat within the perimeter of 1600 Pennsylvania Avenue since 1814, when the British army had stopped by for a light lunch and a spot of arson for dessert.

There were patrols and guards within the building, specifically the detail to which Dora had got herself assigned. But they were there more for show than anything else, to stand by doorways looking serious and imposing when foreign dignitaries and leaders of industry came to visit and, Dora suspected, to provide a constant low-level ego boost to the politicians by reminding them they were important enough to have bodyguards. Meanwhile the internal computer network was incredibly secure, utterly impossible to penetrate from the outside – but give someone with the right skills five minutes alone on a terminal in the building and they could have the run of the systems for ever with little risk of detection. And Dora had the right skills.

By the end of her first week she had a series of discreet little nuggets of code embedded within the White House's internal systems, harvesting data and funnelling it out to a secure server once a day in an info burst disguised as a software update ping. Every evening she would sift through what had been delivered, picking threads of stories out of the chaotic collections of documents, videos and audio feeds generated by the internal surveillance systems, some of which dated back over a hundred and fifty years. She was pretty sure no one knew the old sound-recording infrastructure was still in place, complete with microphones hidden in discreet cornices and picture rails. The recording functions had been disabled long ago, but it had been the work of a stolen hour to reinitiate them, sending pulses down old copper wires that hadn't hummed with power since the time of Ronald Reagan.

And so Dora collected and collated a dossier of evidence. Debates and discussion, decisions and demands, deadlines and diktats – she noted them all and stored them away for future use. But none of that surveillance was any use to her at this exact moment.

She stood rigid and formal by the Oval Office door, the weight of her shoulder-holstered gun heavy and comforting. She liked the suit, too. It was well cut and fitted snugly; it felt expensive. She even liked the feel of the buttoned-up collar and the tie at her throat. The dress code for male and female agents in Abhilasha Patel's White House was exactly the same.

The earpiece irked her to distraction, though. It irritated her inner ear and she had to fight a constant urge to pull it out, shove her little finger in as far as it could go and wiggle it about in a desperate, no doubt hopeless, attempt to scratch the itch. Why they couldn't just give everyone an ENL chip and communicate directly, she didn't know. In fact, anybody appointed to the president's security detail had to have their chip removed, if they had one. There was something oddly Luddite about the attitude to technology here, Dora thought. As if there was an innate suspicion of new things. They used radio earpieces and wore classic suits and ties instead of Kevlar-weave combat clothes. Dora suspected this retro approach came from the president herself, wondered if maybe her own personal experiences with cloning and its aftermath had made her sceptical of anything cutting-edge.

Dora subtly shifted the weight from her right foot to her left. The hardest part about this job was standing still for hours on end – she preferred a more active form of espionage.

Creating the fake identities to get her and Kaz into the

White House had been the most challenging infiltration job she'd ever undertaken. Six months of carefully cultivating contacts, sourcing data, back-door hacks and some good old-fashioned confidence-trickery. Being able to travel in time helped, too. The biggest challenge, though, had been to make herself look credibly old enough to hold this job. A chameleon shroud wouldn't have made it through the first security check, so she'd had to have a little plastic surgery – not much, just enough to get rid of the last vestiges of baby fat and add a hint of laugh lines around her eyes. She was still the youngest agent on the team, but officially she was twenty-six, not nineteen. Didn't stop the rest of the agents from ragging on her about her inexperience and youth, though. On her first day one of them, a big dumb ape, more muscle than man, tried to put her in an armlock as a kind of half-hearted hazing. Dora thought he got off lightly with just the three broken fingers – she could have broken his arm.

And his neck.

The team accepted her now, but they kept their distance, were strictly professional, which was how she liked it. The less approachable she was, the less chance there would be awkward questions she didn't want to answer.

She wouldn't have admitted it to Kaz or Jana, but she was still smarting from her failure on Mars. She'd been in the same room as Quil for all of ten minutes before she'd blown her cover completely and begun the cascade of events that had led to countless deaths. She had been overconfident, and she had to carry the guilt of that. She thought back to what Kaz had told her about not having to be a perfect ninja killbot, or whatever phrase he'd used. Her sense of her own invincibility had certainly taken a knock that day. She'd been trying to compensate for it since by being super-cautious, and trying not to be so prickly with her two friends. But letting her guard down didn't come naturally to her any more.

Dora found her thoughts drifting towards her friends.

Kaz was putting a brave face on the loss of his mother, but she knew how badly he was hurting, and she could see the effort it took for him to remain calm and in control. There had been a few moments during the fight towards the White House where she thought he might have let Sweetclover die, but he had kept his word and protected their frenemy. She hoped he would be able to handle the stress of going undercover here. She thought he probably would, but she wasn't sure. He still had a lot of healing to do. It was clear to Dora that he hoped Jana might be a big part of that healing, but although Jana's affection for Kaz was obvious, Dora didn't think it went beyond sisterly attachment.

In fact, Dora thought she had caught Jana looking askance at her a couple of times, and wasn't sure what the look meant. Was it suspicion? Assessment? Or something more, perhaps? She had an inkling that Jana might be interested in her. Like, *interested* interested; and she wasn't sure how she felt about that. She had filed it away as something to think about when things with Quil were resolved. But standing outside the Oval Office door, shifting her weight from foot to foot and staring at the blank wall opposite her, she lapsed into idle daydreaming about a life beyond fighting and war, and she found she could picture herself sharing that life with Kaz and Jana, somewhere safe and quiet where they could build a home – though what form their relationships would take was a puzzle to her. She imagined various configurations of herself and the other two as lovers and friends, and was mildly surprised to discover that she couldn't find one that didn't seem like it would be pretty great. They were her friends, yes, but since she had made the decision not to return to her own time again, unable to face the dead-eyed ghost of her zealot brother, his puritanism erased by a mind-writer at her insistence, they had become her family. She loved them, but she did not show it, and that love was a new thing, still defining itself, unfixed.

Neither of them wholly trusted her, she knew that. Her refusal to reveal the identity of their mysterious saviour from the future, Steve, was a block to trust. She was looking forward to the time – soon, now – when the truth would be revealed. She hoped that they would understand why she'd made the choices she'd made, but she couldn't be one hundred percent certain.

And there was the other thing she wasn't telling them. The one fact that could unravel everything. She swept that thought away, back under the rug where it belonged. She might never choose to reveal what she had seen during her first journey through time – the implications scared her.

Perhaps it wasn't so much that they were withholding trust because of the secret they knew she was keeping from them – perhaps it was that she didn't feel she deserved their trust because of the secret only she was aware of. Whatever, they were deep into the endgame now. Soon they'd all be dead or free to choose the course of their own lives. Dora was excited, and a little scared, by that prospect. For five years her life had been defined by the fight against Quil. She had turned herself into a warrior and a spy in order to fight that battle, had reshaped everything she was into a weapon. Who would she be when the fight was over? What would be the point of her?

She didn't know, and that was the most frightening thing of all.

The door opened and a cadre of generals filed out muttering

quietly, disturbed and focused. Dora pulled her thoughts back to her present situation. She wondered what had happened in the meeting. Her knowledge of future events allowed her to make some educated guesses. The meeting had been called in response to the ambush on Ganymede, and the call for peace talks would go out in the next twenty-four hours. She expected that the decisions to sue for peace had just been made, and the president was beginning to formulate the plan to poison her abandoned clone child, the plan that would end so badly.

Dora was surprised when Kaz shuffled past, following on the heels of his new boss, Amos Hope. Her initial response was relief that her work had paid off, and he'd got the job, then surprise that he'd been in such a high-level meeting on his first day. Then worry, as he saw her and made eye contact and his surprise and delight at seeing her showed on his face. She scowled at him hard, and he turned away, realising his mistake. Dora held her breath, but none of her colleagues seemed to have noticed the slip.

Three months of this, she thought, and she wished she could just jump forward to the end. But the only way into the shelter below the White House was to take the slow road.

She shifted her weight again, breathed out, stared at the blank wall before her and continued waiting for the war to reach her, anticipating the evening, when she could listen to the conversation that had occurred in secret, in the room she had been guarding.

Northern France, early morning

Jana sprinted as hard as she could for a count of ten, then slowed to a jog.

There was an old Roman road in the north of France that she liked to use for her morning run. It ran straight and true, cutting a line across the landscape uncaring as to rivers, hills, valleys. It was uncompromising in the way it imposed itself on the world, and something about that attracted her.

She liked to feel the burn in her muscles as she powered up an incline; it reminded her that her body was young again. The weeks she had spent recuperating from the after-effects of the timebomb's blast had left her frustrated and irritable. She disliked inaction, and walking around in the body of a deaf, blind, arthritic wreck had driven her up the wall. Once the doctors had said she was as fixed as they could make her – which wasn't completely fixed because her hearing was still muffled in her left ear, and the big toe on her right foot had stubbornly remained achy as all get-out – she had started an exercise regime of punishing rigour.

Not only did it help to banish the bone-deep memory of the pain, she also found the exertion helped to focus her thoughts. When she was running she could let her mind drift, and she was surprised by the ideas, memories and daydreams it would alight upon. She found herself dwelling on Quil as she crested the small hill and powered into the long straight stretch of road that lay ahead of her.

Her travels through Quil's memories had left her with a deep affinity for her clone. She had empathised with and understood her choices and her actions, and would be willing to defend them. She had allowed herself to believe that she and Quil could change history, erase the timeline that contained her evil shadow, maybe bring some justice and peace to the future together. The loss of that dream when she realised they had been deceived by a quirk of quantum mechanics, followed almost instantly by the loss of Quil – the good one, the one she thought of as *her* Quil – had left her emotionally numb. She had come to think of Quil as her sister, her family, the first person she had blood ties to who she actually liked and who maybe liked her back. Getting to know Quil had given Jana a sense of belonging she hadn't even known she'd been missing.

But that Quil was gone now, erased from existence by her monstrous twin, and as Jana had lain recuperating in Kinshasa she had reacted by replaying her borrowed experiences over and over again from her ENL chip's memory. She relived Quil's panicked first moments, her accidental time jump, her stay on the mining ship and the day she had met the resistance. It was like looking at photographs of a dead relative, but infinitely more intimate; comforting and painful at the same time.

She picked a tree by the side of the road in the far distance and burst into a sprint again, pushing herself towards it.

Jana still felt left out.

Kaz and Dora were in place at the White House, but she wasn't able to be there with them lest her mother recognise her. The plan they had agreed upon called for her to jump forward and rendezvous with Dora so that she could be smuggled into the DUCC ready for the final showdown. But Kaz and Dora had one advantage over Jana – they had both been travelling in time for so long that their powers and control had matured enough for them to jump solo, and with a high level of accuracy. Jana was frustrated that her powers were not yet that advanced.

Plus, she missed them.

While they spent three months embedding themselves in her mother's White House, learning the layout, getting to know the enemy and all her accomplices in ways that might help them, Jana was stuck, alone, waiting for her powers to mature.

While she waited, she had set up temporary home in a rented apartment in Portland in the late twentieth century, and buried herself in study. She found she had a ravenous appetite for history – books, films, TV, whatever she could get. For most people, such entertainment provided escapism from the humdrum reality of their daily lives as they imagined themselves living in bygone eras. But for Jana, it was more like a menu, a tantalising smorgasbord of times and places she could visit, people she could meet, events she could witness in person. The possibilities were dizzying, and she intended to take full advantage of the opportunities her ability presented, just as soon as she had taken care of Quil. Just get that out of the way, she told herself as she powered towards the tree by the roadside, and all of history would be hers for the taking.

She passed the tree much sooner than she'd anticipated; she must have been running faster than she thought. She paused for a second, confused by the distance she had covered in such a short time, then shook her head and dismissed it.

Daydreaming. She fell back into a brisk walk, breathing hard, and pulled out a bottle of water. She felt the rawness in her throat and smiled as the cold liquid soothed it. She felt a sad smile come to her lips as she put the bottle top back on, unsure where the sudden tinge of melancholy had come from. Then she resumed running.

She dismissed the thought when she saw a glint of sunlight on metal in the far distance. Romans. Time to go. She promised herself that if she made it back to the right time and place in one jump, she'd gather her things and head straight to the rendezvous with Dora. She slipped the bottle of water back into her pocket, and concentrated on the numbers.

She felt the equations flow around her, as the landscape dissolved into a sea of numbers into which she dived with poise, surrendering her body and mind to the ebb and flow of impossible tides.

She found her destination instinctively, feeling the numbers flowing around and through her, feeling the cracks that sought to channel her out of her fugue state into real time. As the options narrowed, and she found her way through the pathways towards the correct place and time, she had to choose her exit point carefully. The sense of where she was going was still obscure to her. The time was easier than the place of arrival. Time was all numbers, and mathematics didn't lie. But landing in the right place, which she was beginning to realise was calculated in relative distance from the timebomb lodestone, deep under Sweetclover Hall, was trickier. She thought of a place, visualised it in her mind, and this seemed to steer her towards it, but the exact exit point could be some miles distant.

Strangely, concentrating seemed to make the process less precise; the secret to steering, she was learning, was to relax and trust the numbers, to travel by instinct and sensation rather than trying to impose her will upon the process.

Eventually she found the right place. It presented itself as a still point in the equations; a perfect, almost shining sequence of mathematical expression that resonated to her thoughts, drew her magnetically and then spat her out into the brisk, cold air of a Portland dawn.

She smiled her satisfaction and resumed running.

12
8 April 2158, 8:00 A.M.

Washington was eerily quiet, even for a Saturday morning.

At this time on a normal day the streets inside the mighty levee would be bustling with people. Not sightseers – it was still too early for them. This time of day belonged to commuters and locals, bustling between transport stations, coffee joints and offices. Hurrying to their desks to spend another day administering the affairs of a diminished, but still powerful, nation. These streets normally belonged to functionaries and decision-makers, and the lower caste of workers who catered to them – baristas, shoe-shiners, short-order cooks, police.

But not this morning. There were no ordinary vehicles to be seen – no buses, trams or trains were running in and out of this part of town. The entrances to the subway stations were sealed with metal grilles and keep out signs. Heavy concrete barriers lay strewn across the roads at random angles.

There was movement, though. The city wasn't entirely deserted. The tanks that hovered at the intersections of the grid-pattern roads hummed with power, their short, stubby guns a statement of brutal intent. Hundreds of marching feet echoed in unison between the buildings, as phalanxes of troops took up defensive positions at key strategic points, covering the approaches to the White House. Anyone watching the seat of power through binoculars would have seen soldiers hard at work on the roof, securing the metal stands of heavy weapons emplacements, which bristled with armaments.

The city was preparing for war, and Jana would have been lying if she had said it didn't excite her. Not because she enjoyed being in the thick of battle – and anyway, she had already fought in the battle that was to come, shepherding Sweetclover safely through the slaughter to his wife's side. She knew how chaotic and brutal the fight would be, and she didn't relish the prospect of living through it, or anything like it, ever again. Her excitement was for the confrontation that was coming, the final opportunity for her to end the war that she had accidentally caused.

She stopped and thought for a moment, surprised that the thought had bubbled to the surface. Did she really blame herself for all this? Rationally, logically, she knew this wasn't her fault. She had just been a girl when her rebellions against parental authority had set her mother on a course that would change the world. She hadn't known what would happen when she'd jumped off that roof. None of this was her fault, not really.

But that wasn't how it *felt*.

Because the truth was that if she'd behaved better as a teenager, if she'd not given her mother such a hard time, if she'd been good and obedient and all the things her mother had wanted her to be, there wouldn't be a fleet of ships hovering above the Earth right now, ready to slaughter billions at the whim of a monster that wore her face.

It wasn't her fault, but it was a consequence of her actions.

She was culpable, complicit, implicated, whatever you wanted to call it.

It was her mess, intentional or otherwise, and she was going to clear it up if it killed her.

Her arrival from Portland had not been perfect – she had arrived fifteen minutes early and two streets south of the rendezvous point – but it had been good enough. Activating her chameleon shroud so that she looked like a soldier, she had made her way at a brisk running-an-errand pace to the office block on the corner of Virginia and 23rd. The skytown rose elegantly from the road, its huge wooden bones curling up into the cloud base. It would be on fire in a few hours. Jana had watched the flames licking upwards, seen the soldiers jumping to their deaths from the upper storeys rather than face the fire.

There was a bustle of activity around the doors. This was the base of operations of the marine corps, and they were setting up positions on various floors high above the street – missile launchers aiming up, sniper emplacements aiming down. Soldiers were running in and out of the building, but nobody was checking any IDs, partly because the excitement of the coming battle was making them sloppy, and partly because the city was in lockdown anyway. Jana scanned the faces of the soldiers gathered in the lobby and picked Dora out easily – her fitted black suit made her stick out like a sore thumb.

Damn, she looked good.

Jana quickened her pace, reminding herself that she was a soldier on duty and that hugging the friend she had missed so much would draw attention. Instead she stopped when she reached Dora, and snapped out a crisp salute.

Dora smirked as she returned it. 'Follow me,' she said, turning on her heel.

She led Jana to a stairwell doorway beside a bank of lifts, and they pushed their way through. They could hear the soft clatter of boots on the wooden stairs high above them as they descended into the roots of the building.

They had gone down three flights before Dora stopped, turned and hugged Jana tight.

'Good to see you,' she said, squeezing hard.

Jana squeezed Dora back, breathing in the smell of her and feeling a deep contentment.

This was how home was meant to feel.

'You too,' she replied. 'I missed you.'

Dora released her embrace and stood back, her hands resting on Jana's hips. 'I know,' she said, smiling, her eyes narrowed, indicating . . . what? Jana felt a flutter of nerves as they held each other's gaze a second longer than was quite usual.

'But we have to be quick and quiet,' said Dora eventually, reclaiming her hands and snapping into business mode.

Jana forced herself to quell her nerves and refocus on the task at hand.

'Do you have the template?' she asked.

Dora nodded and handed over a tiny data crystal, which Jana took and slotted into the box at her belt that held the chameleon shroud. She knew her external appearance was changing, but she did not know into what.

'How do I look?' she asked.

Dora looked Jana up and down, appraising. 'Like a rugby player who can bench press six hundred pounds and who's been squeezed into a suit so good that it almost hides how uncomfortable you feel in it.'

'Finally, I look the way I feel inside,' joked Jana.

Dora smirked. 'You are now Special Agent Swinbourne, White House security detail.'

'And the real Agent Swinbourne?'

'Won't be bothering us today,' said Dora darkly.

Jana didn't press the question as Dora turned and led her down yet more stairs to a heavy metal service door. It looked like a vault door – a big wheel in the middle rather than a handle, and a biometric access panel beside it.

The security panel scanned Dora's iris, then she typed in a seven-digit code and spun the wheel right, left, right and left again. There was a deep mechanical rumble and the door swung open.

Dora stood in the doorway and turned to Jana. 'From now on, say nothing. You're my partner but everyone we will meet knows that you don't talk much and you tend to take your lead from me.'

'So you've got the real Agent Swinbourne wrapped around your little finger,' said Jana. 'Why doesn't that surprise me? Did you have to wrestle him into submission?'

'Something like that,' said Dora, turning and walking away.

Jana followed, and did not ask the obvious follow-up question as the door slammed behind them. The sound of gears locking bolts back into place underscored the finality of the decision to enter the labyrinth of tunnels beneath Washington DC.

The tunnel was on the fringes of the DUCC, and as such was functional and unappealing. It was entirely made of concrete and there were streaks of orange and white damp on the walls, some crusted with limescale deposits that would one day, many centuries from now, harden into stalactites. Jana wondered why so much of their adventure in time seemed to involve caves both natural and engineered. She was sick of cellars and tunnels.

They walked for about two hundred metres and then came

to another heavy vault-type door. Again, Dora gained them access, and this time they emerged into the part of the system that was actually in use.

The carpet was deep blue and deep pile, the walls painted cream, and the lighting was subtle but welcoming. It felt like a corridor you would find in a five-star hotel, windowless but expensive, with doors that led off to suites and conference rooms. The air was surprisingly fresh, no trace of the musty dampness there had been in the first corridor they had traversed.

Dora stepped away from the entrance briskly while the door was still closing, obviously anxious to put as much distance between them and their point of ingress as possible. Jana fell into step beside her.

'The president and the staff are still upstairs in the White House,' muttered Dora as they walked. 'There's nobody important down here yet, but there are lots of staff checking systems and preparing the DUCC for imminent use. I made sure Swinbourne and I were detailed to check the perimeter for signs of weakness or intrusion.'

'Nicely done.'

'The attack doesn't begin until midday, so we've got' – she checked her watch – 'three and a half hours until the scramble is sounded and the government comes and hides down here.'

'What do we do in the meantime?'

'We sweep the perimeter, I said.'

'For three and half hours? How big is this place?'

'There are ten miles of corridors, and thirty-two separate exits into other underground systems – cellars, sewers, subway tunnels – and a few specifically built points of escape to the other side of the levee.'

'What, underwater?'

'Airlocks, wetsuits and minisubs.'

'Wow.'

Dora stopped and turned to Jana, smiling slyly. 'So our job is important. We have to make sure all the exits are secure, but usable, so the great and the good can make their escapes when the time comes.'

It took Jana a moment to cotton on. 'Oh!' she exclaimed when she realised what Dora was aiming at. 'But we're actually going to be—'

'Sealing them up tight with a little hack I've developed,' Dora confirmed. 'It turns the vault doors into solid metal prison gates. There'll be nowhere for the president and her cronies to run. Quil and the Godless could just sit upstairs and starve them out.'

'But they won't have to . . .'

'Because, if it comes to it, I will pass them the code to open one of the entrances so they can take this place by force.'

Jana smiled with satisfaction. 'She won't realise it, but the moment the president gives the order to take shelter below ground, she's sealing herself into a perfect trap. So let's get on with it.'

13
8 April 2158, 11:52 A.M.

'The scans must be showing *something*!'

President Patel slammed her palm on to the incident room desk as she shouted. The general who sat to the right of her looked nervous as he confirmed that, in fact, all attempts to scan the enemy fleet were proving futile. They had no idea what was happening on the Godless ships.

Kaz, standing at the back of the room behind Amos Hope, could have told them what they wanted to know. They had been relying on their surveillance satellites to monitor activity in the fleet so they would have a warning if the clone troops began assembling in drop-ships preparatory to an assault. But the shielding on the ships was too great, so the only indication of an attack would come the moment the ships were launched, which could be five minutes, hours or days from now.

One thing Kaz had learned was that the president did not enjoy uncertainty.

Kaz knew exactly what was happening up above the atmosphere. Right now the troops were mustered around view screens in full gear, listening to Quil giving a rousing speech about freedom, justice and the harsh necessity of war. He knew, because he was up there; or a younger version of him was, anyway, alongside Dora and Jana, waiting to shepherd Henry Sweetclover through the imminent battle to safety in the ruins of the building that Kaz stood in now, listening to a president who knew she had completely lost her grip on the situation.

He had witnessed the disintegration of her certainty over the last few weeks. It had begun with Mars. Although he had not been made privy to the plans she had put in place – the poison fruit designed to drive her opponent mad, the assassin who had been sent to fail, the expectation of her enemies turning on each other – he knew why she had seemed so confident, but it had puzzled Hope. Kaz's boss had been having meetings with various other high-level officials behind closed doors, away from security and official channels. They had discussed the peace talks, the president's inexplicable decision not to attend in person, the odd confidence she exuded when they knew their defences were no match for the Godless fleet. Opinion in the upper echelons was divided. Many thought the president had a plan that she had not shared with them (which, of course, she did), while the rest were beginning to suspect that she had lost touch with reality and had fallen into denial about how hopeless the situation looked.

If Hope considered Kaz a possible threat to his careful, considered construction of a power base within the White House, he gave no indication of it. In fact, he allowed Kaz to see everything he did, relying on his loyalty in a manner that seemed to Kaz both foolish and kind of admirable. He played up to it, of course; adopted the persona of an eager, compliant, infinitely discreet helping hand, obedient without ever tipping into obsequiousness. Even though the constant mental vigilance was exhausting, he flattered himself that Dora couldn't have done a better job. And every time the pressure got too much and he felt a cluster headache building behind his eyes, Kaz would lock the door of his apartment in the evening, and jump away to spend a weekend on a beach somewhere, recharging his batteries and returning seconds after he'd departed, ready to resume his act.

When the Mars peace talks had descended into violence, Kaz had seen Abhilasha's certainty falter. Her plan, so cunningly conceived and carefully executed, had gone horribly wrong with alarming speed. During the crisis meeting that had taken place in the hour before the destruction of Barrettown, Kaz fancied that he could see her trying to work out how it had gone off the rails, what variable she had failed to account for.

He knew perfectly well what the variable was – him and his friends.

As he, Dora and Jana had improvised their routes to safety through the battle of Barrettown, President Patel had improvised also. Kaz had stood silently in the corner of the incident room as the president had spoken with Quil via comm-link, and he had heard the gasps of astonishment as the nature of the relationship between Abhilasha and Quil had been revealed to the inner circle. When the conversation was over, and Quil was safely imprisoned in a ship blasting its way up through Mars's thin atmosphere, he had watched the president give the order to the captain of the stricken *Redoubtable* to steer his plummeting vessel into Barrettown and destroy it lest it be used as a base of operations by the Godless hordes.

Kaz would never forget the look on the captain's face as he received that order.

His face was streaked with blood, lit by the flashing of the emergency lights and the flames rising from the ruined bridge on which he stood resolute. Something in his eyes as he was ordered to destroy hundreds of thousands of lives chilled Kaz's blood.

It was a look Kaz had seen before – in the eyes of Dora's brother as he'd sought to cleanse his world of popery; in the eyes of a young man sitting in a car on a Beirut street; in the eyes of Quil as she'd gunned down his mother.

If there was one fear that kept Kaz awake at night, it was that his eyes would mirror that same look when he watched Quil, and the monster who had caused her creation, die at his hand, as he was sure they would, in the smoking ruins of the White House on 8 April 2158.

For a few days after the disaster on Mars, the president had seemed once again confident and in control. Quil was safe in custody. The head had been cut off the snake, and there was a sense of cautious optimism in the White House, a wishful notion that maybe the leaderless enemy could now be reasoned with.

Hope had nonetheless continued his covert agitations, exploiting the suspicions that had sprung up following the revelation that Quil was the president's missing daughter, last seen in New York seventeen years earlier, the object of more feverish speculation and conspiracy theories than any other incident in recent history.

Then the optimism faded again when the timebomb was deployed, and Quil escaped to retake her position at the head of the fleet that now hung above the Earth. That had been the last straw for Abhilasha. All her plots and schemes had failed, and she was confronted with the likelihood of defeat and death. All the suspicions of Hope's allies were apparently confirmed – their president had been divorced from reality all along.

And all the while, through the various crises and reversals of fortune, the constant pressure from the lobbyists of IMC and their mining rivals. The endless invocations to stay the course, to 'secure the prosperity of the future' by putting down this piddling uprising of non-human rabble to ensure the resumption of the glory days of abundance and profit and stability. They were relentless, their envoys and executives forever prowling the corridors of power, bending ears, taking meetings, applying pressure.

Kaz had only been privy to their ploys in respect of Hope – who they were blackmailing with video of him and his mistresses enjoying themselves while his wife was out of town – but if they used similar tactics with every representative, he was not surprised at the power they yielded.

There were none of them here now, though, in the incident room of the White House on the morning of the day Kaz knew it would be destroyed. They had been scarce the last few days. Kaz imagined them as cockroaches who had noticed the light coming on, and had scurried away to their hidey-holes in the hope that nobody would come to flush them out.

Now it was just the president, her generals and advisors, and a situation that none of them could hope to control. They gave orders to the army, put missile and air bases on alert, prepared contingency measures of all kinds. But it was futile, and they knew it.

Kaz wondered when and how Hope and his cadre of traitors would make their move. He knew the president would still be in power once the battle had ended and she was penned up underground (and him with her!).

Did this mean Hope would wait until after her speech to the world? Or did it mean that he would try and fail to wrest power from her sometime in the next few hours . . . Kaz suddenly had a horrible thought.

If Hope made his play and failed, then he was a dead man.

And so was his right-hand man.

If he was right, and Hope was planning to try to unseat Abhilasha in the next few hours, he would be facing danger not only from the bombardment and attack of the Godless, but from within the White House itself.

This long-overdue realisation snapped Kaz's focus back to the meeting that was going on before him. The president was still haranguing the general who was failing to provide the intelligence she required. Kaz glanced at his watch. 11.34 a.m. He had twenty-six minutes until the Godless drop-ships launched. Before they had begun this phase of their plan, he, Dora, Jana and Sweetclover had meticulously plotted the timeline of the day up to the moment Sweetclover had jumped back in time.

Kaz reviewed what was to come for the thousandth time. The ships would launch at 12:00. The ones that would survive the barrage would land at 12:11, by which point all White House staff not designated to defence are safe and secure below ground in the DUCC. The White House falls at 12:33, to the monsters whose ship dropped straight through the roof, but the street-fighting in the surrounding area continues for two hours. Quil enters the Oval Office at approximately 14:09. The president gives her speech at 14:30, Quil gives her rejoinder at 14:35, after which Henry leaves to jump back in time. They have no knowledge of events after that moment, but the deadline is clear – they have to force the president out of the bunker within the hour or nuclear fire will rain down on the Earth.

Dora's mission was to lock the DUCC down tight so that

the president could not escape, and then attach herself to the president's personal guard. Jana should be with her, if all had gone according to plan. Kaz would be there too. Their intention was to keep the president alive and force her to surrender to Quil in the Oval Office in front of cameras that would beam her humiliation around the world. They would not let her escape, they would not let her kill herself in her bunker, they would not let her call Quil's bluff. Their job was to deliver her into the hands of their enemy by 15:30 and then walk away.

Kaz did not think it would be as simple as that.

'We should surrender.'

Wait, what? Kaz realised he had let his attention drift again, but Amos Hope's deep, rich voice had brought total stillness and silence to the room.

After such a dangerous pronouncement, Kaz would have expected all eyes to be on the person who had spoken. Not in this room. Here, all eyes were on the president, waiting to see how she would react to her closest ally speaking the unspeakable yet again. She was the grenade in this room.

'Amos Hope,' said Abhilasha softly, after a long, tense silence. Her jaw was clenching, and her knuckles were white where she gripped the edge of the desk. 'I thought I had made it quite clear that there would be no talk of surrender in this room.'

'We are hopelessly outmatched, Madam President,' rumbled Hope. 'The Godless fleet has total mastery of the skies. There is nothing we can do against such odds. If we fight, we only invite destruction. The only way to save lives is to surrender. And that is what I believe we must do.'

'I agree with the chief of staff, Madam President.'

'I also agree, Madam President.'

The chorus of approval went on for nearly a minute. In all the tension, Kaz could feel relief in the room. The moment of internal crisis had arrived and they were relieved to have finally spoken out. Even if this gamble meant their deaths, they were relieved. Roughly half the people in the room, about twenty in total, had stated their support for the idea of surrender.

After the declarations, silence. Until the president spoke.

'General,' she said, her voice trembling slightly, though whether from fury or fear Kaz could not be entirely sure. 'Is it your belief that the coming battle is unwinnable?'

The general she had only minutes before been berating said firmly, 'No, Ma'am.'

'And why is that?'

'They have the superior fleet, this is true, but they have limited troops. Based on information provided by the mining corporations, we estimate the entire clone army numbers only fifteen-thousand individuals. Once we engage them on the ground, we have overwhelming numerical superiority. They are not trying to capture a town or a city, or even a country. They are trying to capture a planet. Which is, by any sane calculation, impossible.'

Abhilasha nodded once, accepting this appraisal.

Kaz knew it was hopelessly optimistic, and the premise was flawed. Quil wasn't trying to capture the Earth, she was trying to subjugate it. And if that meant nuking all major cities from orbit, she was more than willing to do so. The failure in this room was one of imagination – not only had they misidentified her objective, they could not conceive of how ruthless their opponent was.

'Madam President, that appraisal is hopelessly naive,' replied Hope. 'They control the skies. That tactical advantage alone guarantees victory. We have no idea what the weapon they fired at England was, but its destructive power was devastating. If they have more of them, they can wipe us out from orbit without putting a single boot on the ground.'

'Our sources confirm that the weapon fired at England was unique,' countered the general.

'And if your sources are wrong? And even if they're not, we know they have nuclear weapons. They could raze half the world to force our surrender.'

'Only half?' replied the president. 'I'll take those odds.'

Some of the people around the table emitted audible gasps, as did Kaz. She was willing to sacrifice billions of lives if it meant a chance of winning this war and remaining the ruler of an irradiated wasteland.

She and Quil really did deserve each other.

The president nodded to the general. 'General, if you will,' she said.

The doors to the incident room opened and a line of soldiers filed in, weapons drawn. Half the faces in the room blanched. The general stood and pointed out, one by one – slowly, enjoying the moment – those people who had agreed with Hope's call for surrender.

Kaz's heart sank as the finger pointed to him. Even though he had said nothing, he was guilty by association and nobody would ever believe that he had not known of Hope's plans. As each person was pointed out, a soldier came to stand behind their chair. Once the selection was complete, the president stood and addressed the room.

'Those people indicated have been found guilty of treason. By executive order, in time of war, the president is permitted to authorise summary justice. General, kindly take these traitors to the Rose Garden, and execute them all.'

The general saluted crisply, the condemned began to protest, and the soldiers began to drag them from their chairs.

Kaz felt a firm hand on his shoulder and turned to meet the gaze of the soldier detailed to escort him to his death. He looked for any trace of humanity or kindness in the blue eyes of the young man, but he found none.

There was no point in resisting. If he ran, he'd be cut down where he stood. He knew he could jump away into time whenever he wished, but if he did, it was very unlikely he'd be able to make it back to this time and place. He might miss the moment of truth, and he was determined not to let that happen. Of course, he would have no option but to jump if they got as far as the Rose Garden. He wondered how they'd react to his sudden, fiery exit from reality.

The wall of screens behind the president suddenly burst into life, startling everyone.

'Drop-ships are away,' said the general, his voice faltering. 'I repeat, the Godless drop-ships are away.'

The president did not hesitate. 'Soldiers, execute the traitors then report to your stations for duty. The rest of you, evacuate to the DUCC by your pre-assigned routes.'

She turned to the general. 'Sound the siren,' she said, then she turned and strode out of the room.

A shrill, ear-splitting whine burst from speakers mounted in the walls. One woman tried to take advantage of the momentary confusion to make a break for it. The soldier beside her raised her gun and fired once, in a bored kind of way. There were barely audible screams mixed in with the siren's whine, then Kaz and the other prisoners were marched out of the incident room past her smoking corpse.

'I am sorry for this,' said Hope, ahead of Kaz in the line as they climbed the stairs to ground level, shouting to be heard above the siren. 'I had thought, maybe I could do some good.'

Kaz sneered, and decided what the hell, time to drop the mask. The siren stopped just as he began to speak.

'Some good? Are you serious?' he spat. 'You've supported this corrupt, murderous bunch of monsters for years. You turned traitor now, at the very last minute, just to try and save your own skin. Nothing more. Don't try and pretend to be noble. You're just as bad as she is.'

Hope turned to look at Kaz, his mouth agape, astonished to hear such words coming out of the mouth of his meek assistant. Kaz was a little surprised himself. He'd not realised quite how much contempt he had been nurturing for the man he had spent three months shadowing. But in many ways Hope was more contemptible than even Abhilasha or Quil. At least they seemed to believe in something. But this man, who believed only in his own right to power, was a parasite. Kaz would not mourn his loss one jot.

'Surprise,' said Kaz with a grin. 'I have a spine after all. You have no idea what is coming. You're lucky you'll be dead before they get here.'

They reached the landing and were pushed and shoved through the doors into a corridor that led to the Rose Garden. If Kaz was going to make a move, he would have to do it soon. If he could just duck into a side room long enough to jump away, nobody would see how he escaped. He hated leaving Jana and Dora, but he couldn't see a way to reach them safely. They processed along the corridor, various people crying, some begging, some walking tall, proud and stoic. A door just ahead was ajar and Kaz decided that he would step sideways when he came alongside it. He would only need a second—

But before he could make his break, there was the most incredible noise – a cacophony of twisted metal, crumbling masonry and explosive impact.

Kaz was flung sideways by a shockwave, and he lost consciousness.

14

Jana stood guard while Dora locked the final exit, making the DUCC into a huge trap. She finished the instant the siren began to sound.

'Timing!' yelled Dora over the noise.

Jana gave Dora the thumbs-up and then fell into step behind her as she ran towards the main entrance, ready to receive their guests. The intersections of the corridors were marked with letters and numbers that presumably corresponded to a map, but Jana had no idea of the layout and had to trust Dora's sense of direction as she led them around endless corners towards the centre of the labyrinth.

High above them, Jana knew, younger versions of she and Dora were plummeting towards the Earth in the same drop-ship as their enemy and her husband. It was a disorienting feeling, knowing that there were two of her running around at the same time.

The siren had stopped sounding by the time Dora skidded to a halt in a lobby area with large double doors in the far wall. The carpet had the presidential insignia woven into it, and the walls were lined with photographs and paintings of previous presidents. There was already a group of agents waiting patiently in a row, standing to attention. Dora fell into line and snapped to, and Jana followed suit. None of the other agents spoke to them, or to each other; they were all focused on the doors before them, waiting for the president to enter.

Jana stared at the door too, and finally admitted to herself that she was scared.

She had not been in the same room as her mother for many months, and she wasn't sure how she would feel when they were reunited. Of course, she knew Abhilasha wasn't really her mother, any more than Quil was her sister, but knowing something and feeling it are very different things. In all the ways that really mattered, Abhilasha Patel was Jana's mother.

A mother who had tried to have her killed and replaced by a more pliant version; a mother who had planned to kill her father; a mother who had conspired in the demonisation and brutal subjugation of an entire portion of the human race.

And yet Jana knew there was a part of herself, deeply buried but potent and powerful, that would trade her ability to travel in time for one loving embrace from this monster; to have the woman who hated her stroke her hair and tell her everything was going to be all right.

Jana did not know how she was going to react when met by Abhilasha, but she loathed the feeling of panic in her belly. She took comfort in the disguise wrapped around her by the chameleon shroud, and imagined herself a burly, six-foot muscle-mountain, impervious to emotion of any kind.

The door swung open and President Abhilasha Patel strode through. Jana could see that there were lots of people lined up behind her on the staircase, desperate to secure themselves in the DUCC shelter. But the president was in no hurry, and walked slowly up to the man in the middle of the row of guards, presumably the ranking officer, and nodded a greeting.

He replied with a curt 'Madam President.'

'You know the drill,' she said, then she strode past him and away down the wide central corridor.

She was smaller than Jana remembered, that was the first thing that struck her. Was it that she had shrunk with age, or was it that Jana was taller now? Neither seemed plausible, but there it was – she looked smaller. There were deep creases on her forehead and lines around her eyes that had been emerging when Jana was a child, but which had deepened with time, and the cares of the presidency. Most shocking, though, were the grey roots that were clearly visible along the parting in her hair. The mother Jana remembered would rather have died than let her standards slip so far.

'Follow me,' whispered Dora, then she turned on her heel and fell into step behind the president. Jana followed suit, as did two guards from the opposite end of the line. Together, the four of them flanked the president, pledged to guard her with their lives.

Jana really hoped Dora had a plan to deal with them when the time came. Behind them the mass of White House staff, panicked and afraid, flooded into the tunnels.

The central control room of the DUCC sat at the very heart of the complex, and an extra level down, like a bubble hanging beneath the tunnels. This put an extra layer of shielding between its occupants and the surface, and it could be completely sealed if the labyrinth was breached. Jana assumed it had its own escape route, but if it did, it remained unsecured – this room had not been part of the circuit she and Dora had performed earlier. Jana wondered if they'd made a fatal mistake. It was large and open-plan, more like a hall than a room, with desks in widening semicircles facing in towards a central desk, with a podium to the side. Huge screens lined the wall behind the desk.

To Jana it looked like the hall was designed to function as both a control centre for a war and as a form of debating chamber for a government. But the positioning of the main conference table left no doubt who would be in charge, and the agents took stations flanking it as the president took her place at its head. Dora stood at the president's right hand, Jana beside her, so close she could smell her mother's perfume, as various soldiers, politicians and staffers filed into the room and took up their stations at the curved desks, firing up holo-screens and beginning to monitor and communicate with the outside world. The president's table, which could seat twelve people, also filled with generals and advisors, but they seemed unsure of where to sit, and there was some confusion among them, which the president had to handle personally, telling everyone where to sit and which role they had to fulfil, promoting many of them on the spot. This did not fit with the well-drilled process they had seen so far.

Staring out at this hive of concentration and purpose, Jana was filled with doubt. How were she, Dora and Kaz supposed to force the president to surrender herself? The odds against their success were overwhelming. And where was Kaz anyway? Dora had told her that he was on the list of staff guaranteed admittance to the DUCC in the event of an attack, but as she scanned the faces before her she couldn't find him anywhere.

'I think we have a problem,' whispered Dora. 'Half the senior staff are missing, including Amos Hope, the chief of staff.'

'I remember him,' said Jana bitterly.

'Kaz is his PA, so he should be here. I think there's been

some kind of failed coup attempt. They may have been thrown out of the DUCC. Kaz was afraid something like this might happen.'

There was a distant thud from somewhere far above, and everyone in the room momentarily froze and then lifted their faces upwards in fear.

The attack had begun.

After a moment's silence, the room burst into frantic activity. The chatter of voices shouting updates, people running here and there passing information directly, screens flashing maps, diagrams and live feeds. The president sat at the head of the table monitoring four screens of her own, barking commands to her staff, taking sidebars, running a war.

In all the commotion, Dora and Jana were able to talk, as long as they were subtle about it.

'If Kaz isn't here, where is he?' asked Jana.

'I guess he's either upstairs or he's jumped away.'

Jana fervently wished he had jumped into time before any harm had befallen him – he'd already lived through the battle that was going on above ground once; it seemed like tempting fate to try to do so again.

'Confirmed sighting!' yelled one of the generals, flinging his screen to the president's station. Jana looked down and saw a grainy close-up of Quil, weapon firing as she advanced with her troops.

'Masked,' snapped Abhilasha back at him. 'Could be anyone. I've already told you, it's not a confirmed sighting until we see her face.'

Jana could see the president's screens from where she stood, and she began to get a sense of the battle. What she saw mirrored her experiences in the fight – the Earth troops were pulling back, being defeated by masked clone soldiers advancing on all fronts. But the closer she looked, the more she began to worry.

'Dora,' she whispered, indicating one of the maps. 'Those green icons are troop formations, yeah?'

'Yes,' replied her friend, who had been focusing her attention on the positioning of security agents around the room.

'So look at how they're deployed.'

Jana waited for Dora to see it. She didn't have to wait long.

'They're holding back, letting the clones win,' she said.

'Only just, but yeah, I think they are. Why would they do that? Why would they keep troops in reserve just out of sight like this?'

Dora's eyes widened in alarm. 'They want them in the White House. They're letting them take it.'

Jana was puzzled for a second, then she turned to Dora and they both whispered, in unison, 'It's a trap!'

Jana cursed herself for not anticipating this. Her mother, who had played dirty every step of the way, had allowed herself to be cornered too easily. It made perfect sense that this was a gambit. She knew that her younger self, fighting her way to the White House above her, had not felt like this was an easy fight, but that was the cleverness of the trap. The president had to sacrifice a lot of her troops to make her ultimate victory hard-won enough to be convincing. Typically ruthless. Quil hadn't suspected a thing. Jana checked her watch.

'In just over an hour Quil's going to be sitting in the Oval Office issuing her ultimatum,' she whispered.

'Which is right where the president wants her,' replied Dora.

Jana thought furiously. What could the plan be? Could it be as simple as mining the White House and blowing it sky-high once she'd lured Quil inside?

'What do we do?' asked Jana. 'Do we let my mother spring her trap, or do we stick with our original plan?'

'We wait and see what happens. If we make the wrong move, or the right one at the wrong time, we'll be screwed. Just hang tight and don't panic.'

Easy for you to say, thought Jana.

So they stayed there as the battle progressed, beamed down to them from a hundred eyeskys and a thousand individual soldiers' data feeds. They watched the Godless troops cut a swathe through the Earth forces, even as larger units of Earth soldiers stayed hidden out of sight, under-ground or just beyond sensor range, waiting for the order to mobilise, drawing the enemy in deeper and deeper with every minute.

Jana realised, with sudden, shocking clarity, that she and her friends were completely out of their depth. The forces at play here, the plots and counterplots, the sheer weight of lives at stake – how the hell were three teenagers and a dodgy lord from the seventeenth century supposed to stand in the way of all this?

Paralysed by fear and indecision, Jana stood guard as the battle for the White House concluded.

'Where is she?' demanded the president, slamming her fist into the table. 'We need to know where she is.'

Her advisors chimed in their views.

'She could still be in orbit.'

'We have multiple sightings of the woman in the blank mask in this area, I think it's her.'

'I think that's a decoy.'

'Yeah, we're supposed to think she's upstairs.'

'It's a trick.'

'No, she's too brazen for that. It's her.'

'It's not.'

'It can't be.'

'It must be.'

'ENOUGH!' Abhilasha shot to her feet, her entire body rigid with fury. 'Enough of this. We need to know if our lure has worked. We have to get her to reveal her position. Ready the cameras, I'm going to address the world.'

There was a flurry of activity, but it was coordinated and rehearsed. The broadcast team had camera drones in the air within a minute, and the president was standing at the podium drafting a statement with the help of what remained of her communications team.

'She's only giving this speech because she knows Quil will respond in kind,' said Jana.

Dora nodded. 'And when she sees Quil's broadcast, she'll see that she's in the Oval Office and she can spring whatever trap she has planned.'

'It going to be a really big bomb isn't it.'

'I'd be surprised if it was anything more subtle. I would think that Quil has only moments after she stops talking before she's blown to bits.'

'And then the ships will probably just nuke the world from orbit and fly home.'

'Let's see. We don't know how your mother will react to Quil's ultimatum. She might not spring her trap, if she thinks doing so will result in a nuclear strike.'

'We can't afford to take that chance,' whispered Jana. 'As soon as she's finished her speech, we have to make our move.'

Dora looked sideways at Jana and held her gaze for a minute. Then she nodded once. 'I think you're right, we can't take the risk. Anyway, Henry is still up there and I don't want him getting himself blown up.'

Jana was confused by this sudden concern for Sweetclover. 'And Kaz,' she said pointedly.

'Yes, of course.'

Jana knew what her mother was going to say, because she had seen this speech already, but she was impressed that such powerful oratory was prepared in five minutes flat.

'When she's speaking, all eyes will be on her,' whispered Dora. 'So follow my lead.'

The thuds and noises from above that had been their constant companion for two hours had stopped before the president began to speak, so the huge hall was silent as she delivered her speech; it was the focus of everybody's attention. Jana and Dora still stood by the table, out of everybody's direct line of sight.

'Last week, the world watched in horror as Barrettown burned,' began Abhilasha.

Jana felt Dora press something into her hand and glanced down to see that it was a small gas mask. She looked up at Dora quizzically, and saw that she was holding a grenade in her right hand and a gas mask in her left. She passed the grenade to Jana and took another from her pocket.

'As soon as she ends transmission, pull the pin and we gas this place,' said Dora. 'It'll put them all to sleep within seconds. Then we drag your mum up to meet Quil. Simple.'

Jana did not think it would be simple. She knew what Dora wasn't saying – with three grenades thrown from three different points around the room, they would have had solid coverage. But they were a man down, and there was a pretty good chance some of the agents would stay upright long enough to put up a fight. A fight Dora and Jana would have little chance of winning.

The president's speech was holding the room mesmerised.

'This may be my last transmission,' she said. 'But whether I and my staff survive this day is not important.'

I think it's important, thought Jana indignantly. She could see that some of the people watching the president speak in the hall thought so too – there were a few sideways glances between colleagues as she said those words.

The speech was drawing to a close, and Jana looped her right index finger through the ringpull at the end of the grenade's pin. This was it, the moment they'd been waiting for all this time. The chance to take action that would stop Quil and her mother once and for all, end a war, maybe cleanse her conscience of some of the guilt she carried, and then start a new life, free of this madness. Even if their chances were slim, they had to act.

It was the moment of truth.

'To the people of Earth, I say this. Report to your muster stations and prepare to defend your homeland.'

As the president wrapped up her speech, Dora felt the muzzle of a gun pressed up against her spine and heard the voice of the only security agent in the hall who had actually been paying attention to his job whisper in her ear, 'Move, and you're dead.'

Dora moved faster than Jana thought possible, spinning and kicking at once, sending the gun clattering from the agent's hand. Jana rolled forward and brought the gas mask up to her face. It automatically sealed itself across her mouth, nose and eyes as she raised her gun to fire at the agent Dora was already fighting hand to hand. Realising that she couldn't get a shot off without killing Dora, Jana spun and raised her arm to throw her grenade, but before she could release it she was shot straight between the eyes.

Or at least, straight between the eyes of the hologram

generated by her chameleon shroud. Since her disguise was a head taller than she, the beam actually hit her scalp, burning a clean scorched line right down her centre parting and causing her to scream in agony and fire her gun wildly, sending a hot beam of death slicing through the air, chopping down a camera drone and neatly bisecting the main conference table, causing it to collapse into two halves.

Through her watering eyes, Jana was aware of her grenade hitting the ground at her feet and rolling away, the pin still safely in place.

She felt hands grab her and throw her forward onto her face, and then heavy boots began kicking the life out of her. She curled into a ball and screamed for them to stop, certain she was moments from death.

'Wait!'

It was her mother's voice, shouting for calm. Jana felt like one big bruise, and she could taste blood as she opened her eyes and looked up.

She could see Dora, on her knees with a gun pressed to her head.

She could see her mother, looking up at the screen.

She saw Quil on the screen giving a speech from the ruins of the Oval Office.

'She's there! It worked, she's standing right on top of it!' shouted the president. 'Do it! Do it now! Detonate the bomb!'

One of her aides pressed some buttons on a handset and one corner of the wall of screens turned to a black block that displayed a countdown. Five minutes to arm and detonate whatever surprise they had concealed above ground to wipe out the Godless leadership.

And Kaz.

Clapping her hands in satisfied glee, Abhilasha Patel turned her attention to the two traitorous agents who knelt before her with guns to their heads.

She sneered down at Dora, leaned back, and kicked her, hard, full in the face.

'Traitorous bitch,' hissed the president, as Dora wiped away blood from her broken nose with the back of her hand.

'Can't be a traitor, if I was never loyal in the first place. Ma'am,' said Dora, smiling ruefully.

Jana's heart was in her mouth as the president held out her hand to one of her agents. The hulking, black-suited man did not need to ask what she wanted; he just handed her his gun.

The president slowly raised the weapon and pointed it straight at Dora's heart.

'I'm not going to ask why you betrayed me,' she said. 'Whether you're a clone sympathiser, part of Hope's little rebellion, or just some madman who wanted the fame that comes from assassinating a president. But I want you to look me in the eyes before you die, so I can see that you understand how completely you have failed.'

Jana looked up at the woman who had, in two separate ways, birthed her, watching her finger tighten on the trigger that would end her best friend's life.

15

Kaz blinked the blood out of his eyes, tried to get his bearings, and wished for a life where he didn't repeatedly wake from unconsciousness bruised and confused.

He was lying in a pile of rubble, dust and plaster layered over him like a shroud. His legs were pinned under something heavy, but they didn't feel numb or broken, just stuck. He knew that one of the first drop-ships had been targeted straight at the White House, and he presumed it was that impact which had knocked him off his feet.

He also knew that ship had been full of Quil's specially engineered monsters, and that their objective was to kill everything that moved. He had no idea how long he'd been lying there, but while he could hear the sounds of battle in the distance, there didn't seem to be any fighting in his immediate vicinity. He had to assume the White House had been secured, which meant he was alone and unarmed at the very heart of enemy territory. He should have been underground with Jana and Dora by now, helping them subdue resistance and dragging the president kicking and screaming out into the light of day to face Quil's judgement. His absence reduced their chances of success significantly, but there was nothing he could do about that right now. He had to trust that they'd be OK because there was just no way for him to reach them. Which meant he had a stark choice – stick around and risk capture and death, or jump away and leave them to it. Leaving would certainly be the safest course of action.

He could hear Dora's voice in his head, telling him that the strategically sensible thing to do would be to retreat, because he would be a huge liability if he were captured.

But he could also hear Jana's voice chiding him for even considering running away, and making him swear never to run out on them again. Her voice was by far the loudest.

He scanned the area. He was still in the corridor, with the Rose Garden to his left and the collapsed wall to his right. His field of vision was obscured by the corpses of three of his fellow prisoners, so he couldn't be sure there wasn't someone silently standing guard a few feet away, but he couldn't see any movement. He would just have to take the chance.

He locked eyes with the surprised, disbelieving gaze of his ex-boss, Amos Hope, who lay crushed beneath a pile of masonry. He had been this man's shadow for three months, but he did not mourn him. It seemed fitting that Hope should have been crushed by the building he had sought to take control of, as if the system itself had rounded on him and struck him down for his presumption.

Kaz tugged his right leg and felt the beam give a little. He heaved a sigh of relief and began wriggling and pushing his way free, always conscious of the noise he was making, the possibility of discovery, and how completely he was a sitting duck. He was ready to jump away the second he saw a clone trooper, but after a long few minutes he pulled himself free and rose awkwardly to his feet. His legs hurt terribly, but they weren't broken. Crouching down, Kaz rummaged through the debris that smothered another of the nearby corpses – one of the agents who had been escorting him to execution – and found a weapon. The laser fitted snugly in his hand and, although he knew it would be no use at all if he encountered one of Quil's bioengineered monsters, it would make short work of anyone else foolish enough to get in his way.

But what way was that? He struggled to think of a useful plan. There was no realistic prospect of rendezvousing with Dora and Jana – there were just too many clone soldiers between him and them. If only he had a chameleon shroud, he could maybe get close to Quil, or make his way to the DUCC entrance and use the code Dora had given him to open the door . . . And then an idea struck him. Foolish, perhaps, but just maybe he could be of some use after all.

He would have to move quickly and quietly, and avoid detection at all costs. If he could just get to the other side of the building, he might have a chance of doing some good. Taking a deep breath, he limped across the rubble and peered around the half-standing wall of a conference room.

And looked straight into the soulless eyes of one of Quil's porcelain-skinned monstrosities.

For an instant he thought it hadn't noticed him; its face was not capable of registering emotional responses, so there was no flash of surprise, alarm or excitement at being confronted with a live enemy. But a second later its skin began to grind as it moved towards him with alarming speed, raising its weapon as it walked.

Kaz pulled his head back as a laser blast seared through the space it had just vacated, then he turned and ran back down the corridor. He had only a second or two before the creature rounded the wall and had a clear shot at his retreating back, so he couldn't hope to survive a sprint down the corridor's full length. He found himself drawing level with the doorway

251

he had planned to skip through on his way to the Rose Garden, and he vaulted over the rubble and flung himself head first through the splintered doorway. Instinctively he tried to land on his shoulder and roll away, but instead of hitting solid ground, his shoulder hit another pile of rubble, which cascaded away beneath him and sent him sprawling, face first, on the floor.

Knowing he had only moments, Kaz rolled sideways and came up with his gun raised and firing wildly. For the first time that day, he got lucky. The monster's hulking shape filled the doorway and although the beam from Kaz's weapon bounced harmlessly off the creature's hide at a sharp angle, its refracted beam sliced through one of the only ceiling beams still in place, weakening the structure of the room and bringing an avalanche of stone, wood and plaster down on the monster's head.

Kaz scrambled backwards, engulfed by a cloud of dust, keen to get as much distance between himself and his downed pursuer as possible; surely someone (or something) would have heard the commotion and be coming to investigate.

But as he rose clumsily to his feet, Kaz gasped in horror to see the dust cloud clearing to reveal the monster, still standing, with its weapon aimed straight at Kaz's head. In an instant of awful clarity, Kaz knew there was no way he could jump away into time before the beam sliced him in two.

Then, as the rumble of the building's disintegration lessened, Kaz heard a repeated clicking sound. The monster looked down at its gun, then tossed it away. Kaz realised that although its owner had been undamaged by the collapse, the gun had been trashed. He breathed a sigh of relief at his good fortune, but then gave a yelp of alarm as the creature, which stood with rubble and debris up to its waist, simply began walking through it as if all the accumulated debris were merely water through which it was wading.

Kaz staggered backwards, but he was off balance and slowed by his injured legs. The monster was upon him before he could turn and run. Damn, the thing was stupidly fast. Kaz felt cold, stony fingers wrapping around the back of his neck and beginning to squeeze as he was lifted off his feet. No point jumping away now – he'd only take the creature with him.

Kaz squirmed and kicked, but he couldn't loosen the creature's grip. In desperation, as spots began to appear in his peripheral vision, he pulled the trigger of his gun and waved it above him in a rough circle, carving a huge chunk out of the remaining ceiling and bringing it smashing down on them both. Something hard smashed into his head and his senses reeled as he was again engulfed by debris. But his desperate strategy worked because the creature lost its grip, and Kaz collapsed to the floor in the midst of the shower of rubble, stones and bricks clattering around his head, causing him to lose all sense of orientation and space. He felt himself starting to pass out and forced himself to move upwards and forward through the chaos, determined to stay on his feet no matter what. Just as he was climbing to his feet, though, something swept them out from beneath him and he fell again, spinning on to his back, sharp edges jabbing him as he fell, winded.

Blinking away the dust, trying to crawl backwards, he saw a long white arm reaching out of the dust towards him. Too late again. This thing was relentless.

Fingers closed around his throat once more, this time at the front, squeezing his windpipe painfully as he was again lifted from the ground like a rag doll and held at arm's length by the dead-eyed creature that was choking the life from him.

Hopelessly, reflexively, Kaz lifted his weapon and shot the creature in the face, leaving the beam burning on a single point in the vain hope that maybe the stone skin would weaken before he heard the soft crunch of his windpipe collapsing. But the weapon had no effect on the creature, which just adjusted its footing slightly as the rubble shifted beneath it.

The movement saved Kaz's life; as the creature regained its solid footing, Kaz was shaken slightly and the aim of the gun shifted, sending the laser beam boring straight through the creature's right eye.

Kaz felt the grip loosen – not relax exactly, but it stopped tightening – as the laser burned a neat hole through the creature's eyeball. The skull was as impermeable from the inside as it was from the out, so the beam did not burst free through the back of the monster's skull; instead all the heat was trapped inside it, cooking the brain in an instant. Thick, meat-smelling steam began to pour from the creature's ears, mouth, nose and other eye. Slowly, still holding Kaz firmly, it toppled backwards to the ground.

Lying on top of the creature, which twitched and spasmed for a minute before finally lying still, Kaz could feel how solid it was. He had no idea what kind of technology Quil had used to create such a creature, but it was several orders of awfulness beyond any cloning process he'd yet heard of. Head splitting, bones aching, chest burning, Kaz reached up and prised the cold stone fingers away from his throat one at a time. They crunched as they moved. When the last finger was pulled free Kaz took a desperate, wrenching gasp of dusty air, and immediately regretted it as he launched into a huge coughing fit. He levered himself up and away from the creature, and rocked back on his haunches, gun still held tightly in his hand. There was no time to pause; he had to get moving.

He put his right hand on the debris-strewn ground and pushed himself up on his left knee, then repeated the process on his right side. It felt like it was taking for ever just to get upright. Bracing his hands on his knees, he forced himself to rise to standing, fighting the head-rush lightness of incipient unconsciousness as he did so. He felt stupidly pleased with himself when he managed to stand upright without collapsing.

His self-satisfaction ended almost as soon as it had begun.

Another stone-skinned monster stood framed in the wreckage of the doorway, raising its gun. Kaz turned to run, only to find two more creatures standing behind him, also raising their guns.

With sudden, awful certainty, Kaz realised he was a dead man.

16

Jana reached down and switched her chameleon shroud off.

'Mother, stop it,' she said firmly.

Abhilasha Patel found herself staring not into the eyes of a six-foot-tall male, but a five-foot-four Indian-American female. Who looked exactly like the 'daughter' who had mysteriously disappeared seventeen years before.

And her finger froze on the trigger.

'What?' she said, completely thrown.

'It's me, Mother. Jana.'

Abhilasha's face creased in confusion. 'But you're upstairs. You're older. You . . .' She trailed away, lowering the gun, utterly wrong-footed. 'I don't understand.'

'Stop the countdown, and I'll explain everything,' said Jana, looking at the numbers ticking down on the screens at the end of the room.

If she didn't get the countdown stopped, Kaz was dead.

Abhilasha stared deeply into Jana's eyes for a moment, then shook her head firmly.

'No,' she said, raising her gun again. 'This is a trick. You're just another clone sent to mess with me.'

'You're right, I am a clone,' said Jana, speaking fast as the weapon drew level with her chest again. 'I'm the clone whose birth you commissioned to replace your real daughter after she died. I'm the clone that you raised as your own for ten years. I'm the clone who drove you nuts, who got expelled from three schools, who ran away from your security detail over and over, who crashed the car, and got tattoos, and got into fights, and crushed on other girls. I'm the daughter whose disappearance spawned a thousand conspiracy theories. I'm the clone of Christmas past. And I'm here to tell you to stop the countdown.'

Abhilasha hesitated again, overwhelmed.

'You can't be her,' she said, her voice soft, her eyes wide with confusion. 'You're too young. My daughter is upstairs, leading an army of monsters against me.'

Jana thought furiously. They didn't have time for her to prove her identity. The clock was ticking. Her mother was right. The only sensible explanation for her age was for her to be another clone, an agent of Quil's army sent to mess with Abhilasha's head. If she tried to explain time travel, she'd be shot on the spot. She needed some proof, some demon-stration. And fast.

There was only one thing to do, but it terrified her.

She turned to Dora, who was still kneeling beside Jana with a gun to her head, blood streaming down her face.

'Dora,' said Jana. 'I need you to jump.'

Dora turned and looked at her, incredulous. 'What?'

'I need you to show her,' she said urgently.

'Show me what?' demanded the president.

'But you'll be alone,' said Dora, ignoring everyone else, her eyes locked tight on Jana's.

'I can handle it,' Jana assured her. 'Trust me. It's the only way.'

'I won't be able to come straight back, remember.'

'I know.'

257

Dora reached out her hand and Jana took it, squeezed it, lifted it to her lips and kissed the knuckles.

'Mother,' said Jana calmly, still holding Dora's gaze. 'Can you see the sparks where we're touching?'

The red borealis danced around their hands as the time energy within them interacted.

'Weapons down!' shouted Abhilasha. Jana assumed some of the agents had drawn a bead on them, alarmed by the lightshow, perhaps expecting an explosion. She was grateful her mother was more circumspect.

'I see them,' said the president.

'Jump,' said Jana again, releasing Dora's hand, fighting back tears.

'I'll see you again,' said Dora with a crooked smile.

'Be sure you do.'

And Dora vanished in a flash of red fire, leaving Jana more completely alone than she had ever felt.

'That was Dora,' said Jana, aware of the tear that had escaped from her right eye, a tear she would have once been ashamed of, but which she now considered a badge of pride. She turned and looked up at her mother, who stood open-mouthed in wonder. 'She's like me. That's why I'm the wrong age. For me, it's only been about a year since that day in New York. The day you tried to have me killed. The day I found out that I could travel in time.'

She was dimly aware that all eyes in the room were on her. All the agents, the politicians and military leaders, the workers at their terminals – all were staring in wonder at Jana and her mother.

Jana held Abhilasha's gaze for a long time, defiant, pleading, desperate for some response as the countdown ticked towards zero.

'Please!'

As the counter hit five seconds, she got her answer.

'I don't believe you,' said Abhilasha.

There was the crack of a massive explosion from above. The room shook violently, all the lights went out, the screens died, the air filled with dust. The noise was deafening but Jana could make out screams mixed in with the cacophony. The feeling of the room shaking itself to pieces was like nothing Jana had ever experienced, and she fell backwards to the floor, where she tried to hold on and ride out the shock-wave. She felt the carpet ripple beneath her fingers as the floor undulated.

Someone fell on top of her, then someone else, and Jana found herself dogpiled as the rumbling faded and the room began to settle. The darkness was absolute. As Jana fought her way free of the bodies on top of her – who were them-selves trying to stand up – she felt her fingers brush the leather strap of a shoulder holster. Working solely by touch, pretending to help the man to his feet, she found the gun and slipped it into her hand, then backed away. In this total darkness, there was no way for him to pursue her.

There was also no way to escape.

The deep rumbling of the expanding shockwave was fading, but the ground was still undulating slightly, and all Jana's bearings were lost. The room was filled with cries and screams. What kind of bomb had Abhilasha planted up there? A nuke? It would explain the sudden loss of power, caused by the electromagnetic pulse. And this bunker was specifically designed to withstand a direct strike by an ICBM.

Which meant, Jana realised, there would be emergency power systems cutting in at any moment.

Furious despair crashed over her like a wave.

Kaz, Quil and Sweetclover were dead. Her mother had won the war by being the sneakiest, nastiest, most ruthless person in the fight – which was, honestly, never in any doubt.

What more was there that she could realistically achieve here? Their plan had been a complete bust. At least Dora was safe.

The room was suddenly flooded with light as the emergency generators kicked in.

Blinking away her night vision, Jana found herself staring straight at her mother, who was looking away to her left, gun still in her hand but pointing at the floor. And suddenly Jana knew exactly what she could achieve.

'Drop it!' yelled Jana, aiming her weapon at her mother and walking over to her.

Abhilasha looked around at Jana and froze.

Jana had the gun to her mother's temple before anybody could stop her.

Many guns were raised as the security and military personnel realised what was happening, but Jana was already walking her mother backwards towards the nearest exit, keeping her in front of her as a shield.

'Anybody shoots and she's dead,' yelled Jana.

She felt the door handle press into her back and she fumbled for it with her left hand, turning it and releasing the catch so she could back through it, pulling her mother after her.

They had backed into one of the seemingly endless corridors that composed the labyrinth beneath Washington. Jana corrected herself – beneath the smoking crater where Washington used to be. She knew there were countless rooms down here, but doubted any of them would be secure enough for her purposes. Not that she had any choice. She turned and began forcing her mother ahead of her down the corridor, turning to send a few bolts of fire back towards the door to the main hall when she heard it crack open.

She dragged her mother down a side corridor, then another, turning at random as often as she could, trying to lose herself in the maze. Eventually, after a few minutes of wandering, she chose a door and pushed her mother through it. She found herself in a dorm room, a row of three bunks to one side, a series of lockers to the left. Windowless, airless, lit only by the red glow of the emergency lights, it was a cell in all but name.

'You're very quiet,' said Jana through gritted teeth as she pulled one of the bunks across the door as a makeshift barricade. 'Don't you want to make a few threats? Tell me I'll never get out of here alive, that it's all pointless, stuff like that?'

'Would there be any point?' said Abhilasha, who sat on the bottom bunk at the far end of the short room.

Jana turned to face her. 'No,' she said, as she sat on the bunk across the door, facing her mother. 'You killed my best friend. He was above ground when you detonated the bomb. I'm going to make you pay for that.'

'I've killed a lot of people,' said Abhilasha, her voice even. 'What's one more? It was necessary. Without your mad creator leading them, the Godless will come to terms, I'm sure of it. You clones were an aimless rabble before she arrived. You will be again. I've won the war. Everything else is just . . . details.'

Jana sat and looked at her mother, and she didn't know what to say. She had spent ten years living under her roof, being raised by her – officially, anyway. She had inherited memories of six more years; happy, younger years. But the woman who sat opposite her was a stranger in every respect.

She hadn't planned for them to meet like this. The idea had been to hand her over to Quil, prevent the aerial bombardment and leave. Jana had nothing she wanted to say to this woman. Sitting opposite her now, preparing to take vengeance for the lives she had destroyed, Jana couldn't think of a thing to say.

'Aren't you going to kill me?' asked Abhilasha, seeming resigned. 'I presume that's why you were created. A cruel trick, to grow you to this age, fill you with the memories of my daughter and send you down here to die. But clones do not understand emotions, not really, not like real people. They can manipulate them, but feelings? Ha. As alien to them as dreams.'

'I had dreams,' said Jana softly, suddenly finding she had more words to say to this woman than she had ever expected. 'I used to dream that we would take a holiday together. You, me and Dad. Somewhere cold, I thought. Antarctica. Somewhere with snow. We'd build snowmen and have snowball fights. And we'd all go skiing, maybe. But it wouldn't need to be somewhere fancy. Not a resort or anything. Just somewhere we could be together, alone, as a family. No meetings, no phone calls, no urgent consultations. No excuses for not spending time with me. Just us. And maybe, I thought, I'd find a way to leave you alone for a while. You and Dad. You were so cold to each other, so distant. I thought perhaps if you had some time alone, you'd be nicer to each other. That's all I wanted, you see, really. Parents who loved each other, who loved me. A family that spent time together. That was my dream. Other children in my school dreamed of being lawyers or doctors, actors or even, ha, president. I just dreamed about a family that had an ounce of love in it. How pathetic is that.'

If her monologue had shaken Abhilasha, she did not show it. Her face remained impassive.

'These are not your memories,' her mother said. 'These are your, what do you call them? Simulacra, that's it. You think, just because you wear my daughter's face, and have some of her memories, that I'm going to . . . what? What is the point of this? Kill me or don't, I don't really care. I've defeated the clone army. My place in history is secure.'

Jana looked at her, astonished. 'So this was your dream, was it?'

'Always.'

Jana shook her head. 'I don't believe you. When you were my age, you dreamed of being president. I know that. You were always very open about your political ambitions. But what did that presidency look like, in your head, when you pictured it? Did it look like this? A smoking crater where Washington used to be. Cities across the solar system devastated. You, hiding in a bunker underneath the ruins of your office, waiting for death. Was this your dream?'

Abhilasha said nothing, just stared, blank-faced, at Jana.

'What, you're not going to engage with me because I'm not a real person, is that it?' asked Jana. 'You must have thought I was close enough to real once. When you had me made. After your birth daughter died.'

'Don't you talk about her,' snapped Abhilasha. 'Don't you dare.'

'I saw her, you know. Not so long ago, actually. My friends and I, we travelled back to that day. Witnessed the accident. It was exactly how I remembered it. But I saw the aftermath this time. I saw Dad, in shock, refusing to believe it, too horrified to even cry. I saw you too, arriving home, screaming at him, screaming at the doctors. Just screaming. I think it's the only time I've ever seen you express any emotion other than contempt. But what drove you after that? Plenty of parents lose their children. It's awful, but it happens. They grieve, they keep on living. But you. What possessed you to do what you did next? It can't just have been grief. Whatever it was must have already been in you. Whatever made you choose to replace her with me. To pretend that nothing had happened, that nothing had changed.'

'Stop it,' hissed Abhilasha. 'You're not my daughter. You're not even the changeling. You're just a weapon.'

'The *changeling*?' Jana felt a sudden rush of anguish. How was it possible this woman could still hurt her with a word? '*The changeling*?'

Was that really how she thought of her?

There really was no point talking to her any more. Her mother didn't believe Jana could travel in time, so she didn't believe she was who she said she was. One solution would be to grab her and take her back in time, show her the truth, force her to accept it. Jana could try to break her, make her face the reality of her actions, make her cry and weep for forgiveness.

But really, Jana couldn't be bothered. She'd had enough and she was tired and she just wanted this to be over.

'You're a monster,' said Jana. 'You know that, right? You've demonised and subjugated a whole section of the population just to secure power. You've tried to have me killed. You tried to have Dad killed. You killed Quil, and Kaz, and countless others. For what? So you could ensure your place in history. But you fail. I know history. I've travelled further than you could ever imagine and you know what I've learned? History forgets us. All of us, eventually. The only thing that matters is how you live your life. And yours has been an abomination.

You're not my mother. You never were. I never had one. You were just my dream of a mother, and you've turned into a nightmare. Time to wake up.'

She raised her gun and began to squeeze the trigger.

17

Kaz screwed his eyes shut and willed himself away into time. He didn't think he would be able to jump before they fired, but it was his only chance.

Just as the numbers began to swim around his mind, he heard a voice, as if from far away, shouting 'Hold your fire!' and he opened his eyes, pulling himself back into the present.

He was still staring down the barrels of two guns, and knew there was a third trained on his back. But standing behind the two monsters before him was Henry Sweetclover.

'Do not fire,' said Sweetclover. 'This man is a friend.'

The creatures did not lower their weapons, but they did not fire either. Instead they turned, their necks letting out an awful grinding screech, to look at the man giving them orders. There was a pause that seemed to last a lifetime, and then they lowered their weapons, turned and crunched away.

Sweetclover looked at Kaz, raised his eyebrows and let out a deep breath.

'That was a bit too close for comfort,' he said.

Kaz did not like the feeling of owing his life to this man, but he nodded his thanks.

'Thank you, I thought I was a dead man,' he said.

'You would have been,' said Sweetclover. 'If I hadn't stumbled across you on my way back to the Oval Office. What are you doing up here? You're supposed to be underground by now.'

'Change of plan,' said Kaz urgently. 'I was looking for you, actually.'

'Me? But—'

'No time. I need you to get back to Quil and give her the code to open up the DUCC. The entrance is down the hallway from the Oval Office, down the stairs into the basement then it's a big vault door. You can't miss it. It's got all sorts of biometric sensors on it, and a time-lock that will have been activated by now. But there's an override code, programmed in by Dora. If you type 1640 into the keypad, you'll be able to walk right in.'

'But how does that—'

'Just do it, quickly. Jana and Dora are alone and God knows what trouble they've gotten themselves into without me. It's a risk, but it's necessary. Get down there, please!'

'And you?'

'I wouldn't make it there on my own,' said Kaz. 'I'm useless to you now.'

Sweetclover smiled and shook his head. 'No, you're not,' he said, pulling the small cylindrical mechanism of the chameleon shroud from his pocket. 'I used this to disguise myself so I could return here. You take it. Resume your post as my guard.'

Kaz grabbed the device and switched it on, seeing the world blur for a second as the hologram wrapped around him. 'Fantastic!' he said, beaming. 'Let's go.'

Henry led the way back to what was left of the Oval Office, Kaz behind and to his left, playing the part of the dutiful bodyguard.

They entered through the secretary's anteroom and found Quil still sitting behind the president's desk, with her feet up. Around her stood a swarm of Godless troopers and four of her shock troop creatures. Quil was talking to a hologram of her new second-in-command, choosing the cities they would target if the president refused to surrender herself before the deadline.

'Not Paris,' Quil said emphatically as they entered. 'Nobody touches Paris.'

'I should hope not, my love,' said Sweetclover expansively as he walked towards her. 'We made good memories there.'

Quil looked up and smiled at her husband. To Kaz it seemed to be a genuine, loving smile, and once again he wondered how someone so cruel and ruthless could also be so affectionate.

'And we will again, Hank, once this war is concluded.'

'I can help with that, I think,' said Henry, leaning forward with his hands on the desk.

'I'll call you back,' said Quil, dismissing the hologram and then looking up at Sweetclover quizzically. 'How?'

'I found a survivor,' he said. 'He volunteered some information in the hope that it would save his life.'

'Information?'

'The code to open the door to the bunker.'

Quil narrowed her eyes suspiciously. Kaz couldn't blame her – it was a thin story, and Sweetclover was not a practised liar.

'He's telling the truth, Ma'am,' said Kaz.

Quil flashed him a furious glance. 'Of course he is,' she snapped. 'He's my husband.'

OK, thought Kaz, not quite the way I intended to help, but whatever works.

'Then let us try it, darling,' said Quil, rising to her feet. 'Perhaps we can bring this war to its conclusion sooner than I had expected.'

Instructing the troopers to follow her, and calling for backup to meet them in the basement, Quil led the procession to the huge vault door that stood in the concrete surround of the basement wall. There were a variety of sensor pads and scanning devices around the door, and a single keypad on the right-hand side was lit.

Henry stepped forward and made to punch in the code, but Quil placed her hand on his forearms and stopped him.

'Let this one do it,' she said, indicating Kaz. 'Just in case.'

How nice to be disposable, thought Kaz as he stepped forward and keyed in the code, offering up a silent prayer that Dora had done her work well. He needn't have worried. The door gave a series of clicks and thunks as huge bolts retracted, and then it swung slowly open on hydraulic levers.

'Nice,' said Quil, nodding appreciatively. Then she drew her gun and led the party through the doorway. There was a staircase immediately ahead of them, leading down almost to the vanishing point.

With Quil at their head, Henry beside her and Kaz and the troopers bringing up the rear, they descended quickly. At the bottom was another vault door. Quil looked across at Henry.

'Did your little tattletale tell you the code for this door too?'

Henry, unsure how to respond, was foolish enough to flash a helpless glance at Kaz, hoping for assistance. But Kaz hadn't known there was a second door either.

Quil saw Sweetclover's imploring glance and turned to Kaz, her suspicions once more aroused. Frightened that his cover was about to be blown, Kaz quickly stepped forward and keyed in the same code, once more putting his faith in Dora.

His heart sank, though, when the only reaction to the code was the basement-level door above them beginning to swing closed.

'What's is this?' said Quil, angrily. 'Is this some kind of trick?'

Her gun was raised now, and she pointed it first at Kaz and then at Sweetclover. Kaz saw all the colour drain from Sweetclover's face as he found himself on the receiving end of his wife's suspicions. His reaction told Kaz that this was a new development, and one which scared Sweetclover half to death.

'No, my dear,' he spluttered. 'I swear—'

The door above them swung shut with a very final clang.

Quil, Henry and Kaz all stood, frozen in anticipation, waiting for something to happen. Quil had just opened her mouth to speak, the barrel of her gun coming to rest aiming at Kaz, when the door before them gave a groan and the bolts began to retract. Kaz let out a breath he hadn't realised he'd been holding.

'It's a kind of airlock,' he said. 'Security for—'

He never got to finish his sentence. There was a deafening noise and the staircase began to shake, the lights went out and the whole world became a maelstrom of noise and vibration. Knocked off his feet, Kaz fell to the floor in the darkness, his senses stunned by the sheer chaotic assault of noise. It felt like it lasted for ever, and he could feel his senses slipping away from him, but eventually the cacophony faded and he was left, lying on the ground, in the darkness, bleeding from the ears and completely disorientated.

Again.

When the world stopped spinning he could hear muffled voices in the darkness, but he couldn't make out words, or who was speaking. Eventually a single red light burned into brightness and he saw the collected remains of their party. Quil and Hank were sitting with their backs to the vault door, arms around each other. The troopers were sitting or lying scattered up the staircase. Standing tall, seemingly unaffected behind them, ten steps up, were the four creatures that had accompanied them, impassive and ready.

Quil was laughing. She was actually laughing. By leaning in closely and lip-reading, he could make out what she was saying.

'She nuked the White House,' Quil said, amazed and amused. 'The crazy bitch actually nuked the White House.'

She sat and laughed for a while, as the soldiers gradually shook themselves back to some semblance of order. Kaz's hearing slowly returned, though only just enough – everything sounded as if it was being echoed to him down a long pipe.

Kaz turned his attention to the door. The keypad was dead, but the door had opened just a crack before the power had gone. He wedged his fingers around the edge of the metal door and pulled but it was hopeless. He might as well have tried to make one of Quil's monsters crack a grin. Which, come to think of it, gave him an idea.

'How strong are they?' he asked in a lull between Quil's gales of laughter, pointing to the creatures on the stairs.

Gradually Quil calmed herself and, planting a kiss on Henry's forehead, she rose unsteadily to her feet.

'Very strong indeed,' she replied. 'But I doubt even they can punch through a door this thick.'

Kaz pointed to the crack. 'They don't need to,' he said.

Quil smiled at him, nodding her understanding, and gestured

for the creatures to descend. Under her instruction, they lined up, hooked their thick stone-skinned fingers around the edge of the door, and heaved.

The screech of bending metal was loud enough that it made Kaz wince, even with his damaged hearing. The monsters braced and pulled, their muscles bulging obscenely beneath their porcelain-white skin, their eyes popping and their jaws clenched. But gradually the door began to inch open. It had opened a few centimetres when one of the creatures' arms popped out of its socket and hung uselessly at its side. It didn't even pause, but just kept pulling with its one remaining useable arm.

When the door was open wide enough for them to slip through, Quil gave the order for them to stop. The creature with the dislocated shoulder grabbed it with its good arm and wrenched it back into place, then Quil, weapon drawn, squeezed through into the tunnels beyond the door.

18

As Jana felt the tiny resistance on the trigger that indicated the gun was about to fire, there was a sharp knock on the door and she heard, to her amazement, Quil's voice calling in to them.

'Is this a private reunion, or can anyone join in?'

Jana gasped; Abhilasha too.

'Hey, Jana,' continued Quil. 'A little birdie told me you've got our progenitor's mother in there. Don't hog all the fun. Let me in.'

Jana's mind raced and her heart leaped with hope. Quil was alive! Which meant maybe Kaz was too. But how to play this? She'd seen this version of Quil when she'd appeared in the quantum bubble, cancelling the kinder, saner Schrödinger's cat version of Quil out of existence, but the last time she'd had any meaningful interaction with her had been in 1645, and that had not gone well.

'Hey, Quil,' she shot back, keeping her tone light. 'How's it going? Thought you'd been nuked.'

'Don't you mean you hoped I'd been nuked?'

'Nah. Where would the fun be in that? I want to kill you myself.'

Quil laughed. 'You're trapped,' she said, her amusement plain.

'Oh, you know I'm not. I can just grab Mom's hand and jump us both out of here. Then you'd never find us.'

'True,' conceded Quil. 'But without a humiliated president to parade before the cameras, I'd have to make good on my threat to destroy a few cities. Just to save face, you understand. I'm thinking Sydney, Moscow, San Francisco, Buenos Aires, Mumbai, Shanghai. Unless you have any other suggestions? My husband is keen on flattening London.'

Jana cursed under her breath. Quil would do it, too.

'What is the purpose of this charade?' said Abhilasha, her confusion plain on her face.

'Shut up, you,' snapped Jana. 'You know, sometimes you talk like the bad guy in a cheap movie. "What is the purpose of this charade?" Do you hear yourself?'

'Is she giving you lip?' asked Quil, her amusement clearly audible.

'You know what she's like.'

'Do I ever.'

Jana bit her lip, thought hard, and came to a conclusion. 'OK,' she said, 'how about this. Just you. You come in and join us. Let's make this a proper family reunion. I promise not to shoot you.'

There was a moment's pause, then Quil responded, still with laughter in her voice. 'Then Henry comes too. He's family. He should get a chance to meet his not-really-mother-in-law.'

So Sweetclover was alive too. That was good news. Jana still didn't entirely trust him, but he wouldn't be by Quil's side if she knew he'd been fraternising with the enemy.

'Why not?' said Jana, as cheerily as she could. 'I'll open the door and you both come in, unarmed, and slowly. If you try to storm the room, I'll just open fire. Chances are I'll take you down with me.'

'I wouldn't dream of it, darling,' chirped Quil.

Jana leaned forward and aimed the gun between Abhilasha's eyes. 'You don't move a muscle,' she said.

She stood and pushed the bunk away from the door, then stepped back, keeping her gun aimed at the doorway.

'Come in,' she said.

The door opened and there stood Quil. It made Jana's heart jump to see her, unmasked, her skin healed and youthful. This Quil looked exactly the same as the version who had walked Jana through her life story. In spite of herself, Jana felt a tiny twinge of hope – maybe she could save Quil from herself, maybe she could restore the version she had known, somehow.

Quil walked into the room, with Sweetclover at her side. He looked wary and unhappy at this turn of events, and would not meet Jana's eye. Behind them both, Jana could see several clone troopers and one of the monsters. She blinked in surprise. The trooper closest to Quil was wearing the smiley-face mask that Sweetclover had worn during the battle above. But that meant . . .

Smiley-face stepped forward quickly, shoving Quil and Sweetclover into the room and slamming the door behind him. Jana held her fire, unsure what to do, as he replaced the bunk across the door and turned to face her and the two very startled new arrivals.

'What do you think you're doing?' Quil yelled at her insubordinate underling – who shimmered and changed as the chameleon shroud powered down, revealing himself to be Kaz.

Jana ran over to him and hugged him tightly, happier than she could express that her friend was alive. He kept his head up and his gun raised, covering Quil, Sweetclover and Abhilasha.

'Where's Dora?' asked Kaz.

'Jumped back,' said Jana, disentangling herself. 'Trying to prove to my mother that time travel is real.'

'Did it work?'

'What do you think?'

Jana turned so she was standing shoulder to shoulder with Kaz, both armed, their guns pointing at the three people who stood before them.

'Hello, Kaz,' said Quil, with a huge, fake smile. 'Sorry about your mom.'

Jana reached out and placed her hand on Kaz's forearm. 'Don't let her goad you,' she said softly.

'Of course not,' said Kaz calmly. 'That's your job.'

Jana was relieved at this seeming self-control. She had been worried his anger might overwhelm him, but it appeared not. She felt kind of proud of him, and gave his forearm a squeeze.

'I do not understand what is happening,' said Abhilasha, her face displaying a potent mix of confusion and outrage.

Quil turned to face her. 'Do you not, *Mother*? This is your day of reckoning. This room. Here and now, is where you pay for all your crimes.'

'Yours too, Quil,' spat Jana. 'This whole thing ends here. No more killing. Just us, alone at last. And it will be my decision, and mine alone, which of you three leaves this room alive. So sit down.'

She indicated the nearest bunks with her gun. Quil shrugged, making light of things as always, and sat on the bottom bunk, patting the space beside her as an invitation to Sweetclover to join her. Quil sat on the opposite bunk. All three looked up at Jana and Kaz.

Jana finally had them all in her power.

But she had no idea at all what to do with them.

'What was your plan?' asked Quil, leaning forward, a picture of engaged curiosity. 'I mean, the three of you turning up here like this isn't a coincidence. You must have had some strategy, and it must have gone completely sideways for us to all end up in this delightful little bunk room. So spill, what was your endgame?'

Jana couldn't see any harm in letting her know.

'You probably won't believe this, but we were going to help you,' she said, and took some pleasure in Quil's obvious surprise.

'Eh?'

'Kaz, Dora and me were going to drug her' – she indicated Abhilasha – 'and deliver her to you. Figured it was the best way to stop you nuking half the planet. We wanted to stop the war, basically. Let you win.'

'So you are working for the clones. I knew it,' said Abhilasha.

'Oh do shut up, Mother,' said Jana and Quil in perfect unison.

Quil narrowed her eyes, regarding Jana curiously. 'But why? Why would you do that?'

'Yeah, I wondered that,' said Kaz wearily. 'But she can be very persuasive.'

'You were poisoned,' said Jana. 'On Mars. The plums in your hotel fruit basket.'

Jana didn't think she'd ever get tired of seeing Quil wrong-footed.

'No, I wasn't,' protested Quil. 'Not so much as an upset tummy.'

'It was a very special toxin, specially designed just for you. Its purpose was to drive you mad. Make you paranoid and erratic. The idea was for you to go so nuts that your own side would remove you from command, giving Earth a tactical advantage.'

'Bullshit.'

'Mother?' Jana directed her attention to Abhilasha, who sat looking furious.

'It should have worked,' Abhilasha muttered. 'I have never understood what happened at the press conference.'

Quil's jaw fell open.

'We did,' said Kaz. 'We intervened. Derailed everybody's plans.'

'And who the hell are you, anyway?' said Abhilasha.

'I'm the changeling,' said Jana contemptuously. 'I told you that.'

'So, wait, I was poisoned to make me nuts?' said Quil. 'But, well, obviously I wasn't. Because I'm not.'

Every other person fixed Quil with a very hard stare, and said nothing.

Eventually Jana broke the silence. 'We were going to force the president to surrender to you, and then administer the antidote so you'd be in your right mind again. We figured that would be a good end to all this.'

'Antidote?' asked Quil.

Then Henry said, 'I'm sorry about this, my love,' and stabbed her in the neck with a hypodermic.

She didn't see it coming, and she recoiled from her husband.

'Hank?' she said, her face a picture of betrayal, before her eyes rolled back in her head and she passed out.

'Well done, Henry,' said Jana.

Sweetclover was leaning over his unconscious wife, stroking her hair. 'This cure of yours had better work,' he said, his voice low and dark.

'It worked on her quantum twin,' Jana assured him. 'It will work on her.'

'So what do we do now?' asked Kaz. 'Just leave? I mean,

she'll wake up sane. She's won the battle, taken the president captive. The war's over. It's all over. We're done. Aren't we?'

But Jana was staring at Abhilasha, who sat still, confused, angry and powerless but still defiant, her look challenging and unrepentant.

'No,' she said. 'No, we're not done. There's still unfinished business here.'

Jana lowered her gun and knelt down beside Sweetclover, laying her arm on his shoulder as he sat worried vigil over his wife.

'Henry,' she said. 'I want to get her away from here. Give her time and space to recuperate, to get her head sorted out. We can find a way back here, we've done it before. Will you let us take you somewhere quiet and safe?'

Sweetclover looked up, and Jana could see the anguish in his eyes. She wondered if anybody would ever love her the way he loved Quil. She hoped so, but deep down was a little voice that whispered no, because she didn't deserve it.

He nodded. 'If you think that is for the best, I will not object.'

'Thanks.'

Jana stood and held out her right hand to Kaz. He took it, and leaned over to grasp Sweetclover's shoulder, while Jana leaned over and used her left hand to grab hold of Abhilasha's hair.

Her mother yelled in fury and then panic as Jana pulled them all away from the ruins of Washington, to a safer time.

Interlude:
Io Scientific,
Cornwall, England, 2014

Henry Sweetclover was pretty sure he was about to kill himself.

He cast one last look around the central lab of Io Scientific as he prepared for the desperate gamble that would likely cost him his life.

There was Kaz, so young and excited, not yet worn down by the loss and the violence that would nearly overwhelm him in the year to come.

Beside him was Dora, younger still, a girl entirely lost in a terrifying world, yet meeting it with such innocence and wonder, a thousand miles and a thousand years away from the ruthless operative she would become.

And there was Jana, angry and guarded, resentful, closed off, always calculating the angles, as yet unaware of her own capacity for loyalty and love.

They had so far to go, so much to learn and experience, and even though he had thought of them as enemies for so long he knew now that they had never had been. They were just kids trying to stay alive and do the right thing. And he owed them penance for his part in their ordeals. That was why he'd agreed to adopt the role of their protector, travelling back in time to 2014 and taking up a job as a lowly security guard named Steve in order to ensure their escape from the trap he and his wife had laid for them. It seemed appropriate that it should be he who provided the catalyst for their adventures.

Three months he had been in Pendarn, waiting for them to arrive. He had enjoyed living in this time period again. It seemed, if not strictly normal, at least familiar. And after his recent experiences in the distant future, a period of calm and normality was what he needed. A period of mourning too, for all he had lost.

He had sat in that leaky Portakabin watching his old house Sweetclover Hall, and the hole he had cut in the fence, night after night, waiting for them to arrive, ready for one final adventure. He had felt a mixture of fear and relief when he had finally seen Kaz squeeze through the chain-link fence and walk into the abandoned manor house. The circle was closing, and even though he knew what it would cost them all, and who would die as a result of his protection of the timeline, he felt confident it was for the best.

Older Dora's appearance at the Portakabin had surprised him. Sneaking around in the dark like that, checking up on him as he waited for her younger self to appear for the first time. He had thought her trust fully won, but it appeared she still harboured doubts about his resolve. She had left as silently as she'd arrived, but he felt sure she was still around somewhere, keeping an eye on him, making sure he kept his word. She needn't have worried.

It had been good to switch off the chameleon shroud, to drop the disguise of Steve and reclaim his own face as he walked away from the burning motorbike. He had let the three kids believe his face to be another disguise, a mere impersonation of their enemy. They had not imagined that they were actually seeing him as he really was.

The rescue had gone as smoothly as he could have wished. His younger self and his wife had secured enough blood to synthesise an injection that would give him the gift of time travel; they had heard enough of Kaz's life story to identify Beirut as a key event; they had not secured Jana's chip.

He had not anticipated the brief trip to Beirut and the day of the bombing that had eventually led to Kaz's mother's death, but if anything it had sharpened his resolve to do right by the three. He bore a large responsibility for the tragedy of that day, even though Kaz did not understand that yet.

And now here he was, standing by a door that was about to explode, providing an escape for his slightly younger self, trapped in the corridor outside by his yet younger self.

His life had become so complicated, he sometimes felt he needed a flow chart to keep track of it all.

But this was the final loop. He would ensure the three young people escaped into time, as equipped as possible for the challenges that lay ahead of them, even if it cost him his life.

There was no one left to mourn him now, anyway.

He held his fingers to the window in the door and counted down, 5, 4, 3 . . . He stepped back, drew his weapon and braced for the explosion.

There was a deafening roar as the door exploded and flew outwards into the corridor beyond. As he raised his weapon and began firing out of the door into the smoke beyond, Henry knew that Jana, Kaz and Dora were holding hands and wishing themselves away into the past.

The first bullet hit him in the right shoulder, flinging him back and spinning him sideways. The second scored a hot, red line across his belly. He couldn't even count the rest of the bullets as they thudded into him. He felt calm and cold as the world began to slip away from him. He didn't even feel the arms that caught him as he toppled backwards towards the floor.

Kinshasa, 2120

'I must admit, I did not expect it to be you,' said Dora as she sat in the chair by his bedside, regarding him curiously. 'I thought it would be Kaz, or maybe even a future version of me. But you . . . that does not make sense.'

Henry felt like crap. At first he didn't know where or when he was, but the room was bland and functional. A private hospital or a clinic, perhaps?

'Kinshasa,' he said softly, as he realised. This is where he had tracked them to after he had run out on Quil at the White House.

'How do you know that?' asked Dora, leaning forward.

He tried to get his jumbled thoughts in order. It was hard, because the anaesthetic was still leaving his system, and the post-op painkillers had filled his head with cotton wool. He thought hard, trying to fit the pieces of the puzzle together in his mind.

Dora had explained her timeline to him before he'd said goodbye to her in Switzerland. This young woman, the Dora beside his bed now in Kinshasa, had only recently completed her training with Garcia in the twenty-first century. She was jumping through time clearing up messes – rescuing her family from 1614, defusing the bomb he and Quil had left in

Sweetclover Hall; saving him and that security guard from Io Scientific in 2011; intervening to protect Kaz and Jana on the rooftop in New York in 2141. She was doing what he was doing – closing loops, tidying up loose ends. And he was one of them.

'From your future,' was all the explanation he could muster.

'So we become allies?' she asked, her disbelief plain.

Henry managed a weak smile. 'Of a sort. Not enemies, anyway.'

The long silence that greeted his response caused him to turn his head and focus his blurry eyesight on Dora. Older than the girl he'd just rescued in 2014, but noticeably younger than when he'd left her in Switzerland. Still so much that would happen to her. That *must* happen to her.

'I can't – can't tell you the future,' he said. 'You understand.'

Dora regarded him curiously, then nodded.

'Events have to proceed as they did for me,' he continued. 'If you change them, I won't be able to come back and rescue you. So you need to keep my secret. You can't tell the others about me.'

'How do I know this isn't some trick? A long con you're playing on me, moving all the pieces on the chessboard into the right configuration for you and Quil to defeat us in the future?'

Henry was confident that the disbelief on his face was answer enough. But just in case, he asked, 'How many times was I shot?'

Dora bit her lip, narrowed her eyes and, eventually, nodded again. 'OK,' she said. 'Good point.'

'You must promise not to tell them about me, not until it becomes obvious. It's important. The knowledge could change things.'

'I understand.'

'Promise.'

'I promise.'

Henry breathed a sigh of relief. 'Good,' he whispered, before surrendering to unconsciousness.

Dora visited every day, solicitous of his recovery and always discreet. She assured him that his presence and identity were a closely guarded secret, and that he would be free to go as soon as he was fully recovered.

His recuperation took months, even with the benefit of the best medicine 2120 could offer. He came to realise how close to death he had been, and how much he owed Dora for his rescue.

Then one day towards the end of his convalescence, an older Dora slipped quietly into his room.

Henry was sitting propped up on the bed, engrossed in *Pride and Prejudice*. He had taken advantage of his time here to catch up on his reading – continuing a project he had begun during his time in 2014, working his way through the classics of English literature that had been written in the years beyond his time of birth. Austen was his particular favourite.

He glanced up from his book and smiled a greeting, then laid the book across his lap in surprise as he registered the tiny differences in features and deportment from the Dora who habitually visited him here.

'Hello, Henry,' she said as she sat beside his bed. 'Long time since I was here.'

'Dora,' said Henry, smiling, happy to see her. 'Am I right in thinking that you are a lot older than you were yesterday?'

Dora returned his smile, though it was tinged with melancholy.

'You are,' she said. 'I last saw you in Switzerland.'

Henry felt a flutter of nerves as he realised what this visit meant.

'So this is goodbye,' he said. 'The loops are closed, the adventure is over.'

'Almost,' said Dora, gently.

Henry cocked his head, curious. What else could possibly remain for them to do?

'I have one more job for you,' said Dora. 'And then . . . an offer.'

Io Scientific research Centre, Siberia, 2143

Henry had to smile at the appropriate ridiculousness of his life.

He and his wife had started a company called Io Scientific in 2012, the objective being to develop technologies that could help her win the war she was fighting in the future. As an offshoot of that work, cloning techniques had progressed by leaps and bounds. Henry had then travelled back in time and worked for his own company in disguise, as Steve the security guard, in order to frustrate the plans of his younger self. And now here he was, 129 years in the future, working for his old company again, again as Steve, again as a security guard.

The company had changed, of course. Long ago abandoned by its founders and floated on the stock market, it was now run by a board of directors who answered to greedy share-holders interested only in the size of their dividends. The company he and Quil had created was almost single-handedly responsible for the creation and production of the clones who composed the underclass she would one day champion, and the army she would eventually lead. Henry wondered how much his wife had known about the role of Io Scientific in mass-market clone production.

He thought about her insistence on time's will, her certainty that nothing she did during her travels into her past could make any difference to the flow of events. She had always maintained that she had no free will in the past, that everything she did was done only because it had to be done, because time willed it so, because it was her destiny. She bore no responsibility, took no credit, nor bore any guilt for her actions. She would have said that she had no choice but to call her company Io Scientific, that her role in creating the future that would in turn create her was merely a function of time's determination. Not her doing, not her fault.

Henry had never really believed that, and when he had learned of the poison that had unbalanced her mind, he believed that he had found an explanation for her crazy theories. The symmetry of Quil's life bothered him, but he preferred to consider it evidence of God's plan, rather than the mechanistic working of deterministic fate.

And anyway, it was he, not she, who was now closing the biggest loop of all.

Henry sat at the reception desk in the huge echoing marble-floored lobby of the Io Scientific Research Centre in North Siberia. The building was locked up for the night. There were a few patrols wandering the grounds, a team of guards pacing the floors above him, and one particularly dedicated scientist beavering away in the contagious diseases wing, but the building was mostly quiet and dark. Henry checked the company manifest – the secret one, protected by layers of encryption and security, which had opened to him easily once he had typed in a series of codes provided by Dora.

Throughout his time here, Henry had kept a close eye on

the progress of the clone designated KRTV-710. An off-the-books, private commission, this clone was a bespoke piece being created for a rich client who prized privacy and discretion above all else. The conception and growth of the body had been run-of-the-mill, apart from one specific modification designed to ensure that the clone was of a different sexual orientation to the original. The memory edits, on the other hand, had been extremely complex, requiring a level of skill and finesse far above the average. Henry had monitored the work with interest – after all, not everybody has the opportunity to witness the birth of the love of their life.

The cancellation order for the clone had arrived just before staff had closed up for the day, as Henry had known it would. Dipping into the chat logs of staff had revealed a deep anger at the destruction of such fine work, especially by the technician who had performed the memory sculpture. But they were employees, and they did not get a say in such matters. The order was clear – the clone was to be terminated and incinerated before ever being brought to consciousness. The termination was to be conducted first thing in the morning.

Now the building was dark, Henry knew it was time to act. He had been timing the movement of the guards outside, and knew that it took half an hour for them to circle back to the lobby on each rotation. They would acknowledge him with a nod through the huge plate-glass frontage of the building each time they did so. This gave him a thirty-minute window. It would be enough.

He slipped away from the desk, hurried to the stairs – not the elevators, that would leave a record – and climbed to the first floor. The lab where KRTV-710 was being grown was at the end of the corridor, and he pulled out the key card that

Dora had given him as he walked towards it. One swipe, and he was in.

He had not actually been into the lab before, and had only followed KRTV-710's growth through the reports on the system. Seeing her with his own two eyes was a profound experience. She lay there, naked, in a half-tube that stood on four legs, like a table. The tube was filled with clear liquid, and a biomechanical umbilical cord stretched from the clone's belly button out through the glass to a large machine that whirred and buzzed as it processed nutrients fed into it by pipes that hung down from the ceiling.

She looked so peaceful, lying curled up. So young, too. It was strange – she looked like Jana, the Jana he knew, but she was his wife. Before the burns, and the plastic surgery that removed all traces of them and left her looking her age. He knew everything that would befall her, from the first moments of her life to the last.

And he wanted to change it.

He could. He could trigger her awakening now. Smuggle her out of the building before first light. Take her somewhere she'd be safe and cared for. They would have all of time to hide in. Of course, she wouldn't be his wife. That would be out of the question. But maybe they could form a kind of family.

How he wanted to change her destiny. Spirit her away from here and undo it all. But what would happen if he did?

Best-case scenario – they would live the rest of their lives in some distant time and he would have to watch her grow into a new person and make her own way without him.

Worst-case scenario – it would cause a paradox that might destroy time itself.

Either way, he would be undoing their marriage, removing

all the outcomes of all the choices she had freely made, regardless of whether she considered them freely made or not. He would be erasing her, and the love they had shared, from time itself. As strong as the pull of change was, he knew that he didn't have the right.

He placed his hands on the glass by her head and sent up a silent prayer for the girl who would become Quil, then he went to a nearby fridge and swapped a small bottle of poison with a bottle containing a special cocktail that would make her appear dead before delivering a time-delayed jolt that would wake her. It was the only way he could truly save her.

He would stay for one more day, make sure that her awakening and escape went as planned tomorrow night, and then he would be free.

He considered Dora's offer as he looked down at the sleeping clone of Yojana Patel.

Yes, he would take her up on it.

It felt . . . *right.*

Part Four

Dig two graves

Part Four

18
Lake Geneva,
Switzerland, 2005

The sun rose over the villa in a blaze of orange and purple that reflected off the lake. Matched with the yellowing leaves and the autumnal mist, it made the world seem awash with cool fire. Jana liked to be up to see the sun rise. None of the other residents of the villa were early risers, so this was her time. A moment of quiet solitude and calm before the hubbub of the day.

She navigated the steep incline that led down from the villa's terrace to the stony beach below, surefooted and nimble. The rounded stones rolled and clacked beneath her feet as she walked to the water's edge, where the soft waves lapped gently over her sandals. The water was almost perfectly still, a mirrored surface that stretched away ahead of her into the fiery mist. Reaching down, Jana picked up a flat, round stone, hefted it once in her hand to get a sense of its weight, then pulled back her arm and sent it skipping across the water, creating a line of concentric ripples that rippled out into the mist.

'Good throw,' said a soft voice behind her.

Jana jumped slightly and spun around to find Dora standing behind her.

'How do you do that?' she asked in amazement, looking down at the stones that had so loudly announced her own passage to the shore.

'Ninja skills.' Dora winked.

'Freak,' said Jana, smiling, as she began to walk along the water's edge towards the old wooden jetty that hung in the mist like a ghost structure. Dora fell into step beside her.

'I hope you do not mind me seeking out your company at this hour,' said Dora. 'I understand that, at this time of day, you prefer solitude, but I wished to talk to you, before the household rises.'

Jana loved the way Dora fell back into the more formal, English speech patterns of her youth when she was nervous or unsure of herself. It was so endearing, it made her want to squeeze her till she squealed. Instead, she settled for looping her arm through Dora's.

'Of course I don't mind,' she said. 'What's up?'

Dora did not reply, but Jana knew better than to push her. They walked together arm in arm, in companionable silence until Dora finally spoke.

'I have been keeping secrets,' she said. 'And I do not wish to do so any more.'

Jana smiled. She had been wondering when Dora would 'fess up.

'You mean about Sweetclover being Steve?'

Dora stopped in her tracks, surprised by Jana's deduction. Jana tugged her arm gently, and they resumed walking.

'How did you know?' asked Dora.

'Guesswork.'

'Based upon what evidence?'

Jana shrugged. 'A hunch, I suppose. He's never been much of a bad guy, has he, really? Not since 1645, anyway. I think the guilt of how he behaved that day changed him. Really, all he's ever wanted to do was keep Quil safe. And now she is. Her war is won, she's cured of the madness that possessed her. I can see why he would want to travel back in time and ensure that this timeline stays solid. It allows him to secure his wife's recovery, and make amends to us at the same time. He loves her so much. It's, I dunno, humbling.'

'You surprise me,' said Dora.

Jana laughed. 'What, you think I'm too dumb to work it out?'

'No,' said Dora, laughing. 'I merely mean that I would have expected you to say something to me when you worked it out. You are not normally so reticent.'

'I trust you,' said Jana simply. 'I knew you'd tell us when the moment was right. Didn't want to push.'

They reached the jetty and stepped over it, continuing beyond it along the shore.

'I am grateful for your trust in me,' said Dora.

'You earned it.' And more, thought Jana, but she did not voice the thought. 'Why tell me now, though?'

'I began to feel guilty about keeping secrets from you. And I felt that perhaps volunteering a secret to you might induce you to reveal one to me.'

Jana felt a sudden rush of nerves. She could only think of one secret that Dora might be referring to. She did not trust herself to reply, so she bit her tongue and kept walking, feeling as if the world was shifting around her in a way that felt exciting and terrifying at the same time.

Dora did not force the issue, and they walked on together

for five minutes, watching the sun burn away the mist, shake off its fiery cloak and rise into a clear blue sky. Shortly thereafter they reached the point where the beach ended abruptly in a sheer cliff face. They stopped, and Dora unhooked her arm, turned to face Jana and reached out to take her hands.

'Jana,' she said nervously. 'I see the way you look at me, sometimes, when you think I cannot.'

Jana was so overwhelmed with butterflies she didn't dare open her mouth to reply. She felt like all that would come out would be an alarmed squeak. She stared at their joined hands intently until Dora let go with her right hand, raised it and placed a finger beneath Jana's chin, lifting it slowly so that their eyes met.

The soft, kind smile on Dora's face was the most beautiful thing Jana had ever seen.

'I wanted to tell you that I do not object to that way you look at me,' said Dora, who, Jana realised, was as nervous as she was. What did she have to be uncertain about, wondered Jana? What was Dora doing? Was she trying to let her down gently – or, possibly, something else? Jana dared not hope.

'When I was training with Garcia, in the twenty-first century, he taught me to use all the tools at my disposal. *All* of them. A spy, he said, is whatever they need to be in the moment. I didn't question his teachings, not any of them. Save for one lesson, to which I would not submit. I would not . . . I felt able to – with boys. But not – not with girls. It seemed . . .

'You must understand, Jana, that when I grew up, such a kind of love was not spoken of. It was not condemned, or taboo. It was simply not considered. Not among my people, anyway. The idea would not have occurred to them, or to me. And when Garcia suggested that I explore this – as a tool, you understand, a weapon I could use in certain circumstances – I recoiled from the idea.'

Jana waited for Dora to continue, but she did not. Instead, she bit her lip and broke Jana's gaze, staring at her feet. This was the Dora Jana remembered from before her years of training; the young woman uncertain of herself, feeling her way through a world that had suddenly become more confusing than she could ever have imagined. Jana had seen more and more flashes of the old Dora recently, since Mars. Less ninja-killer Dora; more old, sweet Dora. It felt as if she was recovering from a long period of shock and withdrawal, and it was a wonderful thing to see.

Jana took a deep breath and repeated Dora's earlier action, lifting her friend's chin with her hand and meeting her gaze. Dora looked scared half to death.

'And now?' whispered Jana.

Kaz took a sip of coffee, sprinkled grated cheese onto a piece of lavash bread and slipped it beneath the grill. He couldn't stand feta, and the idea of mixing any kind of cheese with jam still repulsed him, but he had developed a taste for grilled cheese on lavash bread for breakfast. The smell of the bread and coffee reminded him of his mother.

He wondered if there would ever come a time he could think of her without a stab of anger and guilt. He had asked Dora, thinking her experiences with her brother might give her some perspective on the process of healing such wounds, but she had refused to discuss it and he had backed off.

'Good morning, Kaz.'

Sweetclover entered the kitchen, hair still wet from his morning shower. He was dressed in jeans and a clean white shirt, nothing formal, relaxed clothes for a man who seemed to have undergone a complete transformation in the time Kaz had known him.

'Morning,' Kaz grunted.

Try as he might, and no matter how profoundly Sweetclover may have changed, Kaz could not feel comfortable around the man.

'Coffee's brewed,' said Kaz, indicating the large moka pot on the stove.

'Excellent,' replied Sweetclover, and he set about preparing himself a cup.

Kaz took his grilled cheese and coffee and went to sit at the large wooden table that sat in the centre of the kitchen. Sunlight streamed in through the windows, both from the sky and reflected up from the lake. Soft wave patterns danced on the ceiling above him.

'How is she this morning?'

Sweetclover turned and smiled. 'Much better,' he said. 'The disorientation has completely passed. She knows who she is, and where. And who I am, thank God.'

'And her memories?'

'Perfectly intact, thank you very much,' said Quil as she entered. She paid Kaz no mind, instead walking up behind her husband, wrapping her arms around his waist and kissing the back of his neck.

'Get a room,' muttered Kaz under his breath.

The outside door opened and Dora walked in, followed closely by Jana. They were in close conversation, giggling over some shared joke. Their cheeks were rosy, their hair was a mess, and there was a conspiratorial air about them that made Kaz's stomach sink.

'You too?' muttered Kaz, rolling his eyes. Why was everyone loved up but him? He could feel a sulk coming on, and determined to try to fight it off. He was getting sick of feeling grouchy.

Jana pulled a chair up beside Kaz while Dora popped some bread in the toaster and put the kettle on to boil. Kaz glanced sideways at Jana, and raised his eyebrows knowingly. He'd been expecting Jana to make a move on Dora for a while, but he hadn't been sure how Dora would react. Looked like it had gone well and, as left out as he felt, he was happy for them deep down. Deep, deep, down, underneath an awful lot of jealousy.

She responded with a smile, a blush and then a wide-eyed glance that said 'Stop it, I'm embarrassed'.

Kaz hadn't ever expected to see Jana self-conscious; hadn't even thought she was capable of it. It was endearing, and it provided a unique opportunity for teasing that he was incapable of passing up; mercilessly teasing Jana would be a good way to take the edge off his grouchiness.

'Oh,' he said quietly, so no one else would hear, 'you were fine stripping off in front of me in Pendarn, but you're embarrassed after, what, a lakeside walk with your new girlfriend?'

'Stop it,' whispered Jana, mortified.

'Make me,' said Kaz, grinning wickedly.

Jana flashed him a look that made it perfectly clear she absolutely would make him, and he really wouldn't like it. Kaz decided that hell, he actually would kind of like it, and resolved to keep teasing as much as possible.

Cheered by the prospect of an enjoyable day of good-natured antagonism, Kaz rolled his cheesy lavash bread into a tube and bit the end off. Delicious.

And then Quil sat opposite him and his momentary good mood vanished.

He and Jana had talked late into the night about Quil,

about how she was not completely responsible for her actions, how the real blame lay at the feet of the president who had poisoned her and driven her mad. And Kaz understood Jana's point of view, and he remembered the other version of Quil, the cured one, and accepted that she wasn't a bad person. But that Quil had still been a ruthless political operator, had still forced millions of people to experience the death of a child knowing that this would lead to violence. Jana couldn't tell him how extreme the action of the poison had been. It was unique, so there was no way to quantify its effects. Had it made her twenty per cent more paranoid and aggressive? Ten per cent ? Ninety per cent? It didn't change her personality completely. She was still capable of trust and love, as her marriage to Sweetclover demonstrated. And what about the effects of being blown back through time, burned and desperate, spending years recuperating? What effect had that had on her sanity?

All Kaz knew for certain was that Quil's finger had been on the trigger of the gun that killed his mother. He was prepared to accept that the president bore some responsibility, but that was not the same thing as exonerating Quil of all blame.

He rose from the table and excused himself.

'Hey, Kaz, we're still doing the thing at ten, right?' said Jana as he made for the door.

'Yes,' he said. 'I'll be there.'

He stepped over the threshold out into the early morning sunshine, felt the first glimmerings of the day's warmth on his face, and struck out for the beach.

19

Jana took a deep breath and pushed open the door of the villa's living room. Quil was already inside, sitting on the sofa, talking to her husband in a low voice. She looked up when Jana entered, then turned and nodded at Henry, who took his cue and rose to leave. He flashed a smile at Jana as he passed her and she smiled back. In the two days they had spent here, she had seen how attentive he had been as Quil had recuperated from the effects of the antidote, which had not been pretty. The undoubted depth of his love for his wife, and hers for him, had made a strong impression on Jana. That kind of marital affection had been entirely absent from her house, and she was touched by it; this was surely how a marriage was supposed to be.

Henry closed the door behind him and Quil beckoned for Jana to come sit beside her. The sofa faced a huge picture window that looked out over the lake, and Jana and Quil sat there for a moment, lost in the view, wondering what to say. Jana felt nervous and self-conscious.

'Henry says that the effects of the antidote have passed,' she said eventually.

'Yes,' replied Quil. 'It was . . . not pleasant.'

'How do you feel now?'

Quil pondered for a moment before answering. 'It is very strange. I have lost count of how many years it has been for me since Barrettown. At least ten, maybe twelve. I've had that poison in my system all that time, messing with my head. But I don't remember feeling drugged, or different in any way. If you'd asked me a week ago if I felt like I was under the influence of something, I would have laughed at you.'

'And now?'

'Now it feels like . . . It's hard to describe. Like there was a tightness in my head, a tension that's been released. I can only identify it by its absence, if that makes any sense.'

Jana nodded. 'I think so.'

Quil turned to face Jana, pulling one leg up under the other and leaning in. 'So Henry tells me that when you rescued me from my interrogation, the quantum generator split me in two. That there was another version of me who stayed in the future with you. That while I was being blown up, burned, lost in time for a decade, she got the cure immediately.'

'That's right. She – that version of you – was erased when you got caught in the quantum bubble. The superposition collapsed, only one of you could exist.'

Quil shook her head and breathed out through her teeth. 'Hard to wrap my head around. Not the science, that makes sense, just the idea that there was a variant version of me.'

Jana smiled. 'Well, you're a variant version of me, so . . .'

Quil laughed. 'Yes, I suppose I am.'

'We spent a lot of time together, that other Quil and me. I showed her my life, she showed me hers. We came to understand each other, I think. So I know everything about your life before you were split in half. And I think I know enough about what you've been doing since then. But there are things you don't know. Things I need to explain to you.'

So Jana told Quil about the death of the real Yojana Patel, the plot by her mother and Amos Hope to kill both her and their father, the reasons it had failed and the consequences of that failure. Quil sat, rapt, as all the missing pieces of her life finally fell into place, hardly saying a word as the story unfolded.

'It's strange,' said Quil when Jana had finished, 'having someone else explain your own life to you.'

'Believe me, I know how you feel.'

'You became friends with this other version of me.'

'Yes. While you and I were trying to kill each other, she and I were trying to understand each other.'

Quil regarded Jana curiously. 'You miss her.'

'I came to think of her as a kind of sister, I suppose. We do have the same mother, after all.'

'Lucky us,' said Quil, rolling her eyes.

Jana had been anxious before entering the room. Kaz had given her a stern talking-to, reminding her that this was not the Quil she had befriended. This woman had lived a different life for a decade, a life soaked in blood. They had no way of knowing how much of her ruthless madness was the result of the poison she had ingested, and how much was innate, caused by the ordeal she had undergone. But as Quil rolled her eyes and smiled, Jana dismissed Kaz's concerns. She may have lived half a life more than the Quil she had befriended, but it was still the same woman, fundamentally.

It wasn't Quil who Jana was worried about now.

'So shall we go get ready to talk to her?' asked Jana.

Quil gave a single, curt nod, suddenly serious again.

'Yes,' she said coldly. 'Let's.'

* * *

305

The main room of the villa was more than big enough for the requirements of the interview.

It wasn't a trial, Jana had made that clear, although Dora wasn't convinced that Quil agreed.

'We don't have the right to put her on trial for her crimes,' Jana had insisted.

'We have more right than anybody,' retorted Quil.

And so on and so forth for about twenty minutes. Jana had told Dora that she trusted this version of Quil, that the antidote had fixed her and they had reached an understanding. But watching them argue about the nature of their mother's interrogation gave Dora pause to wonder whether Jana was being entirely objective. Was Jana so keen to see the good in this Quil that she was being blind to the damage that remained?

Eventually Dora and Kaz intervened and agreed with Jana. President Patel would answer for her crimes before a proper court, in front of the whole world. But that would come later. This was a more personal reckoning. A chance for Jana and Quil to get answers and maybe some closure. Dora thought closure was the last thing they would ever find, but she was prepared to support Jana's plan.

After she and Kaz intervened, Quil clammed up. Dora did not get the impression that she had taken their intervention well.

Dora had laid the room out carefully. At the end farthest from the doors, she had placed a large armchair with its back to the wall. Ranged in front of it were five smaller chairs, and a large TV monitor, hooked up to Dora's tablet. There were also five cameras ranged in a circle, to capture the entire event. Quil had insisted on this, and Jana had nodded her acquiescence.

The stage was set. All that remained was to gather the players.

Dora set the cameras recording, and turned to the door where she found everybody standing ready. She nodded to them and, wordlessly, they left the room, walked down the hall and up the stairs to the landing. Dora held the key – it had been agreed by everybody that she was the best choice for that responsibility. She pulled it from her pocket and opened the door, feeling a flutter of nervousness as she did so.

She pushed open the door. The room was large and light, the windows' shutters open, showing the view of the lake and the mountains beyond. There had been some discussion about locking the windows and shutters from the outside – Quil thought Abhilasha might perhaps have been a suicide risk; but nobody else had agreed. They did not want her to feel like a prisoner, even though that is exactly what she was.

President Abhilasha Patel sat on the bed, hands folded in her lap. The breakfast tray sat on the desk beside her; she hadn't eaten a thing. Abhilasha was still dressed in the clothes she had been wearing when they had captured her – a plain dark suit with white blouse – and she looked composed.

'We'd like you to come with us, please,' said Dora. Jana had insisted from the start that their prisoner be treated with care and respect, and nobody had disagreed. They had forced her into this room, but no coercion had been required in the three days since. Dora was prepared for physical resistance, but she was relieved when the president rose to her feet and indicated that she was ready.

Quil and Jana led the way, the president behind them, with Kaz, Dora and Sweetclover behind her. Together they paraded down to the main room and took their seats. They sat silently for a long moment, then Dora began.

'We've not been properly introduced,' she said, addressing

the president. 'My name is Dora Predennick. I was born in 1626 in England, and I am a time traveller. I've been asked to chair this meeting because it was felt that I had the least personal involvement with you, and am most able to remain impartial.'

'I do not recognise your authority,' said Abhilasha calmly.

'You have no choice in the matter,' said Dora firmly. 'We are not a court, not exactly. But the two women sitting either side of me' – she indicated Jana and Quil – 'have many questions. And I have some evidence to which I would like a response.'

'Where are we?' asked Abhilasha. 'How did I get here?'

'You are in Switzerland. This is a private, rented villa. Nobody knows that you are here because you have not yet been born. It is 23 April, 2022.'

Abhilasha scoffed, but did not speak.

Dora sighed. 'We have demonstrated our ability to travel in time. Once when I left your bunker, and once when we brought you here. I do not know what other evidence we could provide, short of taking you into a city. And we are not prepared to take that risk, so you will simply have to take our word for it.'

Dora wondered what explanation Abhilasha offered herself for her transposition in time and space. Had she convinced herself that she had been teleported in some manner? It didn't really matter, but her recalcitrance gave a clear indication of how strong-willed she was.

'For your sake, and for the cameras, we're going to introduce ourselves properly.' Dora indicated for Jana to start. She wanted to take her hand and squeeze it for support, but felt that this would reveal too much to Abhilasha, who she remained wary of.

Jana cleared her throat nervously and began to speak, holding her mother's gaze.

'My name is Jana Patel. I am a clone. I was created in 2128 as a replacement for the recently deceased daughter of Abhilasha and Prabal Patel. I was implanted with the memories of their dead daughter and, for many years, I lived with her parents, believing I was her. I came to understand my nature and origins sometime after my thirteenth birthday.'

Dora studied Abhilasha's face as Jana spoke. The older woman studied Jana, trying to feign lack of interest but unable to entirely mask her fascination and curiosity.

Quil spoke next, as they had agreed in advance.

'My name is Quil,' she said. 'I am a clone. I was created in 2140 as a replacement for Jana, who had disappeared. I was implanted with an edited composite of her memories and those of the original Yojana Patel.'

Abhilasha allowed herself an obvious sneer of contempt for the woman who had led the army that had brought her down, but made no comment.

'My name is Kazic Cecka,' said Kaz. 'I was born in 1996, in Poland. Like my friends, I am able to travel in time.'

'And I am Lord Henry Sweetclover of Sweetclover Hall. I was born in 1606 in England, and I am Quil's husband.'

Abhilasha regarded Kaz and Henry with mild interest, but said nothing.

'Good,' said Dora, trying to maintain an air of brisk efficiency. 'Let us begin. Abhilasha Patel, World President. We've brought you here because Jana and Quil have many questions they want to ask you. Kaz, Henry and I are here to support them. I'll ask Jana to begin.'

Dora looked left to Jana and offered her a nod and a smile

of support. Jana looked back, wide-eyed and nervous, but she smiled weakly before turning to face her mother.

'I've thought a lot about what I was going to say to you,' said Jana. Her hands were clasped tight in her lap and Dora could see that her knuckles were white. 'But I suppose the first and most important question is: why do I exist?'

Abhilasha sat and looked at Jana, her face giving nothing away, offering no answer.

Jana continued in the face of her silence.

'Dora,' she said. 'Could you please run the first clip?'

Dora touched her tablet and the screens came to life. The screen showed the back garden of the Patel house, the fruit trees stretching away into the distance. It was raining slightly. Prabal stood halfway up a small ladder, picking plums from the tree and dropping them into a bucket held by his daughter, Yojana Patel, who stood in her raincoat and boots at the foot of the tree.

Abhilasha gasped slightly in surprise. Dora found herself pleased that they had got a reaction out of her at last.

'For the record, this footage was recorded in the garden of your family home,' said Dora.

Abhilasha glanced at Dora, her disbelief, shock and pain clear on her face.

'How did you get this?' she breathed.

Dora did not answer. They had explained that they were time travellers often enough. Maybe now Abhilasha would start to believe them.

On the screen, events played out as they always had. The slip, the fall, the scream of anguish from Yojana's father. The ambulance that came so quickly but not quite quickly enough. When the screen showed only an empty kitchen, its floor scattered with plums and blood, Dora ended the clip.

She knew she should not feel pity for the woman sitting before her, that her actions stripped her of any right to compassion. But she was a mother, and she had just been forced to watch the death of her child, and Dora felt sorry for her in spite of herself. Quil had insisted that they begin with this footage, arguing that it offered the greatest emotional shock and was therefore most likely to break through Abhilasha's façade. She had been right. Dora could see that Abhilasha was shaken to the core. Her lip trembled, and her eyes were wide and brimming with tears that she was fighting to hold back.

'Why would you show me that?' she eventually asked, her voice a whisper.

'Because we want to understand,' said Jana, her tone softer than when she had spoken before. '*I* want to understand. I can't imagine what it was like to lose your child. I really can't. But I also can't understand why you would have me created to replace her.'

Abhilasha sniffed, wiped the back of her right hand across her eyes, took a deep breath and looked at Jana. Dora held her breath. This was a key moment. Would Abhilasha accept that Jana was who she said she was, or would she cling to her denial?

The silence lasted for a long time, maybe three or four minutes by Dora's reckoning, as Jana and Abhilasha stared at each other, one pleading, one seemingly calculating.

'Because I could,' said Abhilasha eventually. 'We had Yojana chipped at the earliest possible age. We had her memories and experiences stored. The doctor who approached us after she died explained that he could bring her back to us. It was expensive, and illegal, but we had enough money to make the obstacles go away. It was easy for them to grow her a new body, and put her inside it. It would be her, he promised. In every way that mattered, it would be our Yojana, returned to us.'

Dora breathed her relief. Abhilasha's façade had crumbled and she was speaking honestly. They might get some proper answers after all.

'Do you expect us to believe,' interjected Quil, 'that you had Jana created out of *love*?' She spat the word furiously.

Abhilasha turned her gaze to Quil, seemingly confused by her question. 'Of course,' she said, as if it were the most obvious thing in the world. 'What other reason could there be?'

Quil's sneer was answer enough.

'We didn't know, not then,' continued Abhilasha, 'that the doctor was lying. We wanted to believe him, so much. He promised to return our daughter to us. How could we say no? But the thing he gave us. It was . . . not right.'

Dora waited for Jana to respond, but when no word came she glanced to her left and saw Jana's jaw clenched tight, her breaths short and tense.

'Not right in what way?' said Dora, asking the question Jana could apparently not bring herself to.

'It's hard to explain,' said Abhilasha hesitantly. 'I was Yojana's mother. I knew her better than anyone I had ever known. And the changeling wasn't *right* behind its eyes. Something different. Older. Darker. I couldn't look at it.'

'She thought she'd nearly died,' said Quil, her voice full of quiet anger. 'She was traumatised. Of course her personality changed. She was growing up.'

Dora was surprised and grateful that Quil was standing up for Jana, who seemed to have been struck dumb by her mother's revelation.

Abhilasha shook her head once, firmly. 'I carried Yojana

312

for nine months, she was a part of me. The way she felt, the way she moved, the way she smelled. I knew these on a genetic level. The changeling was wrong.'

'Jana,' said Quil, leaning across Dora to speak to her clone sister, her tone almost accusatory. 'Don't you have anything you want to say?'

Jana had plenty that she wanted to say, but she didn't trust herself to open her mouth.

The woman she had always thought of as her mother sat before her, unable to meet her gaze, repudiating her, referring to her as a changeling, saying that she was an unnatural creation and a mistake. She couldn't have given a name to the turmoil of her feelings, but she was almost overwhelmed by the mix of anger, disgust, loss and self-loathing that churned in her.

She tried to think of an answer to Quil's question. *Was* there anything she wanted to ask her mother?

Of course there was. But she couldn't bring herself to form the words. Not yet, maybe never.

She looked across at Quil and shook her head. The look in Quil's eyes was hard to pin down. Was she angry at Abhilasha or Jana?

Quil turned away and focused her attention back on Abhilasha.

'She was wrong, you say,' said Quil. 'OK, suppose you're right. Suppose a mix of new body, edited memories and trauma made her seem slightly different. Was it right to punish her for that? To reject her? Avoid her? Leave her upbringing to security guards and a school that didn't care? You may have regretted having her, but you created her. Didn't you owe her something? If not love, then at least care. Didn't you have a responsibility?'

Abhilasha looked at Quil with a mixture of disgust and condescension. Jana felt an involuntary shudder as she saw that look on her mother's face.

'It's not really alive, you know,' said Abhilasha. 'No more than you are. It's a toy, really. A made thing. I don't owe it any more care than, say, a car or an oven. You buy a car and it turns out to be faulty, you can return it to the shop, get your money back. But I couldn't do that, you see. Having it made was against the law, so I couldn't admit to anyone that it was a faulty replacement. And I couldn't throw it away without risking being arrested for murder. So I was stuck with it.'

Silence fell after this disclosure. Every 'it' had felt like a physical blow, and Jana reeled at the force of the assault. She was aware that her friends were sitting open-mouthed in horror at what had been said, but nobody spoke.

Jana thought she might vomit, but then she felt fingers on hers as Dora's hand softly enclosed her tightly gripped fists.

'If you refer to Jana as "it" one more time, I will not be responsible for the consequences,' said Dora, her voice low and more menacing than Jana had ever heard it.

Abhilasha looked momentarily surprised at the threat, then her gaze fell upon Jana and Dora's hands, and the faint sparks that danced in the air where they touched. She sneered.

'And that was the final insult,' she said, her tone one of pure disgust. 'When it began manifesting its aberration.'

Jana felt Dora tensing to rise to her feet, so she untwined her fingers and laid a restraining hand on Dora's forearm.

'It's OK, Dora,' she said. 'Let her speak. I need to hear this. What aberration do you mean?'

Abhilasha answered with a flick of her eyes towards the place where Jana's hand touched Dora. She couldn't even bring herself to say it.

'That I like girls?'

'My beautiful daughter was normal,' said Abhilasha. 'What more proof did I need that you were faulty goods?'

'What makes you think Yojana wouldn't have grown up to be exactly the same?' asked Quil, leaning forward, her face hard and furious.

'My daughter was raised properly,' responded Abhilasha with fierce pride. 'She would never have . . . The only explanation was that they got the cloning process wrong.'

'How did her father feel about this?' asked Kaz, speaking for the first time. 'You've not mentioned him at all.'

'You saw the film,' said Abhilasha. 'It was his fault that our daughter died. The guilt made him weak. He took more and more jobs away from home. Within a year we hardly saw him any more. It drove him away, you see. Its wrongness drove him away.'

'Or your madness did,' said Kaz. 'Jana told me that sexual orientation and gender identity wasn't a big deal in your time.'

'One of the corruptions that led to the disintegration of the old USA. One of the moral failings I took office to correct.'

'Was that the reason you eventually decided to have me killed?' asked Jana, finding her voice.

'I don't know what you mean,' said Abhilasha dismissively.

Jana turned and nodded to Dora, who hit her tablet and played the footage of Abhilasha commissioning Jana's death, and her father's.

When the footage finished, Abhilasha simply said, 'Illegal wiretap, not admissible in court,' and held her chin high.

Abhilasha had been momentarily shocked by the breadth of their knowledge, but Jana could take no pleasure in it. She was already growing tired of seeing her 'mother' wrong-footed. Her defiance and lack of humility were causing Jana

315

to question what the point of this interrogation was. She had hoped for some emotional response, some acknowledgment of guilt or at least culpability. But all they were getting was anger and contempt.

'You're not claiming that it's faked, though?' said Quil.

Abhilasha said nothing.

'How about this?' Quil nodded to Dora, who played footage of Abhilasha commissioning Jana's replacement.

Abhilasha clenched her jaw.

Then footage of her ordering the replacement's destruction following Jana's disappearance.

No response.

'That's me, you understand?' said Quil. 'The replacement that wasn't supposed to wake up – that was me. Full of doctored memories designed to make me the perfect president's daughter. It's interesting, the memories you gave me. The fake ones of you being so kind and loving and patient, always there for me, helping me through the aftermath of Father's death. All a lie. But I'm interested – is that how you saw yourself? Is that the mother you wanted to be?'

'It is the mother I would have been. To my daughter. My *real* daughter.'

She said nothing more after that, folding her arms and staring into the middle distance. Jana studied her mother as she sat there, trying to make sense of her. The loss of her daughter had been a blow, and coming hard on the heels of that, somehow Jana's perceived differences had triggered a full psychotic break. Jana wondered how firm her mother's grip on reality really was. She had thought that the demonising of clones had been a political ploy, but what if Abhilasha really believed the propaganda? What if she had become so paranoid and felt so persecuted that she had believed the lies

316

her madness had told her? Jana began to think there was no way of reaching her, that her emotional core was too buried, that she was too far gone. She decided to try a different tack.

'Corruptions,' she said. 'One of the corruptions that led to the disintegration of the USA. That's what you said. What were the others? What other so-called diseases were you going to cure?'

For a moment she thought Abhilasha was going to maintain her silence, but in the end she couldn't help but rise to the bait.

'America went soft,' she said, obviously parroting a speech she'd delivered countless times. 'Lost its core values. Family, duty, hard work. The neoliberal consensus of the late twentieth and early twenty-first centuries broke the spine of the country, set brother against brother and destroyed the union.'

'And you were going to reunify the USA?'

Abhilasha nodded.

'By any means necessary?'

'Absolutely.'

'And a war has always been a great unifying force, hasn't it?'

'I did not start the war.'

Quil laughed, a short bark of contempt that Abhilasha ignored.

'This is getting us nowhere,' said Sweetclover, his frustration plain in his voice.

'I agree,' said Kaz.

'All right,' said Dora. 'How about we take a look at your war, Madam President?'

She tapped her tablet and up popped footage of a room Jana didn't recognise. A long table at which sat men and women in military uniform alongside older civilians. At the head of the table sat President Abhilasha. The camera was looking down the table over the president's shoulder. On the far wall were a variety of screens; it only took Jana a moment to realise that they were all showing footage from the battle of Barrettown.

The hubbub of argument, orders and reports from the front line were deafening. This must be the incident room in the White House, Jana realised.

Dora had obviously cued up the footage for the key moment, because within a few seconds of it starting, the president shouted, 'Bring up *Redoubtable* full screen!'

The far wall turned into one massive window showing a room full of fire and confusion – the bridge of the *Redoubtable* during the battle in the skies above Mars.

'Captain, report!' yelled the president.

The face of a desperate man appeared in front of the flames. He was bleeding from a gash across his forehead and the right side of his face was freshly burned, the skin peeling and raw.

'Weapons gone,' he shouted. 'Multiple hull breaches, engines barely working. We're going down, Madam President. I've given the order to abandon ship.'

'How much manoeuvrability do you have, captain?' asked the president.

'Minimal, ma'am.'

Jana wished she could see the president's face, because all eyes in the room were on her.

'Captain, as soon as the last escape pod has departed, I want you to take the helm and aim your ship at Barrettown.'

Cries of protest and horror from the assembled military command. The president shouted over them.

'The leader of the Godless forces is trapped there. The city has fallen to the enemy. If we destroy the city, we destroy them. Your sacrifice will end this war.'

The captain didn't hesitate. He gave a crisp salute, a single 'Understood', and the screen went dead.

Jana felt sick to her stomach. This was the first she had heard of this, that Abhilasha was ultimately responsible for the destruction of Barrettown – Dora hadn't shared this with her.

'My God,' breathed Sweetclover. 'There were tens of thousands of people down there.'

'It was a sound tactical decision,' said Abhilasha. Her composure not even vaguely ruffled.

'Forget all the personal stuff,' said Dora. 'The way you made and cast aside daughters as if they were toys. The way you treated an entire section of the population as if they weren't even human. Forget commissioning the execution of your daughter and your husband. This footage alone is enough to have you locked up for the rest of your life for war crimes. Couple it with the footage of you ordering the nuclear detonation in Washington, and your presidency is over.'

Abhilasha considered this for a second and then shrugged. 'I won the war. That's all that matters. The clones lost. They won't be able to infiltrate the Earth the way they infiltrated my family. History will judge me right.'

And then she folded her arms and met Dora's stare without flinching.

'Wait a minute,' said Jana. 'Infiltrated your family? What? Are you seriously saying that you think I was some kind of spy?'

'Sent to undermine my rise to power,' said Abhilasha. 'I didn't realise it at the time, of course. But it became obvious the older you grew. The more rebellious and disobedient you became. What other explanation could there have been? My true daughter would never have behaved in such a manner. I had to get rid of you, you see. I couldn't let you win. And then, when I rose to power, I was free to take my revenge on the whole Godless mess of you.'

'Wow,' breathed Quil. 'You're completely insane. How do you think your sainted daughter would have grown up, hmm? You don't think she'd have disagreed with you? Maybe been a little rebellious, pushed the boundaries a bit? That's what children DO! And I'm here to tell you I've seen the work they did to "fix" me, and your daughter would have grown up as gay as the day is long.'

'Nonsense,' spat Abhilasha. 'My daughter was obedient and normal. She showed no indication at all of the kind of deviance you're suggesting.'

Jana couldn't help herself. She rose to her feet and shouted in her mother's face as hard as she could, 'SHE. WAS. SIX! She hadn't even started growing up yet. You have no idea how she would have changed. She wasn't a prop, not like I was supposed to be. She wasn't some kind of political Band-Aid, designed to make you palatable to voters. She was a person. She would have grown into a woman with her own thoughts, her own ideals, her own values. She wasn't your damned property.'

'She was my daughter,' shouted Abhilasha, rising to her feet defiantly. 'Don't you dare speak of her like that! You don't know her, you never met her!'

'We have her memories!' Quil retorted, also rising to her feet. 'If anyone can speak for her, we can. And I'm telling you, she would have been disgusted by what you've become.'

'Damn you!' screamed Abhilasha, and she flew at Quil, grabbing her hair and violently shaking her head from side to side. Jana dived across and grabbed her mother's shoulders, trying to pull her off Quil.

Then there were hands on her, shouting, a melee, a confusion of limbs, and then . . .

. . . Freefall.

Philadelphia, 27 May 2155

Jana hit the ground hard with her right shoulder, her hands still grasping her mother's shoulder. The impact was jarring and she felt her shoulder socket almost pop right out. There was deafening noise and confusion. Cheering, shouting, chanting. She rolled away from the point of impact, yelling in pain and fury, but she was free of the immediate struggle. She pulled herself into a crouch and assessed her surroundings.

She was in the midst of a huge crowd of people; some kind of demonstration. A few of the protestors had noticed the arrival of Jana and her travelling companions, and were looking down in astonishment, but the majority were shouting defiance to the skies, unaware of the fight happening on the ground. Before her, Jana saw Quil and Abhilasha locked in a furious fight, and Dora trying to separate them. Red sparks danced and flew around the struggle.

Jana was about to move forward and help Dora when a detail registered and she suddenly snapped her head upwards and looked at the nearest protestor.

Who was wearing a white mask.

Panic filled her as she realised where they were. She had felt someone take control of their journey as they had left Switzerland; now she knew it must have been Quil. The scale of her miscalculation made her gasp as if she'd been punched. Quil may no longer have been poisoned, but her need for revenge on Abhilasha had driven her as mad as her mother.

'We have to go!' she yelled as she scrambled towards the fight. 'We really have to go!'

Just as she reached out to grab Quil, who was straddling Abhilasha, her clone turned, brandishing a gun at both Jana and Dora. Where had she gotten it? She must have jumped away from the villa in a quiet moment and armed herself. Jana understood with cold horror that Quil had never intended to let Abhilasha live.

'Get the hell away from me!' screamed Quil, her voice barely audible above the noise of the crowd. Jana grabbed Dora's hand and pulled her back.

Quil leaned down over Abhilasha and shouted into her dazed and bloodied face.

'Welcome to your war, Mother!' she cried, grabbing Abhilasha by the hair and pulling her upright.

Abhilasha looked dazed and disorientated.

'Where am I?' she asked, as she was jostled by the ebb and flow of the crowd that engulfed them.

'Don't you recognise it?' yelled Quil. 'I brought you here so you could see what it was like for the people you slaughtered.'

Abhilasha looked around her in alarm and then rising panic. The masked faces of the Godless protestors, the chanting.

Jana saw her mouth something, maybe 'This is impossible'.

'Quil, this is pointless,' shouted Jana, reaching out to her clone sister. 'This isn't achieving anything. We need to go. Please, I'm begging you, enough.'

'Why?' replied Quil. 'So you can show her some more home videos? And then what? Return her to the future to face justice? *This* is justice.'

She illustrated her point by punching Abhilasha hard in the stomach with the hand holding the gun. The older woman doubled over, gasping for air.

'Quil, come on. You're better than this,' pleaded Jana.

'No she's not,' yelled Abhilasha, her voice full of hatred. 'She's a monster, just like you. My monsters. My mistakes.'

Quil began raining punches down on Abhilasha, each blow punctuated with a word.

'We. Are. Your. Children!' she screamed.

Jana leaped forward and grabbed Quil by the shoulders. 'Enough!' she cried. 'We have to go. They're going to open fire any minute.'

Quil shook herself free of Jana's grasp and turned, raising her gun as she did so, turning it towards Jana.

'NO!' screamed Dora, raising her arms and moving to stop Quil, but too slowly, far too slowly. She reached her and grabbed her gun arm, forcing it upwards as Quil's finger depressed the trigger. A white-hot beam lanced out, skywards. They struggled and slowly Quil moved her arm down, the beam cutting downwards towards the crowd, towards Jana, who stood rooted to the spot in horror.

The world exploded with gunfire, and the staccato noise shattered Jana's senses until the world was delivered to her in flashes.

Abhilasha lying on the ground, blood bubbling from her mouth and nose.

Quil's face, distorted with mad fury.

The beam slicing through the air, then arcing down, towards her.

Dora, red-faced, struggling and shouting.

Screams.

The sun overhead.

Gunfire.

The shoving of the crowd.

She raised her arms and took a faltering step towards Quil but then something happened. She couldn't quite work out what, but something splashed across her face. She flinched, wiped her eyes, looked down at her sleeve to find it covered in blood and grey stuff. Blinked, looked up again to see Quil toppling forward, the right side of her head completely gone.

Dora falling away from her, recoiling, sprayed with gore, mouth open in a silent shout.

The world suddenly returned to Jana in an overwhelming maelstrom of noise and motion.

Abhilasha threw herself forward, reaching for Quil's discarded gun. She grabbed it and raised it before Jana, still on her knees on the ground, had a chance to react.

Even above the noise, Jana could hear Dora's anguished cry as she realised she wasn't going to be able to stop Abhilasha firing.

There was a bright, burning flash, and Jana felt something punch her in the shoulder. Her brain struggled to process what was happening, but even in the furious, overwhelming struggle, Jana experienced a moment of clarity.

I remember this feeling, she thought.

Images and sensations flashed across her mind.

Abhilasha, back arched, arms thrown out, bullets bursting from her torso.

The taste of a plum, cold and sweet.

Dora, looking down at her, screaming.

A kiss that made her feel complete.

The feel of cold, wet kitchen tiles beneath her face.

Then darkness.

20
Northern France, early morning

Jana picked a tree by the side of the long, straight Roman road and burst into a sprint again, pushing herself towards it.

She was so lost in her thoughts that the sudden arrival of Kaz and Dora, burning into existence directly in front of her, made her jump and give a small, embarrassing yell of alarm.

'Jeez, guys, you made me jump,' she said redundantly, once she had skidded to a halt.

She put her hands on her knees and bent over, catching her breath, looking up at her friends. They looked solemn and serious.

'Who died?' she joked, then immediately wished she hadn't.

'You did,' whispered Dora, a single tear escaping to roll down her cheek.

Jana felt a thrill of fear and alarm as she slowly stood upright. She tried to think of a response, but nothing would come. She just stood there, dumbstruck, as Dora stepped forward and embraced her, squeezing her tightly, sobbing into her shoulder.

She was even more surprised when Dora broke from the hug and kissed her hard on the lips. Taken completely off guard, Jana reacted instinctively and pulled away in shock.

'Dora!' she said, eyes wide.

The tide of self-recrimination that crashed down on her moments later was literally staggering. Why the hell had she broken that off? Hadn't she been dreaming about that kiss for practically ever?

'Sorry,' said Dora from behind a blushing half-smile. 'I forgot, we haven't done that yet.'

'Oh boy,' said Jana, her emotions a roiling mixture of joy and terror.

She stumbled to the side of the road and sat down, hard, on the grassy verge. Kaz and Dora sat either side of her and, to Jana's alarm, they each took one of her hands in theirs. She felt like a patient receiving a terminal diagnosis. Which, she supposed, she kind of was.

'We need to tell you—' began Kaz.

'No, you really don't,' replied Jana. 'Just give me a second.'

Kaz fell silent. Jana sat between her two best friends, holding their hands, gathering her thoughts and calming her emotions. After a few minutes, she felt ready to speak.

'I died?'

'Yes,' said Kaz.

'OK,' Jana nodded, forcing herself to remain calm and in control. 'And you're here to, what? Prevent it? Warn me? What?'

'We're here to tell you a story,' said Dora.

'And to ask you a question,' said Kaz.

'But haven't you already messed with the timeline?' asked Jana urgently. 'Just by being here? Now I'm forewarned, so the paradox is . . .' She trailed off as Kaz unhooked a knapsack from his shoulder and opened the flap to reveal a mind-writer inside.

'We'll erase your memory of this conversation before we leave,' he said. 'The timeline is safe. We just needed to talk to you.'

Jana felt a flicker of hope she hadn't even been aware of die in her chest.

'Oh, I see,' she said. 'How?'

'Quil,' said Kaz. 'We thought she was better, not mad any more. We were wrong.'

Jana didn't need any more detail than that.

'I should have stopped it,' said Dora, looking sideways at Jana, her face a mask of misery and regret. Jana squeezed her hand tightly.

'I'm sure you did everything you could,' she said, amazed that she was comforting someone about their guilt over her own death.

'I haven't, though,' said Dora. 'Not yet. That's why we're here.'

'We said we had a story to tell you,' said Kaz.

'Is this the story of how I die?' asked Jana. ''Cause I'm not so sure I want to hear that.'

Dora shook her head. 'No,' she said. 'It's the story of how I died.'

Jana cocked her head. 'Eh?'

Dora took a deep breath. 'Professor Kairos has always been very clear that there are three possible explanations of how the timeline works,' she explained. 'First, it could be self-correcting. Any attempt to change events would fail, because it's impossible.'

'Second,' continued Kaz, 'you could change events, but by doing so you'd be creating a new timeline. So we could save you, but it wouldn't really be you, not exactly. We would all be living in a new timeline where you survived. The timeline where you died would still exist, we just wouldn't be in it any more.'

'And third,' said Jana, 'a change could create a paradox and destroy everything. And we don't know which of these is the right model of time, because any experiment designed to prove it would carry the most enormous risk.'

'Right,' said Dora. 'But there's one final secret I've been keeping all this time. Something I've not told you.'

'She only just told me,' said Kaz, a flash of anger in his eyes.

Jana looked at Dora curiously. 'So . . .?'

'What if there's a fourth model of time?' said Dora. 'All of Kairos's theories are based on a traditional understanding of the universe, on the established laws of quantum physics. But science didn't work out the rules of the quantum realm for decades because they kept trying to understand the quantum realm using the rules of Newtonian physics, which just didn't apply. The idea that the macro and micro universes could operate on such different principles was inconceivable to them.'

'OK, following you so far,' said Jana.

'We think Kairos has been making the same kind of mistake,' said Kaz. 'We think he's been using the wrong paradigm because the rules of time are as different from the quantum laws as they, in turn, are from Newtonian.'

Jana screwed up her face in puzzlement. 'So you're saying that the rules of time are, what? Totally weird?'

'For want of a better word, yeah,' said Kaz, nodding. 'There must be rules, but whatever they are, they're completely uncharted because everybody's been trying to understand time using the wrong basic assumptions.'

Jana shook her head. This sounded like guesswork to her.

'Based on what evidence?' she asked. 'What's your secret, Dora?'

Dora stared at her feet and Jana realised she was nervous.

'When I first travelled through time,' she said, not looking up, 'I saw something I can't explain. Something impossible.'

'Tell me.'

Dora looked up and met her gaze. 'I was only there for a moment. It was night-time, there was fire. I might have been mistaken.'

'Tell her, Dora,' said Kaz.

Dora sighed, and spoke reluctantly. 'I saw myself being burned at the stake,' she said, almost in a whisper.

'What?' asked Jana, amazed. 'Like, literally? Like a witch?'

'Exactly like a witch,' said Dora. 'You see, even before I met either of you, I not only knew that I was going to die, I knew how I was going to die.'

And suddenly so many of Dora's actions made so much more sense to Jana.

She knew she was sitting with her mouth open like a guppy, but she didn't care. She was about to say she couldn't imagine what it must be like to know you were going to die, but then she stopped herself, because, as of five minutes ago, she knew exactly what that felt like.

'But here's the thing, Jana. I didn't die like that. The me that I saw burning was fifteen at the oldest. I'm older than that now, and it still hasn't happened. I kept telling myself that maybe the fire made it hard to see, that I missed how old she, I, was. But no. She was a girl. The me that I saw burning was a girl.'

'But that's . . .'

'Impossible, yes,' said Kaz. 'None of Kairos's models of time travel allow for that kind of thing.'

'Did I jump to a different timeline? Stop by some kind of parallel universe? Or something else, something we don't even have words for yet? I just don't know.'

'Did you ever tell Kairos this?' asked Jana.

Dora shook her head, looking ashamed and embarrassed. 'I was afraid he'd tell me it was inevitable. That I couldn't escape my fate, no matter what I did. Despite all my training and preparation. And I didn't want to hear that. I was afraid. Sorry.'

Jana pulled Dora into a hug. 'Don't be silly,' she said. 'You've done nothing wrong.'

'There's something else,' said Kaz.

Jana released Dora, but kept tight hold of her hand.

'What's that?' she asked.

'How the hell are we travelling in time?' he asked.

Jana was confused by the question. 'We know that. Kairos told us. Like Quil, we will at some point in the future spend a lot of time with the asteroid that made up the timebomb. Some of the mineral will seep into our bloodstream. We'll be affected by it, and the effects will echo back down our time-lines.'

'Yeah,' said Kaz. 'But that hasn't happened, has it? And I can't see any way it's ever going to happen, not now.'

Jana shook her head on confusion. 'It must do. Other-wise . . .'

'Otherwise how are we travelling in time. I know. But we are. So . . .'

'So what?'

'So I think,' said Kaz, excited, 'that we got our powers in a timeline we've already erased. I think we've changed our destinies already. At some point we made a decision, took some action, that deleted the future where we get our powers.'

'Then how are we travelling in time?' asked Jana.

'Exactly! How? I think we are, literally, paradoxes. I think the fact that we are travelling in time at all proves that Kairos was wrong. That time is weirder and more complicated than he ever guessed.'

'And so here we are,' said Dora.

Jana looked between the two of them, her mind reeling. The implications of what they were telling her were huge and baffling.

'We think this means we can save you, Jana,' said Dora.

'We think we can save everyone,' said Kaz.

'We could undo everything,' said Jana, feeling a thrill of nerves as she voiced the unthinkable. 'We could stop me jumping off the roof. We could save Quil. Confront my mother before any of this started.'

Dora and Kaz both looked nervous and shifty when Jana said this.

'What?' she asked.

'You don't want to confront your mother,' said Kaz.

'Trust us,' said Dora. 'There's no version of that scenario that ends well.'

'OK,' said Jana. 'But the other stuff. We could, couldn't we?'

Dora and Kaz exchanged a long, meaningful look.

'That's the question we came to ask you,' said Dora at length. 'Should we? Do you want us to?'

Jana thought they must be mad to ask. 'Are you kidding me?' she said, aghast. 'Why wouldn't we?'

Dora looked pained. 'It sounds selfish, but if we undid everything, I wouldn't be me any more. I'd be some girl in a kitchen in the seventeenth century. And that'd be my life, Jana. I've seen so much, changed so much. I don't want to go back to being her. Her world was so small, and mine is vast. I'd have to grow up all over again and it was hard enough the first time.' Dora paused, took a breath, and then said, 'And, most importantly I wouldn't meet you and Kaz.'

Jana felt a tug in her chest and suddenly felt short of breath. The idea of never meeting Dora and Kaz was the most awful thing she could imagine. Kaz had opened up parts of her she'd never acknowledged before – friendship, trust, the ability to be vulnerable and honest with someone. And as for Dora, well . . . it seemed like she was going to be a very important part of her (short) future. Was she willing to sacrifice the things that she'd learned, the ways in which she'd grown as a result of meeting these two?

'What about you Kaz?' she asked.

He shrugged and winced. 'It's tough. I love you guys. Truly. You're my best friends and I don't know where I'd be without you. If I thought I could save my mum, maybe I'd be more gung-ho. But Quil didn't set that bomb. I think my mum would have died in Beirut even without Quil's intervention. But am I willing to sacrifice knowing you if I know, when making the choice, that it would save your life, Jana? You bet. No question.'

'Not to mention all the lives lost in the war,' said Dora. 'Barrettown, Philadelphia, Washington.'

Jana bit her lip, thinking hard. 'Washington? Did Quil win her war? Are the clones free?'

Dora and Kaz nodded. 'Yes,' said Kaz. 'We didn't travel that far into the future, but I think we saw enough to say that they won't go back to slavery.'

'So if we undo Quil, we maybe condemn the clones to heaven knows how many years of subjugation and mistreatment.'

'Whatever we do – change things, or leave them as they

are – there are consequences that spread far beyond us,' agreed Dora.

'So in the timeline you just left, the war is over, the clones are free, and you two are both fine.'

'Yeah,' confirmed Kaz. 'But—'

Jana held up her hand to stop him. 'And the choices that we made to get to that outcome, they were all freely taken? Nobody forced us, manipulated us?'

'We don't think so,' said Dora.

'And if I correctly understand your point about how we got, or didn't get, our powers, it's possible we're already in a timeline that's the result of previous interference, maybe by our younger or older selves?'

'I think so,' said Kaz. 'Dora's less convinced, but . . .'

'It's possible, yes,' said Dora, reluctantly.

'Which means that this might already be the best possible outcome,' said Jana. 'We might have already gone back and tried over and over again, and never managed a solution better than this.'

'Well . . .' said Kaz.

'So what if we try to fix things and create a timeline where you're both dead and only I survive? Or worse, one where we all die, so there's no chance for any of us to come back and change things?'

That stopped Kaz and Dora short.

'Crap,' said Kaz.

'I hadn't considered that,' said Dora.

'If time is as weird and changeable and fluid as you think, we don't know what the consequences of our meddling could be.'

'You'd be alive,' said Kaz.

Which led Jana to only one conclusion, and she couldn't

quite believe she was opening her mouth to say, 'But I'm not worth it.'

Kaz and Dora began to protest, but Jana cut them off abruptly. 'No, I'm not,' she snapped. 'We can't undo Quil, and we can't risk the timeline. So, can you save me without risking either of those?'

Jana was looking at Kaz as she said this, but he said, 'Ask Dora, she was there.'

Jana turned to look at Dora, whose face told a clear story. 'I don't think so,' she said, her voice barely even a whisper. 'The fight that killed you was historically important. If Quil doesn't try and shoot you, the whole history of the war could change.'

'Historically important?'

'Philadelphia. She fired the first shot in Philadelphia.'

Jana felt sick to her stomach as she nodded her understanding.

Could she really talk them out of saving her life?

'Then I have to die,' she said firmly.

Kaz and Dora sat there, speechless.

'I think I just killed myself,' said Jana, trying to make a joke out of it, even though she thought she might vomit from fear.

Dora was crying, looking at Jana, unable to speak.

Kaz just looked stunned, like he couldn't quite believe what was happening and any moment he'd wake up.

Then Jana had a thought.

'There is one way you could save me,' she said. 'Kind of.'

So she told them the plan that she had been mulling over for some time, and they nodded, and agreed to do as she asked. But although their agreement brought a kind of comfort to Jana, it brought little to Kaz or Dora.

When she had finished talking, Jana stood up, forcing herself to be resolute. She pointed to the rising sun and said, 'I think you should go now. Any longer and I'll notice how much time has passed and realise that something's happened.'

Dora and Kaz also rose to their feet and stood awkwardly, not knowing how to say goodbye. Jana decided to do it for them.

She stepped forward and took Kaz into a tight embrace.

'You're a sulky pain in the arse,' she said. 'But you're my best friend. You're kind and good and brave and loyal. You deserve a good life, Kaz. Live it for me, OK? I love you. Not like *that*, but, y'know, I love you.'

'I know,' he sniffed. 'I love you too.'

She kissed him on the cheek and released him. She took a deep breath and turned to Dora. Dora, who had changed so much; from scared, innocent young girl to emotionless killing machine and, now, to a young woman learning to love and care again after a long, dark period of grief. Jana hated to think what her death would do to Dora.

'And you,' she said. 'Don't let losing me make you go all Dark Side again, all right?'

Dora nodded, her chin wobbling.

'Promise?'

'I promise,' said Dora.

Then Jana stepped forward, cupped Dora's face in her hands and kissed her. And it was a good kiss, a *great* kiss, long and deep and full of all the love and passion in her heart. She felt it from her toes to the tips of her hair, and she felt loved and complete and happy in a way she'd never known before.

But eventually it had to end. She broke away and stepped back from Dora, whose eyes were wide with surprise and desire. Jana smiled the most content smile she'd ever smiled, and said, 'Goodbye. And don't worry about me. I've died once before. It's not so bad.'

Then there was a hum of power from behind her as Dora and Kaz reset her memory.

Jana passed the tree much sooner than she'd anticipated; she must have been running faster than she thought. She paused for a second, confused by the distance she had covered in such a short time, then shook her head and dismissed it. Daydreaming. She fell back into a brisk walk, breathing hard and pulling out a bottle of water. She felt the rawness in her throat and smiled as the cold liquid soothed it.

She felt a sad smile come to her lips as she put the bottle top back on, unsure where it could have come from.

Then she resumed running.

Epilogue:
Poland, 23 October, 2015

'You pick them like this, watch.'

Kaz leaned over, grabbed a large, ripe strawberry and gave it a tug while twisting at the same time. It came easily off the stem. He lifted it to his mouth and took a bite, closing his eyes in exaggerated delight, letting a little juice drip down his chin. Then he opened his eyes, smiled a big red smile and held the strawberry out.

'Go on,' he said. 'Take a bite.'

Yojana Patel leaned forward, opened her mouth as wide as it would go and swallowed up the remaining strawberry, and Kaz's fingers too. He pantomimed surprise and pulled his wet fingers away and waggled them in the air as if he'd been bitten.

'You cheeky minx,' he said, frowning.

Yojana frowned back. The frown-off continued for a minute before they both collapsed laughing.

There is one way you can save me. Kind of. I've been thinking about it a lot.

I've been thinking about Yojana.

Zbigniew held Yojana's hand as she stepped up on to the stool and leaned over the cooker.

'Now, you hold the spoon like this,' he said, demonstrating how to hold the long-handled wooden spoon so as not to burn herself on the edges of the large pot. 'And you stir like so.'

Yojana reached out for the spoon, lost her balance for a fraction of a second, cried out in alarm, flung her arms around Zbigniew and clung on for dear life, staring down at the kitchen floor in fear.

'It's OK, sweetheart,' he reassured her. 'The stool is steady and I'm here to catch you. You're fine. I promise. Trust me?'

Yojana relaxed her grip, looked up at Zbigniew and nodded, biting her lip.

'OK,' she said.

Then she turned back, took hold of the spoon and began to stir the boiling jam.

I've been thinking that we can save her. Like we tried to do with your mum, Kaz, only this time there'd be no one to stop us. It always bothered me how quickly the ambulance arrived. What if it was waiting, around the corner, because it knew something was about to happen? What if the two paramedics were you guys? You could pull it off, Dora. I know you could.

'You don't need to grasp quite so hard with your knees. Just settle into the saddle and keep your back straight. That's it.'

Henry stepped away from Yojana, who sat atop the horse wide-eyed with nerves, but managing to keep them under control.

'Ready?'

She nodded mutely, making her best brave face.

'Remember, don't pull the reins, just hold them loosely in your hand. Off we go then.'

Henry stepped forward and tugged gently at the rope. The horse stepped softly forward, almost as if it was concerned for the girl on its back.

Yojana gave a little yelp as the animal, so much bigger and stronger than her, began to carry her around the paddock. When Henry looked up at her a moment later, her smile was blinding.

No lies. Just tell her the truth, that her parents loved her very much but couldn't look after her any more. Find her a home, be her family. Take out that damned chip. Let her grow up how she should always have grown up. How I should have grown up. How Quil should have grown up. Safe and loved for who she is, not who someone else wants her to be. Free to do the one thing Quil and I could never do.

Dream.

'And the princess took her mighty sword and lopped off the dragon's head, saving the kingdom, and fulfilling her destiny. The end.'

Dora closed the book and placed it on the bedside table.

'That was a good story,' said Yojana, barely stifling a yawn and shuffling down under the covers as Dora stroked her hair.

'Have you had a good day?'

'Mm-hmm,' murmured Yojana, her eyelids drooping.

'Good. There'll be plenty more like it. I promise.'

Dora leaned forward and kissed Yojana on the forehead.

'Goodnight Yojana.'

'G'night Auntie Dora.'

Dora switched off the bedside lamp, rose to her feet and walked to the door. Just as she was pulling it closed behind her, she heard Yojana call her name. She peered back around the door.

'Yes?'

'Auntie Dora,' said Yojana drowsily. 'Do I have a destiny?'

Dora paused for a moment, catching her breath. When she was sure she could speak without betraying her emotion, she answered softly. 'No darling. You can be whatever you want to be.'

'Good,' replied the sleepy girl as she closed her eyes again and drifted off to sleep.

And her dreams were *magnificent*.

Acknowledgements

Writing a trilogy, especially one with a plot as complex as this one, is a marathon not a sprint, and I would've collapsed in a dazed heap before the halfway point if not for my amazing support team.

Anne Perry is the platonic ideal of an editor; insightful, supportive, and always focused on making the books better. It's been a pleasure and a privilege to be in her stable. Oli Munson is a terrific agent, and the publicity team at Hodder shepherded the books to the world with care and attention. Justin Rowles was an invaluable one-man readthru crew, and an army of book bloggers and reviewers generously supported the series over the last few years.

Finally, my wife Emma kept the home fires burning while I madly tried to write this series at the same time as holding down a series of particularly . . . let's say *challenging* 9-5 jobs. It is entirely down to her efforts that our house is not a smoking ruin, and I'm eternally grateful.

Enjoyed this book?
Want more?

Head over to

CHAPteR 5

for extra author content,
exclusives, competitions – and lots
and lots of book talk!

Our motto is
'Proud to be bookish',

because, well, we are ☺

See you there . . .

 Chapter5Books @Chapter5Books

WANT MORE?

If you enjoyed this and would like to find out about similar books we publish, we'd love you to join our online SF, Fantasy and Horror community, Hodderscape.

Visit our blog site
www.hodderscape.co.uk

Follow us on Twitter
 **@hodderscape**

Like our Facebook page
Hodderscape

You'll find exclusive content from our authors, news, competitions and general musings, so feel free to comment, contribute or just keep an eye on what we are up to. See you there!